THE TRIDENT SERIES

STITCH

Book 5

Jaime Lewis

TABLE OF CONTENTS

CHAPTER ONE

"Okay, you little rascals, try not to give Lou any trouble tonight," Mia playfully warned the five chocolate and tan Dachshunds puppies as she gave each one a gentle scratch behind the ear before securing the crate. They were the cutest little furballs, especially as they burrowed close to each other. Lou was the clinic's night time cleaning guy.

Mia stood and adjusted the room's lighting, so it wasn't too bright or too dark. After checking on a couple of the other animals, she made her way down the clinic's main hall, flipping off light switches as she passed by exam rooms. It had been another busy yet productive day at New York's Riverside Animal Hospital. She sighed. She had been hoping to go for a run after she got off work, but once again, Dr. Walters had called and asked if she could cover his appointments. The last few weeks, it had become the norm—the first one in and the last one to leave.

She had only been a couple of months into the job, and she already had begun to feel burned out. Dr. Walters had done a phenomenal job building the facility to be the city's top-rated animal hospital. The schedule was insane as they dealt with various cases, from routine check-ups to evasive surgeries. She was definitely getting the experience she had hoped to gain by accepting the job that Dr. Walters had offered. With the holidays approaching, it seemed as if they were double booking appointments to squeeze everyone in before they shut down for the four-day holiday weekend.

She would never let on how she felt, as she didn't want to disappoint Dr. Walters. He had taken a gamble on her through word of mouth from one of her professors. Plus, she heard from a few staff members that a few doctors before her never even lasted a full year. When she questioned why, they told her it was because of the long working hours, and when they complained about it to Dr. Walters, he found reasons to terminate them. That wouldn't look good on a resume for someone like her, fresh into her career.

What kept her going was the drive and determination to become the next great veterinarian. It didn't matter if she was a workaholic; it wasn't as if she had a life outside of work anyway. She had a few friends from the clinic, and they would get together for dinner or drinks every so often, but that was the extent of her social life. At least in the city. When she could get a weekend off, she'd usually spend it at her soon to be sister-in-law and brother's house in Virginia Beach. It was there she felt at home. She always made sure that her brother was in town, because that meant the odds of seeing the one man who had captured her heart was guaranteed.

Evan "Stitch" Watson was a member of her brother, Ace's SEAL team. She had met Stitch a couple of years ago. The team had been on leave for an extended weekend when Ace invited Stitch to spend it on their ranch in Oklahoma.

Stitch possessed every quality she had looked for in a guy. He was polite, funny, caring, and not bad on the eyes. Their paths had crossed a few times after their initial meeting, but when she moved to New York to continue her studies, they hadn't seen much of each other until last Christmas when she spent the holidays with her brother and Alex. Those two weeks had been a whirlwind yet eye-opening. She and Stitch had been seated next to each other during Christmas dinner, and the conversation between them flowed so smoothly. The more they spoke, the more she realized how much they had in common. There had been a connection with him that she never felt with any other man. They had spent practically every waking moment together in between his work schedule the days following Christmas. When she went back to New York, they had kept in touch.

At the time, she had been dating Terek, her now ex-boyfriend. Mia knew before the holidays that their relationship had fizzled out. In the last few months, the relationship had become monotonous. When he wasn't working, he would grab take-out and bring it over to her apartment. Even then, his mind seemed elsewhere. Granted, he held the top security position at one of the busiest buildings in Manhattan, and she understood the stress he was under, but there just wasn't any spark left between them. Being around Stitch during Christmas and seeing what she could have in a relationship had solidified that it wasn't fair to either her or Terek to continue seeing each other. One night after work, she went to his apartment to talk to him, but she surprised him and herself when she found another woman in his bed. Sadly, she wasn't even really that upset, proving that she had made the right decision to end their relationship. Terek had been the one who seemed most affected by it. Whether it was guilt or the realization of what he had lost, she didn't know, nor did she care.

As the months went by, she and Stitch danced around the attraction they had for one another. The problem was that her brother Ace was not only Stitch's teammate, but his team leader. From what she had heard, there was an unwritten rule that teammates don't date other teammates' family members. In her opinion, it was a so-called asinine rule.

Thanksgiving was just a few days away, and Mia was spending it in Virginia Beach. She had already hinted to Stitch that there was something she wanted to talk to him about. She'd had enough and wanted to come clean with her feelings about him. Hopefully, he was on the same page and hadn't led her on. That would be humiliating as everyone could see there was chemistry between them. Well, maybe not her brother, but together perhaps they would convince Ace to accept it.

Mia flipped off the last light switch sending the main waiting room into darkness except for the one light that stayed on all the time. As she walked toward the side door that the employees used, she heard a noise from across the room that caught her attention. With her hand on the door, she looked across the dimly lit room and waited to see if she heard it again. Suddenly, something slammed into the main entrance. Mia jumped and felt an uptick in her heartbeat. She pulled her cell phone from her purse and dialed 911 but didn't hit the call button. Slowly she approached the main door. She was halfway across the room when the handle on the door started to jiggle as if someone was trying to break-in. Seconds later, the lock disengaged, and she froze. She was stuck and had a decision to make. She had three options; stand where she was and confront the intruder, run to the other exit and call the police in the safety of her car, or hide in the closest room available. She chose option two and took off running toward the door. Suddenly, all of the lights turned on, and brightness temporarily blinded her, causing her to trip over a row of chairs. She screamed as she hit the floor.

"Mia!"

Her body shook as she looked up from the floor in the direction of the deep familiar voice and saw Dr. Walters hurrying over to her. A gush of air was expelled from her body. She tried to calm her racing heart as Dr. Walters knelt next to her and rubbed her arm.

"Jesus, Mia. I'm so sorry. I thought everyone would've been gone by now. Let me help you." He helped her to stand. She was so shaken she didn't think her legs would hold her up. Once she was on her feet, she looked up at him. His eyes held hers, showing signs of remorse. "Are you okay?" He asked, appearing very concerned.

She nodded her head before she found her voice. "I'll be fine." She took another deep breath. "You scared the life out of me. I thought someone was trying to break-in."

He smiled. "That damn door gets stuck all the time. Why are you still here? It's way after closing time," He asked. She wanted to laugh at his ridiculous question.

Before she could answer, a whimper pulled her eyes away from his and toward the door. That was when she realized they weren't alone, and she met the gaze of a gentleman holding a carrier—his eyes were fixed on her. She looked back at Elijah, and he must have anticipated her question because he gestured toward the stranger.

"Mia, I'd like to introduce to you a friend and business associate of mine, Demitri Barros."

Demitri walked over and set the carrier down. Mia turned toward him and looked up to meet his eyes. He was tall, black hair with a sliver of gray at his temples. But what drew her in were his dark blue eyes. He was a good-looking guy, probably in the same age range as Dr. Walters. The casual light blue pantsuit with the white dress shirt's top two buttons undone, added to his appeal. He could easily be a model on one of the ad marquees in Times Square.

"It's is nice to meet you," she said, holding her hand out.

4

Demitri took hold of her hand. "The pleasure is all mine, Mia. Elijah has had nothing but high praises for you and your work here at the clinic."

She smiled, then took a knee to look inside the carrier. "Who are these little guys?" She asked, as there must have been around ten puppies stuffed in the medium-sized carrier.

"Demitri found them in the alley behind his office."

Mia stood up. "Someone just left them in the alley?" She was angry, and it seemed as if it was becoming a trend of dumping puppies here in the city. Same thing which happened to the Dachshunds they were holding.

"I'm afraid so," Elijah answered.

"This is what—the third or fourth litter of puppies that have come through here in just the last three weeks? What are you going to do with them?"

"I'd like to examine each one and make sure they're healthy enough to send to the rescue organization across town."

"Are you just dropping them off tonight?" She questioned, hoping that wasn't the case because, with strays, you never knew if they were carrying any diseases.

"I'd feel more comfortable looking over them before housing them in the kennel with the other animals." She smiled, getting the answer she was looking for.

"I can help you. That is if you'd like the help. I mean, two sets of hands are better than one. It would make the process quicker."

Elijah glanced over at Demitri, and Demitri nodded his head, which Mia found odd.

Elijah smiled. "As long we aren't keeping you from anything, then yes, I'll accept the offer. With two of us, we should be able to knock it out pretty quickly."

She nodded and set her purse and bag on the reception desk, and followed Elijah.

"Let's use exam room six since it has more space," Elijah said as he led the three of them down the hall with Mia between the two men. Mia had always felt self-conscious when someone walked behind her. Especially a

5

man. During her early years of college, she had been harassed by guys while walking the campus. Even though she knew it was Demitri behind her, his presence still made her uneasy. She took a quick glance over her shoulder, and he pinned her with those dark blue eyes before he flashed her a smile. Something about his demeanor gave a warning. What that warning was, she wasn't sure, but she'd be sure to keep an eye on him.

Even using the larger exam room, it was a little cramped with the three of them. Demitri stood off to the side and typed away on his phone most of the time while she and Elijah examined each puppy. At one point, Mia swore she saw from the corner of her eye Demitri hold up his phone as if he was taking a picture. She wanted to question him on it but didn't want to add any tension, but the thought added to her suspicions about the man.

She tried not to let his presence rattle her, and she pushed aside the uneasy vibe and focused on the pups. She was pleased and felt relieved that all the pups seemed in perfectly good health. Her only concern was their size. They seemed too small to be removed from their mom.

"I wonder where their momma is. These little fellas seem awfully small to be on their own." She asked as she cuddled one of the blue French Bulldog pups close to her chest. He was the cutest little thing. They were all cute. Mia couldn't believe someone had dumped them in an alley, considering breeders fetched an average of $2,000-$3,000 for a blue French Bulldog. A well-documented pedigree could fetch even more—over $3,500.

Elijah approached and stood in front of Mia. He looked at the pup then into her eyes. "French Bulldogs are small. I wouldn't worry too much about their size. They all appear to be healthy. I'd say the odds of them finding a nice home are very high." He scratched the puppy behind the ears, and in doing so, the back of his hand brushed against her scrub top, coming close to her breast. Not knowing if his move was intentional or not, she repositioned the puppy in her arms. There were already rumors amongst the staff that Elijah had the hots for Mia. She paid no attention, although she had noticed he had been very attentive lately. He didn't seem to notice what he had done, so she let it slide. Accidents do happen.

"What are we going to do with them, now?" She asked, taking a step backward to put some space between the two of them. As she went to turn to put the puppy back into one of the other carriers, she bumped into Demitri and gasped when his hands landed on her waist. *When the hell did he move from the corner of the room?*

She looked up into his mysterious eyes. The dark blue orbs were intense, like a fire burning beyond them, and again she sensed he wasn't a man to be messed with. She imagined he was full of dark secrets, maybe even dangerous. His expressions alone gave her an unsettling feeling. Without saying a word, he gave her waist a slight squeeze before moving past her, letting his hand brush her backside, sending a chill up her spine.

As if paying no attention to what just happened, Elijah answered her, "Tonight, we'll keep them in the kennel, and then tomorrow I'll have Willow contact the rescue organization we use to place available animals."

Satisfied with his answer, Mia picked up the two carriers and started walking toward the door. "I'll take these guys and get them settled for the night while you finish up with whatever you need to do?" She needed a breather, still feeling on edge with the two men and their actions tonight.

Elijah nodded his head. "When you're finished, stop by my office before you leave. There's something I'd like to talk to you about."

Before she could question him, he turned his back and started talking to Demitri. As she walked to the kennels, she heard the two men laughing. She shook her head. She just wanted to get the puppies settled and go home. She scooped up each puppy, gave them each a little hug, and placed them in the oversized cage. She hoped that those responsible for leaving the puppies out in the cold were eventually caught and prosecuted to the fullest extent of the law.

Elijah watched out of the corner of his eye as Mia walked out of the room. She had no clue the effect she had on him or Demitri, for that matter.

Demitri whistled low once she was out of earshot. "You hit the jackpot with that one. I'll be honest, I'm fucking jealous."

Elijah grinned.

"Where in the hell did you find her? She is the whole package; brains, beauty, and personality."

"I owe Professor Collins for the recommendation. I normally wouldn't waste my time on a recent graduate, but there was something about the way she spoke of Mia that intrigued me, so I took a chance. And I'm glad I did. You know I like to interview job candidates in a more informal setting, so Professor Collins invited me to speak at a lecture for her class. After class, she introduced Mia to me, and I'll admit, I was blown away by her professionalism and intellect within the first five minutes of speaking with her."

"You offered her a job on the spot?" Demitri asked with a raised eyebrow.

"Of course not. I called her the following week and asked her out for coffee to discuss her post-education career. When she told me she was still applying at clinics in the city, I told her not to look any further." He chuckled, "I think I surprised her when I told her I was offering her the job at my clinic." Elijah motioned to Demitri to follow him to his office. "She asked the right questions, like what her role would be here. She's a go-getter, and you know, I like that quality in a person, especially a member of my staff. I think I shocked her when I told her she could start taking patients her first day."

"She's really that good? You aren't just looking for a piece of ass?" Demitri joked, but Elijah could sense there was some seriousness there as well.

"I know a lot of veterinarians, including those who've been around for a while, and believe me when I say that Mia can run circles around them."

They each took a seat in the chairs in front of Elijah's desk.

"Just to make sure she'd take the job, I sweetened the compensation package."

Demitri grinned. Elijah could tell that Mia had caught Demitri's attention. He wasn't sure how he felt about it. Demitri wasn't a one-woman man. Demitri used his charm, money, and good looks to hook the woman he was interested in, and then once he satisfied his needs, he'd kick her to the curb. What many people didn't know was that Demitri had a dark side. He owned several businesses, both in the United States and in Europe. Buried beneath those legit businesses were illegal dealings. His European business was his money maker. He was the majority stakeholder but silent partner of the top lingerie design firm in all of Europe. Rumor was he ran a small but profitable high priced prostitution ring using some of the models. However, it wasn't as if Elijah could cry foul, since he, too had his own dark secret.

"Are you attending the Fur Ball gala tomorrow night?" Demitri asked.

"I am. I've got a few people I need to catch up with. I'm going to ask—"

"Excuse me, Dr. Walters," Mia said from the doorway, and Elijah smiled. *Right on time,* he thought to himself. "I'm sorry to interrupt, but I wanted to let you know the puppies are tucked in for the night. If you don't need anything else, I'm going to head out for the evening."

"Mia, please come in for a minute." He motioned to her. She came closer but appeared nervous. She looked toward Demitri, who was eating her up with his eyes. Elijah cleared his throat, drawing her attention back to him.

"Do you have any plans tomorrow evening?"

She drew her eyebrows inward and shook her head. "No. No plans."

He smiled. "Well, if you are interested, I have an extra ticket to the Fur Ball. There will be numerous clients and associates of the clinic in attendance that I'd like to introduce you to. It would be a great networking opportunity for you."

"Really? I've heard that it is one of the hardest tickets to obtain here in the city. As far as galas go, that is."

Elijah nodded, "It is the hottest ticket in town, and I'd very much like to allow you the opportunity to attend. I'll be attending." He stared at Mia, and a thought came to mind. Maybe tomorrow night would be an opportune time to get a little closer to Mia. Maybe give her a taste of what it could be like being with him and a chance to find out more about her. "I'll even pick you up."

Mia's eyes widened, almost making Elijah laugh. "You don't have to pick me up."

9

Elijah smiled. "So, is that a yes to attending as my guest?"

Her face lit up, and he knew he had sold her on it. "Yes! Thank you so much."

"You're very welcome. And, I do insist that I pick you up. You'll be thanking me once you see the line to the valet. It is a nightmare. I'll be at your apartment building around six-thirty. Take tomorrow off if you need to." He didn't leave any room for an argument. He knew from past functions such as this one that women needed a whole day to prepare.

"Okay. If you really don't mind me sharing a ride with you, I'd appreciate it."

He gave her a soft smile. "Go on and get out of here. Great job tonight, and I mean it, take tomorrow off. You've earned it."

She nodded her head and then turned toward Demitri. "Demitri, it was nice meeting you."

Demitri smiled, "I'm sure our paths will cross again. Take care, Mia."

With one last wave over her shoulder, she exited the office. Elijah waited until he heard the side entrance door close before he spoke. As the metal door slammed shut, he turned toward Demitri, who had a wicked grin growing on his face.

"Well, my friend, it looks as if you have a date tomorrow. And if I'm honest, I'm pissed at myself for not beating you to the invite. It would have been a joy to have that beauty on my arm."

Elijah smirked. Typical Demitri. He needed to make sure he kept Mia out of Demitri's grasps. If not, it could possibly lead to trouble.

"I'd say Mia bought your sob story about the puppies being thrown out with the trash."

Elijah ran his hand through his hair. "I think so, but she's not the one I'm concerned about."

"You've got a snitch?"

"I think so, but I need to set a trap."

"Someone here at the clinic."

Elijah stared at Demitri. He knew he could trust him; hell, Demitri would probably help set the trap.

"Willow."

Demitri looked surprised. "The receptionist?"

"I think so."

"Holy shit. That woman is like a mouse. She hardly says anything or makes eye contact with anyone. Are you sure?" Demitri questioned.

"She gossips. And lately, she's been asking some questions that shouldn't concern her."

Elijah shook his head. "I've got some of the guys keeping an eye on her."

CHAPTER TWO

Mia felt that tingling sensation start to creep along the back of her neck. She always got that feeling when she felt something felt off. She pushed the creepy feeling aside as she tried hard not to appear disrespectful in the middle of what had to have been the most challenging conversation she'd ever had. The sad part was the person she was trying to engage in conversation with had been an idol of hers ever since she'd started to take a serious interest in becoming a veterinarian.

Dr. Oscar LaRoache was a world-renowned veterinarian. Or should she say he used to be? She'd heard rumors circulating the last few months regarding his health and how it had deteriorated. After listening for the last ten to fifteen minutes and hearing the same story about the German Shepard who ate thirty-six of his owner's socks for the fourth time, she realized they weren't rumors. The poor man was suffering badly from dementia, and it was heart-wrenching to witness because the man had been brilliant in his prime.

The gala itself so far had fared well. Even though she wasn't really into the whole city social scene, she was grateful for Elijah's invite because, with his connections, she'd been able to do a lot of networking in just the two hours she'd been there.

Just as Dr. LaRoache started to tell his story again, she felt her phone vibrate in her clutch. Glad for the interruption, she excused herself and exited the ballroom. Down the hall and out of earshot of the loud music, she spotted a couple of chairs.

She smiled when she saw Alex's name flashing on her phone screen. Alex was her brother's fiancé. "Your timing couldn't have been any better," she answered, and her smile grew when she heard the two sets of laughter on the other end. Not only was Alex on the phone, but Alex's best friend Tenley was there too. Those two women were a wrecking ball when they got together. Not in a bad way; they just fed off each other and could make for some really good and entertaining times, especially when there was alcohol involved. However, Tenley was on a break from the poison since she was pregnant with twins due in a few weeks. God help Potter, her husband—and member of Ace's SEAL team—if those two babies are anything like their momma.

"I know you're at the gala right now, but Tenley and I had to call you."

"Why is that?" She asked, taking a seat in one of the chairs. She almost groaned, taking a load off her feet.

"You look amazing!" Alex said in excitement. Alex had asked her to send a picture of her in her gown. The dress was floor-length, mermaid style in snow white with a plunging neckline that showed more cleavage than she normally would and was comfortable with. It was just enough for a classy yet sophisticated look. The back was the main attention-getter, and honestly, she had been a little gun shy about wearing it at first, but the sales lady at the store along with the other customers in the small boutique convinced her that she rocked it. The back was completely open and dipped down so low it stopped just above her rear. It was a dress she never would had picked out herself. But the sales lady apparently did her job because she had been complimented on the dress all night.

"What Alex means to say is you look hot, Mia! I'm sure you've had men swarming you all evening."

These two were hilarious, but Tenley was right—she'd had plenty of offers already, but she wasn't interested. The only man she was interested in was nowhere near New York City.

Mia laughed dryly. "You two are something else."

"Hey…you sound different. Is everything okay?" Alex asked, and Mia couldn't help but grin. Alex had a knack for knowing when something was off. She was very intelligent, and even though she was retired from the government, agencies still tried to recruit her. The guys on the team swore she had been a SEAL in her former life and carried all the training and knowledge into her new life.

"I'm good. You called at a good time. I needed a little break. Who knew networking could be quite tiring, not to mention repetitive." Mia thought back to Dr. LaRoche.

"Well, we don't want to take up your time, but we wanted to call and tell you that you look beautiful," Alex said, and Mia appreciated it.

"Thank you. I have a few minutes to chat. What are you ladies up to tonight?"

Alex sighed. "Tenley and I are bored. Ace has the guys over for their weekly team-building gathering. They kicked us out of the room when we turned off their football game in favor of *How to Lose a Guy in 10 Days*. Guess they weren't in the chick flick kinda mood." She said laughingly.

Mia chuckled, then scrunched up her nose up. "Why do they need to meet every week for a team building thingy? Don't they see each other every day, especially when they're out on their SEAL thing-a-ma-jigs? Sheesh, you'd think they'd be sick of one another."

Alex started laughing. "They're called missions or ops, and I honestly think he just told me that so he could have a night every week that he can have the guys over, and I can cook for everyone." Mia laughed. Knowing her brother's manipulative ways, she wouldn't doubt it.

"Speaking of the team, Alex showed the picture of you in your gown to *everyone*," Tenley stated with emphasis on everyone, and Mia's heart pounded in her chest. If all the guys were there right now, that meant Stitch was there, and he saw the photo. She wondered what he thought of the picture.

"Mia? Are you still there?"

Mia shook her head. "Yeah, sorry. You showed the guys my picture? Why?"

"Why not? You look great. Stitch thought so too. He even got pissed off when Dino commented on your back ass-ets."

"Oh, geez."

"Oh, come on, Mia. Everyone knows you and Stitch have the hots for one another," She paused. "Well, maybe everyone except for your brother. Although I think he knows but is just in denial. Does that make sense?" She asked, laughing.

"Even if we did, it could never work. He works with my brother."

"So?" Alex replied.

14

"So, that's why. You know, the secret unwritten rule. Ace even lectured me when I was younger and he first joined the teams and brought guys home when they were on leave."

Alex made an odd noise with her mouth. "I don't know, Mia. Your brother may surprise you. Look, just have fun tonight. And just think a couple more days, and then we can all hang out together," She squealed in delight. "Plus, I need a drinking partner. Tubby here next to me still has a few more weeks before she can have a drink."

"Hey! I resent that." Tenley interjected but laughed along.

"What about Autumn and Bailey?"

"Autumn's been busy with Cody, plus I think she and Frost are trying for a baby," Alex whispered. "But you didn't hear that from us. And with Bailey still recovering from her ordeal, Irish has a short leash on her, so alcohol for them is definitely out of the question. And, I hate to drink by myself. It's no fun."

Mia was laughing so hard her abs started to hurt. Right at that moment, she turned her head and locked gazes with Elijah. He stood at the other end of the hall, watching her. He looked so authoritative in his stance and the way he just nodded his head as people passed by him. But he never took his eyes off of her. Her smile faded at the thought that he could be upset because she disappeared for a little bit.

"Listen, ladies, as much as I would love to stay on the phone and chat, I really need to get back. My boss is staring at me."

"Oh…he is sexy too. You know, the tall, dark and dangerous type," Tenley said, and she wasn't wrong. Elijah was very attractive. A little out of her age range as he was in his mid-fifties. He was fun to look at, but that was all she was willing to do. She and he had a pure working relationship. Her dad had taught her long ago not to shit where she eat.

She said good-bye to Alex and Tenley. She put away her phone as she walked toward Elijah. Elijah met her eyes, and he flashed her that sexy smile of his. Tenley wasn't wrong; he was a good-looking guy, and the tuxedo he wore added to his appeal. The way it molded against his body, she knew it had to have been custom made and probably cost a fortune.

15

"Is everything okay?" He asked, placing a hand on her waist and giving it a little squeeze. It was a repetitive gesture he had done most of the night while he escorted her around the room, introducing her to the City's finest.

She smiled up at him. "Yes, sorry about disappearing. It was my brother's fiancé, and I wanted to make sure everything was okay."

"No worries. With the way you were smiling, I'm assuming everything is good?"

"Yes, she just called to say hi."

"Good. There are a few more people I'd like to introduce you to. Shall we?" He asked, gesturing back toward the ballroom with one hand while his other was glued to her lower back.

"Sounds great. Lead the way, boss." She joked and gave him a grin.

He smirked before taking her hand and leading her through the double doors back into the ballroom. Elijah waved to people as they passed through. They were headed toward the bar in the far corner of the room when she noticed a group of men standing just to the left of the bar. When one of the men turned, Mia's eyes widened as she locked gazes with her ex, Terek. Instantly she felt sick. He did a double-take and looked taken back by her presence, but quickly masked his shocked expression.

She had met Terek a little over a year ago at a bar not too far from her apartment. They exchanged phone numbers, and soon after, they started dating. Though they were compatible with one another, and he treated her well, the relationship never blossomed. There just wasn't a "wow" factor. She hadn't seen or spoken to him since the night she had caught him with the other woman.

As they joined the group, Elijah introduced her to everyone. She recognized a couple of the men who worked for the City and were clients of the clinic. Demitri was there as well, and when he took her hand and brought it to his lips, she thought Terek was going to make a scene. He tried to hide his displeased expression by taking a drink from his glass. When Elijah turned to Terek, Terek was quick to extend his hand for a shake.

"It's nice to meet you, Mia." He told her, acting as if they had never met before, and it confused her. *Did he just speak with an English accent?* She went to question his greeting, but something in his gaze told her to keep her mouth shut. She shook his hand and gave him a questionable look, but he ignored her reaction and went back to his conversation with the guy next to him. His rejection pissed her off.

She took a step back, feeling somewhat rejected by Terek's actions, and found herself between Demitri and Elijah. Demitri bent down and whispered in her ear, "You look ravishing."

She smiled up at him. "Thank you." She replied.

"Have you enjoyed yourself this evening?"

"I have. It's been a wonderful experience."

"I hope Elijah has taken good care of you."

Elijah looked over at Demitri. "Cool it," He told Demitri, and Demitri smirked before looking down at her and winking. The men then went back to their conversations. As the minutes ticked by and the men showed no slowdown with the business talk, Mia turned her attention toward the bar and ordered a drink. As she waited for the bartender to mix her cocktail, she couldn't stop thinking about the man who stood just a few feet from her. Her surprise run-in with Terek had put a damper on her mood, and she was now ready to call it a night. It pissed her off that his presence had ruined an enjoyable evening. The bartender handed her the glass, and she took a big gulp, feeling the burn of the alcohol down her throat.

"Did we bore you?" Elijah whispered in her ear.

She jerked her head around and found Elijah grinning at her. "What?"

His smile grew, and his eyes held a wicked gleam. "I thought we might have bored you."

"Oh. No. I just didn't really have anything to contribute to the conversation, so I got myself a drink." She grinned and held up her drink before downing the rest of it. As she lowered her hand, Elijah took the glass from her and placed it on the bar.

"Well, I didn't bring you here so you could feel ignored. Come." He commanded, taking her hand and leading her away from the group. Sensing eyes on her, Mia took a quick look over her shoulder. Terek was leaning against the bar staring directly at her. He wasn't happy, and she couldn't

17

understand what his deal was. Was he jealous? The thought of it made her smile. She could easily act like she and Elijah were an item, but she quickly dismissed the idea. It wasn't fair to put Elijah in the middle of her personal issues. Nor was she one to play games. For now, she would just go with the flow and smile like she'd done all evening and hope she'd seen the last of Terek.

CHAPTER THREE

"Stitch!"

Stitch looked up from where he was standing with his hip leaning against the pool table. Ace and Potter stared at him. "Are you going to play or what?"

Damn, he hadn't realized he had zoned out. Ever since Alex and Tenley had shown him Mia's picture, he couldn't get the image of her in that fucking dress out of his head. She looked like she had just stepped off the cover of a fashion magazine, and knowing she'd be in a room filled with wealthy businessmen who probably used their manipulative boardroom ways to get a woman into bed had his head spinning. If she was going to sleep in anyone's bed, he wanted it to be his.

Before his dick got any harder and made a fool of himself, he stood and pointed to the corner, right pocket, and lined up the easy shot. He cursed when the ball went wide to the left. Christ, he was definitely off his game.

"Dude, what is with you tonight?" Ace snickered, then grabbed another handful of peanuts and shoved them into his mouth.

"He needs to get laid," Potter said, leaning on his pool stick. "Oh, but she isn't around, is she?"

Stitch shot Potter a look that told him to shut the fuck up. When Potter grinned, Stitch knew the giant got what he intended. And that got him riled up.

"What? Are you dating someone?" Ace questioned, looking confused. The team shared pretty much everything with one another. But he couldn't very well tell Ace that the woman Potter was referring to was Ace's baby sister. Stitch was pretty confident that wouldn't bode well for him. And it was a huge problem because he not only was interested in Mia, but he was already in love with her. Ever since Christmas of last year, the two of them started talking more and really got to know each other. Even when she was back up in New York, they kept in contact. They both knew they were walking a slippery slope keeping their "friendship" a secret from Ace.

Stitch glanced back at Potter, who suddenly found something to entertain himself with so he wouldn't have to endure Stitch's death stare. Looking back at Ace, he waved him off.

"No. Potter's just messing around."

Just then, Alex made her entrance bouncing her way over to Ace. He opened his arms, and she walked right into them. That right there was what Stitch wanted. He wanted a woman who knew they were loved by their man, just like Alex knew that Ace would move heaven on earth for her.

"You okay?" Ace asked her. Stitch grinned, knowing Alex had a little too much to drink and was currently in her happy place, as she called it.

She scrunched her nose up at Ace. "Yeah, but you need to convince your sister to find a job here in Virginia Beach or close by."

Ace chuckled and wrapped his arms around her. The man was so pussy whipped it was hilarious, but equally humbling to watch a man like Ace, who was fierce and commanding, not to mention so set in his ways as a SEAL, fall so hard for a woman. He couldn't be any happier for his team leader and his best friend.

"Why's that? She seems happy in New York." Ace replied.

Oh, big brother. *You are clearly mistaken*, Stitch thought to himself. If Ace had been within an earshot of Mia during her last visit, he would have heard the somberness when she spoke about New York. Just because she didn't come right out and say she was unhappy, didn't mean she wasn't. A person's body language could give away many clues.

Alex wrinkled her nose up again and Ace's intense expression softened a smidge, and Stitch thought it was hilarious.

"She would be happier here with all of us," she said, pinning her gaze on Stitch, and Stitch squinted his eyes at her. He just shook his head when she grinned. He got her message loud and clear.

"You think so?" Ace asked, seeming utterly oblivious to Stitch and Alex's silent conversation, which was a good thing for Stitch.

"I know so because Tenley and I just talked to her."

Ace furrowed his eyebrows. "I thought she was at that fancy event."

"She is, but Tenley and I were bored since y'all wouldn't let us watch our movie, so we called her to see how things were going."

"And...?" Ace asked, raising an eyebrow.

Alex shrugged her shoulders. "She said it was okay, but that she had met a lot of people."

"Yeah? What kind of people?" Ace asked with a questionable look. Stitch, from conversations with Ace, knew Ace worried about Mia living in New York by herself.

Stitch was curious too and stepped closer to hear.

"You know the types of people that hang out at those types of functions. Rich, some famous people, guys just looking for a good screw."

Stitch felt his eyes widen, hearing the last part of Alex's statement. Oh, she was so going to get an earful from him when he got her alone. She was intentionally baiting him into saying something in front of Ace. Well, she had another thing coming.

"Sweetheart...Are you trying to piss me off intentionally?" Ace asked and, thank god that Stitch wasn't the only one feeling the urge to possibly take a trip to New York City and save Mia from the throng of men wanting to take her to their bed.

"No, I'm just giving you examples of why you should talk to her and convince her to move. Or maybe we all should," She said with a smile, then snuggled against Ace's chest. She turned her head in Stitch's direction and winked. Potter saw her and chuckled. Stitch was glad that his predicament with Mia was this evening's entertainment for some. While he had plans in place to talk to Mia this weekend, if Alex didn't put a cork in her large mouth, he was going to have to have a discussion with Ace before Mia even arrived.

Potter changed the conversation putting the talk of Mia to rest.

"Alex, where is my wife?"

Stitch thought it was funny because it wasn't like Tenley was hard to miss considering she was carrying around twins and looked ready to give birth any day. Not to mention the whining the woman did. Granted, Stitch

21

never carried around a baby in his stomach, but Tenley took it to the extreme sometimes, and Stitch knew it was just to get Potter to do something.

Alex giggled, and it made Stitch snicker. At least she was a happy little drunk.

"She said she was tired, so I rolled her into a chair in the living room, and she fell asleep. She said for you to wake her up when you were ready to leave."

"Great…that woman is impossible to wake up."

"Oh, just wave one of those cinnamon rolls I made in front of her nose. I guarantee she'll wake up." Everyone laughed. Tenley had a bit of a sweet tooth lately. Her doctor had even told her she needed to watch her diet, which pissed her off because now, when Potter was home, he monitored everything she ate. Well, most of the time, that is. When she thought nobody was looking, she would sneak a few treats here and there, like the entire bag of jellybeans Stitch saw her take out of the room with her, but he wasn't going to squeal on his friend.

While Potter went to fetch Tenley, Stitch thought it was a good time for him to call it a night as well. Especially the way Alex's mouth had been running tonight. It was better to quit while he was still ahead.

He pulled Alex into a big hug and whispered in her ear. "You are such a little shit."

She giggled and pulled back. "But you love me." She kissed his cheek.

He did love Alex like a sister, and always would. Stitch, Alex, Frost, and Tenley had been the best of friends since they all met in the first grade. After high school, they had all gone their separate ways, and now, years later, they were back together. In a way, it was just like old times, except they were all wiser and more responsible.

He reached over and shook Ace's hand. "I'll see you tomorrow morning."

Ace nodded. "Remember, if we get through our training simulation tomorrow and Wednesday with no hiccups, we won't have to report in on Thursday unless we're needed."

"Yes, sir." As he walked out to his Jeep, he pulled up the picture of Mia that Alex had texted him. She took his breath away with her beauty. He shot a quick text off her.

"You looked beautiful tonight. Be safe, Mia."

CHAPTER FOUR

Mia stood off to the side in the room and tried to stifle a yawn as she looked around the decorated ballroom. It seemed that the later it got, the more the crowd grew. She was tired, and her feet were starting to ache. Wearing four-inch heels for the last five hours would do that if the person wasn't accustomed to wearing them. From her perspective, she had met everyone she had anticipated meeting, along with other prominent people. She knew Elijah was well-liked, but she hadn't realized exactly how popular of a man he was until she witnessed how everyone flocked to him, vying for his attention—especially the ladies. She had been on the receiving end of some harsh glares from some of the women. However, Elijah showed them no interest except for a polite hello as he escorted her around the room, making introductions. Women like them were the reason she avoided social gatherings like this. She wasn't interested in competing for the prettiest gown or hairstyle or even the best looking man on her arm.

She had locked gazes with Terek a few more times throughout the evening, but she dismissed him. His attitude toward her still nagged her. His appearance made her question his relationship with Elijah, because Elijah didn't seem like the type of person Terek would hang out with. The Terek she knew was more uptight, probably brought on by his military background. He was a skilled military operative, just like her brother. The only difference was that he served in the Army. She would never have imagined him attending a function like this.

Her phone vibrated again, and she shook her head, knowing it had to be Alex and Tenley again. She pulled the phone out of her clutch and took a quick peek. A smile spread across her face seeing it was Stitch. As she read his message, warmth spread through her body. With both of their work schedules the last few months, it had been challenging to find time to talk. She missed his voice, his laughter; hell, she just missed him.

She thought back to her last visit. It had been right after Irish's fiancé, Bailey was kidnapped, shot in her lower belly, and nearly died. Irish served on the SEAL team with Stitch and her brother. It had been a really difficult time for everyone, wondering if Bailey would recover from her injuries.

Add in Mia's stress dealing with her residency, prepping and sitting for the North American Veterinary Licensing Exam, along with job hunting; she had been a little moody during that timeframe. She thought she had hidden her struggles, but Stitch had seen right through her façade, and one night he had pulled her to the side and questioned her. She tried to play it off as if everything was fine, but when he gave her that stern look of his, she knew she was busted and ended up spilling everything to him. They had sat alone outside on the patio talking for almost an hour, and somehow, he managed to ease the uncertainties facing her. Before they went back inside, he took her hand and placed a key to his cabin in her palm, telling her he bought the cabin so he had a place to escape the stress and worries of life, especially after returning home from a mission. He told her she was welcome to use it any time she wanted. Now that everything was falling into place, she had been considering taking him up on his generous offer. Especially now that Elijah had informed her last week that he was planning on cutting back his hours at the clinic, which meant more responsibilities were falling on to her.

She had to remind herself not to get too worked up about it, considering he paid her an impressive salary, especially for someone fresh in their career. However, if you don't have time to enjoy those benefits, then there seems to be no point of slaving yourself. She would talk to Stitch this week and see if he would mind if she used the cabin for a weekend in December before Christmas. Who knew, maybe after her conversation with him over the Thanksgiving holiday, he would perhaps join her for a romantic weekend in the mountains. Stitch may be a hardass Navy SEAL, but from her interactions with him over the last year, she'd bet her life that he was a true romantic under all that armor.

She typed a quick reply, thanking him and telling him she was looking forward to seeing him this weekend. As she pressed send, a large body pressed up against her back, startling her. She looked over her shoulder and gasped, seeing Elijah there.

"You disappeared on me again." He teased, whispering the words in her ear. His mouth was so close to her ear; she swore she felt his lips brush against her skin as he spoke.

She stared at him for a moment. He stood just shy of six feet, physically fit, with a thick head of dark wavy brown hair, and dark eyes; he was most women's idea of a perfect man. The women at the clinic all drooled over him when he would come to work straight from the gym, still wearing his workout clothes. She'd admit, he did look amazing in his tux this evening, and he chose not to shave, so the five o'clock shadow on his cheeks made him look that much sexier.

She smiled but chose to ignore the "disappeared" comment. It wasn't like she had been ordered to stand by his side all night. She was grateful for the invite, but she sensed things were getting a little weird between them.

"I had a wonderful time. Thank you again for the invite." His large hands traveled down her bare arms to her hips, where they rested. The move was intimate and made her uncomfortable and unsure of what his intentions were. In the last few weeks, there had been a slight change in his attentiveness towards her in the office. But after tonight with his blatant flirting, she was beginning to think that Elijah may be interested in her more than just a colleague. She wasn't about to venture down that path. Most women would call her crazy, but he just didn't do anything for her.

A waiter appeared with a champagne tray, and she used that opportunity to step out of his firm hold. Taking a glass from the tray, she thanked the waiter before swallowing about half the glass in one gulp. She had been careful to limit her drinks. This was only her third and final for the evening. Elijah never took his eye off her. There was a gleam in his gaze, and she recognized it. It was the same look guys at a bar or club would give her before they'd try and charm their way into her pants. She wasn't an easy lay and had even punched a guy for insisting she was.

"There wasn't a man in the room that couldn't take his eyes off you."

She lowered her eyes, wishing the floor would swallow her up. She drank the remaining champagne in her glass. She wasn't sure how to respond to his comment. Maybe it was the alcohol, but she smiled and looked up at him.

"I could say the same for you. There were quite a few women who appeared put off that you ignored them."

His eyes grew darker, and he licked his bottom lip.

"That is because I only had eyes for one woman in the room." His gaze was intense. He had a fire in his pupils, and she knew he was speaking about her. It put her on edge. She swallowed hard and wished someone would use this exact time to interrupt them.

She noticed he looked at his watch again. It was the third time in the last couple of minutes.

Elijah glanced at his watch again.

"Is there somewhere you need to be?" She asked, hoping to change the atmosphere surrounding them.

His lips twitched. "I do need to head out. I have a client meeting me at the office."

She nodded her head, but then his words registered.

"You're meeting a client this late?" She asked him, now rather curious who he was seeing at this time of the night.

"He's been a client since I opened the practice and has a new litter of puppies that were born prematurely. Two of the pups have some issues, and I'd feel better if it were me who saw them instead of the emergency clinic.

She immediately became concerned for the pups. "Do you need any help?" She asked, setting the champagne glass down on the table next to her.

He smiled down at her. "This is why you are my favorite. So eager to lend a hand. Thank you for the offer, but I can handle this one alone. I'd rather you stay and enjoy yourself."

If he was leaving, she wasn't going to be too far behind. She shrugged her shoulders. If he wanted to go into work this late, more power to him. She should be thankful he said no.

"Just remember I offered." She told him in a teasing way.

He reached out and took her hand, pulling her closer to him. The move caught her off guard, causing her to fall against his chest. He kept one hand

27

on her waist while the other hand slowly slid down her bare back, stopping just above her ass. She swallowed hard, and her breathing increased. Her face was against his chest. He pulled back slightly, and when she looked up, his dark eyes were focused on her. Slowly he lowered his head and kissed her cheek, letting his lips linger against her skin. She was stunned by his actions and afraid to move as one slight shift to the right, and his lips would meet hers.

"I wish I didn't have to leave," He whispered, but she didn't know how to respond. Before she could think of a reply, he gave her hip one last squeeze and stepped back. "As soon as I get to the office, I'll send the car back to take you home."

She took a step backward, putting more distance between them. She felt frazzled.

"Don't worry about the car. I don't mind catching a cab."

"Nonsense. I brought you tonight, and I have to see that you make it home safely. I'll see you tomorrow morning at the office."

She nodded her head, and he smiled again before turning and walking toward the exit. As soon as he was out of sight, she let out a big gasp of air. *What in the hell just happened?* She was trying to process everything when someone behind her spoke.

"Mia?"

When she turned, she smiled from ear-to-ear. She needed to see a friendly face right now.

"Dr. Vineberg. I was wondering if I was going to see you this evening." Mia looked toward his wife standing next to him, and she stepped forward to hug her. "Mrs. Vineberg, it's so nice to see you. How have you been?"

The grey-haired lady gave her a warm smile. "Mia, how many times do I have to tell you to call me Estelle?" Estelle leaned in and hugged her. "How have you been, dear?"

Mia adored the Vinebergs. She had done an internship in Dr. Vineberg's clinic during her last year in school. Dr. Vineberg had offered her a position at his clinic, but it was too far of a commute. She had heard a rumor that he was looking at retirement and considering selling his clinic. It was a shame because he was a rare breed of veterinarians. He was old school going so far as to do house calls still. That was precisely what she wanted to be. She wanted to be that doctor who everyone trusted their animal with. In the few months she'd been working for Elijah, she had already made a name for herself. But she didn't see herself there long-term. She wanted to work alongside and learn from someone who was hands-on and a team player. That was definitely not Elijah. He was a nice guy, treated his staff well, but his work ethic sucked. He was either late or never even made it into the office, which was why she'd seen an uptick in her workload.

"I've been okay. Just trying to get through tonight."

Dr. Vineberg furrowed his eyebrows, and a disappointed expression crossed his face. "Where is Dr. Walters? I heard he was going to be attending this evening."

"Oh, he was here. He left just a few minutes ago."

"Well, I'm glad I got to see your smiling face. So, tell me, how is everything at the clinic? Are you happy? He's not working you too hard, is he?" Oh, if he only knew. But she wasn't going to throw Elijah under the bus.

"I'm making do. Still learning the ropes some, but overall I'm enjoying it." She hoped her slight fib didn't show in her expression.

"Are you here alone, dear?" Estelle asked, changing the subject.

"Yes, ma'am. I came with Dr. Walters." When she looked at Dr. Vineberg, he raised an eyebrow as if indicating she was on a date with Elijah. She quickly followed up that statement. "I just found out yesterday that I was coming. Dr. Walters was given an extra ticket, and he thought it would be beneficial if I attended and did some networking."

Dr. Vineberg nodded his head in acceptance. "Well, this is definitely the event to be seen at, especially in our field of work."

"I'm glad that I got to see you. I was considering sneaking out and heading home."

"Well, we're getting ready to head out ourselves. Would you like to walk out with us?" Dr. Vineberg asked her.

29

She was about to answer yes and call it a night when she felt a hand against her lower back. When she turned and saw Marlon, Elijah's cousin, her first instinct was to run fast in the opposite direction. The guy totally hit the top of her creep-o-meter. She swore every time she'd seen him out socializing, he was with a different woman. If the rumors were correct, the majority of those women were prostitutes. That thought had her quickly stepping away, making his hand drop to his side. *Ewww.*

"Marlon, I was just about to leave." She said, gesturing toward Dr. Vineberg and Estelle, who were both watching closely.

Of course, the first place that Marlon's eyes centered on was her chest. He licked his lips, and she wanted to cringe. He was so disgusting and inappropriate. She didn't want the Vinebergs to wait on her, plus who knew what obscene remark might come out of Marlon's mouth, so she hugged the couple and told them to go ahead without her and that she would make plans to call them in a few weeks.

Once they were gone, she turned back toward Marlon, crossing her arms, and staring at him.

He ran the back of his hand down her arm, making her drop her arms to her side. "What's with the attitude, baby?" He winked. "You and I could have a lot of fun together. After all, we're both here alone. What do you say, wanna dance back to my place?" He reached for her hips, but she was too quick and pushed him away, putting some much-needed space between them.

"Not interested." She stated curtly and gave him a dirty look. He smirked, but thankfully he backed off.

"Soon enough, you'll come to your senses and realize what you're missing."

She held back her eye roll at his idiotic comment. Marlon had been sniffing around since she started working for Elijah. But his words and tone of his voice sent an uneasy vibe up her spine. It wasn't so much of a threat but rather a promise.

He pulled a thick white letter envelope and a larger envelope folded in half from his suit jacket. "I need you to give these to Elijah. It's important. I thought he was coming tonight."

"He was here but had to leave. I can make sure he gets it tomorrow." She said as he handed them over to her.

Marlon shook his head. "No, he needs it tonight."

"Tonight? It's almost eleven o'clock. If it's that important, you take it to him."

A sleazy smile spread across his face. "I've got other plans to make now that you won't join me." He winked again, and she wanted to smack him upside his head.

"Where am I supposed to drop this off? I don't even know where he lives."

"Well, you told those people he was meeting a client. You can swing by the clinic on your way home."

"And, if he's not there by the time I get there?"

"Just leave it on his desk. Be sure you text me so I can let him know."

She hated knowing the scumbag had her phone number. She knew that Elijah hadn't given it to him. Knowing him, he snooped and got it from the personnel files. But if this got her away from his clutches and out of the event, she was all for it. She grabbed the envelope.

"Thanks, doll." He winked again and walked away like a cat on the prowl, seeking out his prey for the night.

She took a deep breath and exhaled. She strongly considered saying fuck it and would give Elijah the damn envelopes tomorrow morning at the office. But knowing Elijah was expecting the delivery, she'd suck it up.

She had almost made it out of the hotel when another voice called her name. She mumbled under her breath. Why now, when she was trying to leave, did everyone want to talk to her? Turning in the direction of the voice, she almost stumbled in her heels when she made eye contact with Terek. *Oh, for heaven's sake.*

As he moved toward her, she felt her belly tighten. He didn't look happy, and she didn't need any bullshit—not tonight.

As Terek stepped closer, she tilted her head to look up at him. He had let his hair grow out a little more than usual. It didn't matter because he was still good-looking. She shook her head. What was she thinking?

"Terek, I was just on my way out," She told him, hoping he'd get the hint that she didn't want to stick around and reminisce.

"I am too. I'll walk you out." He said, taking her elbow and leading her toward the exit as if he was in a hurry. When they were outside, he didn't stop at the valet. She protested, but he ignored her and guided her down the sidewalk away from everyone waiting for their cars. Once they were at a distance from others, he turned her to face him.

"What did Marlon want with you?" He demanded, and not in a friendly way. He looked fierce. His hard expression reminded her of her brother when something upset him.

"You know him?" She found herself asking him.

"I do, and he is not someone I would expect you to associate yourself with."

"Well, it's a good thing I'm not then, right? He's Elijah's cousin. I only know him from the clinic." She fired back at him with a little attitude. Sure, she didn't care for Marlon, but what was it to Terek whether she knew the man? She didn't have to stand here and explain anything to him. She was a big girl who could take care of herself.

"Well, what did he want?" He snapped as if he was getting annoyed with her, and it really pissed her off. She almost opened her mouth and told him what Marlon really wanted—her in his bed, but she clamped her mouth shut and instead held up the envelope in her hand.

"He asked if I could drop this off to Elijah," She looked away, but when she looked back up at him, he seemed to be biting the inside of his cheek.

"Terek, what is with the third degree?"

"Are you seeing Elijah?"

"What?" The line of questioning was now getting ridiculous.

"Are you seeing Elijah, yes or no? Because the way he had his hands all over you tonight, he was clearly making a statement to every man in that room that you were his."

She stared up at him in disbelief. Was he jealous? Why would he care? He had been screwing some other woman behind her back.

"Who I do and don't sleep with doesn't concern you anymore." She shook her head. "I don't have time for this. Good-bye." She turned to walk away.

"Mia...dammit, wait." He grabbed her arm and spun her around. She jerked out of his grasp. He shook his head and ran his hand down his face as if he was frustrated. "Look, I'm sorry. I just don't want to see you get hurt."

"What are you talking about? Why would I get hurt?"

"Despite what happened between us, I still care about you. Just be careful. You don't know Elijah like I do."

"Terek, Elijah is just my boss, okay?"

"So, you aren't involved with him?" He asked, looking instantly relieved.

"No, dammit! It is strictly a working relationship." At least, that is what she considered they had. However, Terek wasn't wrong; after being on the receiving end of Elijah's flirting, he may beg to differ. But she didn't want to talk about Elijah. "Look, Terek, I'm tired and just want to go home."

He grinned at her. "Want some company?"

"You are such an asshole."

He chuckled. "I'm just kidding." He cupped her cheek with his large callused hand and looked into her eyes. His gaze was intense but also held a look of concern. "I am not kidding about Elijah. Be careful and watch your back."

She went to ask what that was supposed to mean, but her car pulled up, and Terek released her, but not before he hugged her and kissed her cheek. He opened the car door.

"It was nice seeing you tonight. Maybe one day, when my workload isn't keeping me occupied, you and I can get together and just talk. There is a lot I need to explain to you. Actually, I owe it to you."

It was almost as if he spoke in some type of cryptic code. She really didn't want to meet him, but maybe it was something he needed to do to

33

move on. She had certainly moved on, and hopefully, after Thanksgiving, she would officially have herself a new man.

He leaned down and kissed her cheek, and again, she felt nothing.

"Bye, Mia."

"Bye, Terek."

CHAPTER FIVE

Alex pulled on one of Ace's t-shirts before walking out of the bathroom. Her alcohol buzz from earlier had worn off. Ace had already showered and was lying on the bed with his hands laced behind his head, staring at the ceiling. From the serious look on his face, she knew something was on his mind. She smiled, knowing she could take that look off his face by just removing her shirt. He did look scrumptious, laying there in only his boxer briefs that molded against his muscles. That thought was short-lived the moment he turned his head and his eyes met hers; she knew sex was going to have to take a back seat because it was obvious he needed to talk.

She climbed into bed and curled into his side. He smelled so good.

"How can I help?" She asked but didn't get an immediate response, so she waited him out.

"Do you think Stitch is good for my sister?"

Alex closed her eyes and smiled. *Finally!* She thought to herself.

"I love Stitch like he's my own blood, and if I had a sister, I'd be very happy if she chose someone with a reputation and character like him."

"This sounds awful because Stitch is like a brother to me, but I think I'm trying to find his faults." Ace admitted.

"And, how is that working out for you?"

"I got nothing." He admitted and blew out a breath.

"Then I think you have your answer. As long as they're happy, be happy for them. I've watched your sister and Stitch for close to a year now, and I really believe they are good for each other. Any time either of them walk into a room where the other is, both of their faces light up."

He wrapped his arms around her and rolled her to her back. He nudged his thigh between her legs and let some of his weight press her to the mattress. Now, this was what she had in mind; she smiled up at him.

"You're amazing," He told her, and she rolled her eyes. He cupped her cheek, tracing her bottom lip with his thumb. "I'm serious, Alex. I still don't know how I managed to find you, but every day I wake up, and I thank god for putting us together on that mission. I love you so much."

She ran her hands up and over his shoulders. Even with his battle scars, his body was a work of art.

"I love you too."

He kissed her again, and she wrapped her arms and legs around him.

"I need something," she told him.

He raised an eyebrow, and she gave him a coy smile.

"What?"

"You inside me."

He smirked. "I think I can oblige."

"Good, because I am about to explode."

CHAPTER SIX

"Is tonight's shipment still on schedule?" Elijah asked Claus as he sat at his desk, reading over the stack of paperwork in front of him and making sure everything was aligned for the cargo to leave. He hated to leave the gala early, but a lot was riding on this shipment, and he needed to make sure it went off without a hitch.

Claus looked up from his phone and pushed off from the wall. "As long as your dipshit cousin comes through with the documents in time, we'll make it." He walked over and took a seat across the desk. Claus played multiple roles within Elijah's business network and was the only person who Elijah trusted with his life and business.

Elijah studied the pictures scattered across his large desk. He hadn't been lying when he told Mia he had to leave to meet a client. It just wasn't a client that Mia thought of. The so-called client was a member of the puppy trafficking ring that Elijah had formed a few years ago. The guy was meeting Elijah at the clinic to pick up the puppies that were in the kennels. Some were the same puppies that Mia had helped examine. He felt awful lying to Mia, but there was no way she could know the truth. It was best she just believed the puppies were abandoned and eventually adopted out.

Elijah had a turn-key operation that made him millions. Each week, puppies arrived from various foreign countries. Elijah would match each canine with forged birth and vaccination documents before being shipped to eager buyers across the country. The buyers were clueless about the puppy's background. The papers provided to the new owners verified their puppy was born in a small town just outside of the City.

He had a warehouse across the Hudson River in New Jersey. The warehouse's interior mirrored a large scale kennel that included two exam rooms stocked with various veterinarian supplies and equipment. Within the last three months, Elijah purchased several warehouses in coastal states near seaports, with hopes of expanding the trafficking business to include shipments to overseas. In fact, his first overseas shipment was tonight's shipment.

Last night had been a close call with Mia when he and Demitri brought the Blue French Bulldogs to the clinic to examine. There were times when he brought a litter to the clinic after hours to give them an exam, and it wasn't unusual to find abandoned puppies in the city, so using that cover worked for his explanation to Mia.

Puppy trafficking was a growing business, and it was Elijah's main source of income. He didn't become a multi-millionaire by just owning an animal clinic. The clinic was a front to cover his ass while he conducted business.

With Mia being hired on at the clinic, she'd been able to cover many of the hours he would have had to work, letting him focus more on the business currently at hand.

He sat back in his chair and reached down to adjust himself. Just thinking about the gorgeous doctor made his dick hard. He couldn't get the image of her in that white dress out of his head. The material clung to every delicious curve her body offered. He couldn't resist touching her silky, smooth skin every chance he got. She was enticing. Not only was she beautiful, she had a brilliant mind. He was twenty years her senior but damn if that would stop him from sinking his dick into her when he got the chance. And he would eventually. He laid some groundwork at the gala by sticking by her side most of the night, along with the few hints he dropped here and there in conversation.

He pictured her splayed out naked, against his satin bed sheets. She had a set of legs he would love to have wrapped around him while he pounded in her petite body. He itched to run his fingers through her jet-black hair as those big brown eyes framed by thick black eye-lashes gazed up at him in lust. He was a dominant lover who enjoyed delivering a little pain to his women. But with Mia, he needed to tread carefully and not come on to her too fast. The last thing he wanted to do was scare her off. With the profit he was bringing in, he couldn't afford to lose her at the office. Eventually, once his bank account hit a magic number, he'd shut it all down and live the rest

38

of his life jet-setting around the world. And if he played his cards right, he would have a stunning woman to keep him company.

Usually, Claus handled all of the shipping logistics, but because of a tip from a source inside the NYPD, he had to change tactics with the puppies' storage and movement. The police had beefed up their patrols along the docks, specifically the rows of warehouses, due to an uptick in crime in the area. Just last week, the cops exposed a massive crack cocaine ring in a building two blocks over from his warehouse. He wasn't willing to take the chance of getting caught, so that was why there were currently sixty puppies in the basement of the clinic. A truck was on its way to pick them up and take them to the shipyard to be loaded onto a cargo ship. The ship had a secret compartment in the bottom of it where the puppies would be stowed during transport. Once the ship was off the coast of Portugal, it would anchor, and the puppies would be offloaded and transferred to a private boat then taken to a location where they would be inspected before being put on the market.

He looked at his watch and again wondered where in the hell Marlon was. The ass-hat should've arrived by now. Marlon had a connection to a guy who handled all of the paperwork needed for the puppies. The guy was instrumental in keeping the business flowing without having to worry. Knowing Marlon, he probably had his hand up some woman's dress. Marlon never went a day without fucking someone.

Elijah was also aware of the way Marlon had been eyeing Mia lately. Every visit to the clinic, Marlon made sure he got the opportunity to see Mia. His blatant actions were starting to piss Elijah off. If Marlon continued to show an interest in Mia, he would have to step in and give Marlon a warning to back-off.

He was ready to tell Claus to get Marlon on the phone when the back door opened and then slammed closed. "About fucking time," Elijah mumbled under his breath. Only it wasn't Marlon's voice he heard. Instead, a woman's voice penetrated the quiet office space. He looked at Claus, who was already up and out of the chair, walking toward the doorway.

Elijah couldn't make out what the woman was saying. He motioned to Claus to stay quiet as they both stood in the doorway and listened. It was difficult to hear, given they were at the opposite end of the hallway. The woman mumbled again, and Elijah nodded his head in the direction of the reception area. Claus went first, and Elijah followed close behind. Since nobody should have been in the building this time of the night, both he and Claus had their hands on their firearms. As Elijah entered the waiting room, he almost faltered the same time his jaw hit the floor.

He recognized the ass that was bent over the reception desk. His cock hardened at the sight of her backside, pressing against the silky material. Mia stood out like a million bucks. He wanted nothing more than to keep her bent over that desk and fuck her until she came screaming his name. She was literally testing his patience.

Getting his thoughts under control quickly, he cleared his throat. Mia jumped and shrieked. She turned, holding her hand over her heart.

"Elijah! Holy shit! You scared me."

He saw he truly frightened her with how wide her eyes were and how fast she was breathing.

"I'm sorry. I was in my office when I heard the door and came out to see who it was." She glanced over at Claus as he holstered his weapon. Mia knew Claus carried a weapon, so her seeing it hadn't been a complete surprise.

"What brings you by? I thought you would still be at the gala."

She dropped her hand and huffed dramatically. He fought back his laughter because she looked so flustered. It was cute.

"I ran into your cousin as I was leaving, and he insisted that I drop these off to you tonight. I didn't see any lights on and thought you had left already, so I was writing you a note and going to leave everything on your desk. But since you are here, these are for you."

She passed him the two envelopes, and he gritted his teeth to hide his anger. How in the hell could Marlon be so stupid and irresponsible to put something this important in the hands of an innocent? Hell, all it would have taken was for the envelope to open, and his little operation would have been exposed. He'd be facing jail time for probably the rest of his life.

He handed the envelopes to Claus, who turned and walked back toward the office. Elijah knew he'd start finalizing the paperwork so they'd be ready when the truck arrived. They only had a small window of time to get the puppies loaded on the ship.

He turned back to Mia. "Thank you, and I'm sorry that my cousin dumped his responsibilities onto you. That was irresponsible of him."

She waved him off. "It's fine. It actually gave me a legitimate excuse to leave the gala."

He frowned. "Didn't you enjoy yourself?"

"Oh, I didn't mean for my words to insinuate I had a bad time. I definitely enjoyed meeting everyone you introduced me to. Plus, it allowed me to get all dressed up," She said as she smiled. "I'm just really tired." She followed up, and now he wondered if he had been working her too hard. The last thing he wanted was for her to be unhappy and ultimately drive her away. An idea hit him. She was planning on spending the Thanksgiving weekend with her brother—maybe offering her a few extra days of vacation would be beneficial. He wasn't sure where her brother lived as she kept her personal life well-guarded. He did overhear her talking to Willow, the receptionist, and thought she mentioned her brother was in the military. It would be easy to get details out of Willow, though with the information he uncovered today, Willow's time at the clinic was limited.

Suddenly, the sound of a door banging behind him had him spinning around, and his eyes widened as one of the larger puppies jumped through the doorway leading up from the basement. The whining and grunts of puppies traveled up the stairs. Claus came running out of the office and scooped up the small white and gray puppy before heading to the basement and closing the door behind him. Elijah's heart raced as he tried positioning his body to block Mia's view, but it was too late.

"Elijah, was that a dog?" Mia asked, trying to look around him, but he reacted quickly, placing his hands on her waist and pulling her back in front of him. He played it off as he glanced over his shoulder, hoping the few

41

seconds would give him enough time to make up a justified excuse. "That little rascal was one of the puppies of the client I met here tonight. I have the litter downstairs in the spare kennel. I want to run some additional tests on them tomorrow."

She tilted her chin up at him and gave him a questionable look. "You have them in the basement? I thought you said there was nothing down there but storage. Why didn't you use the kennel in the backroom?"

"They have symptoms of Parvo, and without knowing for sure, I didn't want to put the other animals in the other kennel at risk."

"Oh no." She stated, and the look on her face told him she had bought the story. She relaxed a little, and he had to hide his smile because she hadn't pulled away from him.

"I think we caught it in time. With a little TLC, they should be fine."

She looked up at him and smiled, and he used the opportunity to pull her in closer. He heard her intake of breath as their chests met, and it aroused him. They were so close, and her light and sweet perfume drew him in. He couldn't stop himself as he lowered his head and pressed his lips against hers. As he started to kiss her deeper, she tightened up and immediately pulled away from him.

"Mia..." He started to say, but she shook her head and took another step back, closer to the door.

"Why did you do that?"

He closed the distance between them and clutched her chin. "I'm not going to lie; I've wanted to do that since I first laid eyes on you."

"You shouldn't have. I mean, we can't. It's unprofessional."

"Not if we both want it."

As much as he would have liked to stand there and convince her that what they could have between them would not be unprofessional, he was pushing it on time by her being around. The sooner he got her out of the building, the less chance he had getting busted.

"Mia, just think about it. You have a long weekend coming up. Try to relax, and we will talk when you get back."

He took her hand and led her to the door. As he pushed the door open, he brought her hand up to his lips and smiled at her wide-eyed and shocked expression. The woman was too smart not to realize they could be a power couple together. She would be foolish to turn him down.

"Let's get you home so you can get a good night's sleep, and I will see you tomorrow." He gave her a little nudge. As she walked toward the waiting car, she glanced his way one last time before getting in, and he waved. She didn't wave back before she closed the door. He watched as the car pulled out of the parking lot and down the street. Once it was out of sight, he took a deep breath. That had been too close. But, on the plus side, he discovered Mia was just as sweet on the inside as she was outside. She tasted so good that there was no way in hell he was going to let her slip away.

"Sorry about that, boss," Claus said, walking up to stand beside Elijah.

"No worries, I think we're okay. We just need to come up with part two to the story by tomorrow morning, because I can assure you that Mia will check on those puppies as soon as she walks through those doors," Elijah said as they walked back inside.

"I'll call our contact across town and make arrangements to make it look like we transferred the litter over there."

"That would be a good idea. There is another potential problem I need you to deal with."

"What's that?" Claus asked, raising a questioning eyebrow.

"Willow."

"I mentioned it to Demitri the other night. She's been poking her nose in places she shouldn't. I received a notification that someone tried to access a password-protected file I keep on my desktop. When I checked the log, it showed Willow's credentials were signed on to my computer in my office."

"What would you like for me to do?"

Elijah pondered the question for a moment. She'd been an employee for a couple of months now, but his gut warned him that something was off with her. He always trusted his gut. He shook his head.

"I don't trust her," He admitted. "There is something about her that strikes me odd. Have Oscar and Jules take care of her."

"Done."

Elijah hated to think any of his employees weren't loyal, but something didn't sit right with Willow, and he wasn't willing to chance it. She needed to go away.

The next day, Mia was dragging ass. It had been after midnight by the time the car dropped her off at her apartment. She thought about going straight to bed but nixed that idea when she took down her hair and felt all the goop her stylist used to make her hair stay in place for the evening. After washing and rinsing not once but three times to get all the product out, it had been well past one in the morning when she slipped into bed. Once she was settled under the covers, her mind wouldn't shut off.

Elijah had crossed a line that had Mia questioning her future at the clinic. He had made it clear what his intentions were, and she wasn't on board with them. She had a lot to contemplate. She loved her job, but if Elijah didn't respect her wishes, she'd be forced to leave. Normally she'd call her brother when she needed to bounce things off of him, but she wasn't so sure he was the best person to debate with on this one. He'd tell her to quit tomorrow. She rolled over and sighed. The long weekend couldn't come quick enough. She just needed to get through one more day, and then she could breathe a little easier. She smiled, knowing Stitch could probably ease some of the worries floating around inside of her head. The thought of him on her mind, she closed her eyes and drifted off to sleep.

When Mia arrived at the clinic, she went straight to the kennels to check on the Blue Goblins. As she entered the back room, she frowned when she saw most of the cages were empty, including the large bottom one where the French Bulldogs were.

Willow walked in, and Mia stood up.

"Do you know what happened to the Blue Frenchies that were here?" Mia asked her.

Willow nibbled her lip nervously. "Dr. Walters had them transferred to the rescue organization first thing this morning."

"And that's a bad thing?"

Willow looked around, again seeming nervous. Her behavior was off, and Mia wondered what was going on with her.

"Willow, is everything alright?"

"I don't want to talk about it here. Are you free tonight after work to meet me for a drink?"

"Sure. I just need to finish packing, and I really want to get in a run. Would eight o'clock work?"

"Yes, that works."

Willow then handed Mia an envelope.

"What's this?"

"Don't open it here. Bring it with you tonight."

"Ok," Mia said but wanted to question her further on why she was acting so secretive. She hoped everything was okay.

She walked into the breakroom and smiled when she saw her friend and co-worker Danny sitting at the small table eating his usual cheese and mayonnaise sandwich with a bag of sour cream and onion chips. How a person could eat the same exact food for lunch every day was a wonder to her, not to mention boring.

Danny was her only "real" friend in the city. The two had met when she was interning at Dr. Vineberg's practice. She and Danny had hit it off immediately. Their personalities were similar, although he was a little more outgoing than her. He was quite the character. He reminded her of a surfer dude with bleach blonde hair. He attracted women everywhere he went, but unfortunately, Danny wasn't interested in what they had to offer. He was more interested in his male counterparts. It always made her laugh when women would hit on Danny, and then he'd tell them that he was a fruit loop in the middle of cheerios.

Danny was also the only person besides her family who she had allowed in her apartment. He would apartment-sit for her when she traveled out of town, and sometimes he would crash there. She didn't mind. He was a neat freak, so she never had to worry about him messing up the place, plus he was a master in the kitchen. So, when he did spend the night, she could count on a gourmet meal for breakfast.

She plopped down in the chair.

"Hey, sweet cheeks." He said, smiling before taking a drink of water.

She unzipped her lunch bag and pulled out leftover baked chicken and mashed potatoes from two nights ago.

"So, how was Dr. Walters today? Has he asked you to come to his office for an important meeting?" Danny asked using air quotes. He smirked, knowing it annoyed her that people were beginning to think she and Dr. Walters saw each other outside of the office. Thank goodness nobody had seen him kiss her last night, although she did confide in Danny.

"Sorry to disappoint, Danny Boy, but I haven't really seen Dr. Walters, much less spoken to him today." And, what a relief if was. After his blatant show of possession last night, she had been a little worried about how he would act at the office in front of the other staff. He had told her last night they would talk when she returned from Thanksgiving, but it didn't mean he wouldn't try today, so she had hoped to avoid him at all costs.

Danny shocked her by placing his hand over hers. "Hey, you know I'm just messing with you, right? I know there's nothing between you two." She must have given him an odd look because he quickly followed up with, "The look on your face gave you away."

That didn't surprise her. She definitely didn't have a face for poker. She'd be broke before the game even began. Her mom and sisters always used to tease her that her face gave away her emotions.

She shook her head and smiled at Danny before stabbing a piece of chicken with her fork and shoving it in her mouth. Once she swallowed, she noticed he was still staring at her.

"What?"

He held up his hands in surrender. "Nothing. Nothing at all, but you do seem a little uptight today. Maybe a little late-night action could release some of that pent-up stress."

She couldn't help but laugh out loud at the way Danny gyrated his hips in the chair while making inappropriate sounds. But that was why she loved him. He could turn the shittiest day into a glorious one just with his personality.

She cocked an eyebrow. "I take it you're heading to Knots tonight?" Knots was an okay club not too far from her apartment. They played good music, and most of the patrons seemed normal. She had learned quickly that her idea of normal wasn't normal in New York City.

Danny played with his soda can. "I'm leaning towards it. Jasper said he would meet me there." He waggled his eyebrows, making her laugh again. Jasper was Danny's on-again, off-again boy toy. "So, do you want to meet me there? Oh, you can wear that new sparkle and shine dress you bought last week. You totally rocked it in the dressing room," He made a face then said, "Scratch that. Don't wear it because then all the men will flock to you, and I'll be left to slim pickings."

"I can't tonight."

"Hot date?" He asked. She never told Danny about Stitch. So he had no idea that she wasn't in the market for a guy.

She shook her head. "No, I need to finish packing, and I promised Willow I'd meet her for a drink."

Danny put his sandwich down and wiped his mouth with the napkin. "Speaking of Willow, have you talked to her today?"

"I did this morning. That was when she asked if I could meet her tonight for a drink. She mentioned she wanted to talk with me about something."

"Did she seem off to you?"

"By off, do you mean acting nervous like something or someone was going to jump out and scare her?"

"Yeah. Weird, huh?"

Mia shrugged her shoulders. "I'll find more out tonight when I meet up with her." Mia didn't tell him about the envelope that Willow gave her. It definitely piqued her interest.

"Well, if you change your mind about Knots, I'll be there all night."

"We'll see." She replied and finished up her lunch so she could get back to work. She planned on leaving the office on time.

Mia breathed heavily as she slowed her pace to a recovery jog. It was chilly out, but a good run always felt refreshing and was exactly what she needed after the last few days. She had a lot of stress she'd been carrying around, and the cardio workout helped to defuse some of it.

She came to a bench along the pathway and stopped to stretch her legs out. She needed to get back into her running regiment, but with the amount of hours she spent at the clinic, she'd be lucky if she got two days of exercise in. During her run, she decided to use the upcoming break from the office to ponder her future at the clinic. Sure, the money was good, but she now felt awkward around Dr. Walters, which wasn't how she wanted to feel every day. The rest of the day at work, everyone had stayed super busy, so Elijah hadn't had much spare time to talk to her. She hoped he realized that she meant it when she said he shouldn't have kissed her and that it couldn't happen again.

Claus had come into the office and stayed the afternoon, which was unusual. He seemed very focused on Willow the entire time, which was odd. Mia then wondered if that was why Willow wanted to talk to her. Maybe there was something between the two of them. Now that would be interesting, considering they each came from a different end of the spectrum. Willow was a sweet, kind, and shy person, whereas Claus was hard and very abrupt.

Her phone chimed, and she rolled her eyes as she pulled it from her armband. Terek had called her three times earlier in the day and sent her two text messages. She wasn't in the mood nor the right mindset to deal with him. She'd wait to call him back until after the holiday.

She swiped the screen, expecting to see another message from Terek but smiled when she saw the text was from Alex.

She shook her head as she read the text. Alex seemed just as excited as Mia was about getting together for the long holiday weekend. She laughed at the meme of a turkey holding a countdown clock showing the time remaining until Mia's plane arrived in Norfolk.

She was so engrossed in texting Alex back that she hadn't seen the man in the black ski mask approaching from behind. As she rounded the corner of the block her apartment building was on, the guy made his move. He grabbed her around the waist and lifted her off her feet. She screamed, but

48

he quickly clamped his hand over her mouth to muffle her cries. She kicked her legs and fought with him as he pulled her into the dark alley between her building and the building next door. Frantically she looked around, searching for anyone to get their attention, but the only thing she saw was a van sitting idle about twenty yards away, and her eyes widened in fear. She flung her arms up and hit the guy in the head. His hold loosened, but he didn't release her. When his hand fell from her mouth, she screamed for help. He lifted her again, and the van pulled up beside them, and the side door flung open.

"Get her in the fucking van." Another voice shouted, and Mia turned to try and get a look at him, but the guy holding her moved his hand from her mouth to her throat and squeezed.

"Make another fucking sound or try to fight me, and I'll break your pretty fucking neck." He spoke close to her ear with a prominent New York accent, sending a jolt of fear through her and making her still. She was thrown into the van and landed on her side. The pain momentarily stunned her, but that hadn't stopped her from trying to escape. As the big guy went to climb in behind her, she kicked him in the chest, and he fell backward into the alley. She scrambled on her hands and knees toward the door on the other side, but his partner was too quick and pounced on her, slamming her face down onto the metal floor.

"Get the fuck into the van!" He shouted to the other guy. Mia's head spun from the blow. Before she could focus, a blunt object struck the back of her head, and she fell victim to the darkness.

Mia's muscles seized, and she shivered as another bucket of ice water was dumped on her. It was the third time in the last hour or so. She had a massive headache, and if her body shook any harder, she'd knock over the chair she was sitting in. She was blindfolded which caused her to be surrounded in darkness. The hoodie she had been wearing had been removed along with her shoes and socks, leaving her in a long-sleeved running shirt and black running pants. Her teeth continued to chatter, and she felt the goosebumps crawl along her skin. Wherever they had taken her wasn't

49

heated. She could feel cold air blowing in from an open door or window. The place had a musty, earthy smell that reminded her of a warehouse or basement. God knew there were plenty of warehouses in the city. That thought scared the daylight out of her. Who would find her in a warehouse? How would the police know which warehouse to search? She started to hyperventilate until a hand slapped her in the face. Her head rolled to the side. Everything felt as if it was happening in slow motion. Besides the pain in her head, she felt nauseous.

"Damn, are you sure this is the one the boss wanted?" A deep snarly voice said to the right of her. She envisioned the voice came from the big dude who had grabbed her initially. What had he meant by was she the one the boss wanted? Had someone been watching her? Had she been targeted? Another gust of wind blew in, and she caught a whiff of someone's god awful cologne. It wasn't one she was familiar with, but it was strong and pungent. Her stomach started to churn. She gagged and felt the bile rise.

"Shit! She's going to puke." Another guy said.

"Well, you're the dumb fuck who hit her in the fucking head instead of just using the damn needle." It was a different voice from the other two, and she started to wonder how many guys were surrounding her.

"I did give her the drugs."

"Yeah, after you had already knocked her out, genius."

She swallowed the acidy bile, and she took a deep breath. No wonder she felt the way she did. Not only had the asshole hit her in the head, he had injected her with some sort of drug.

The fear of everything hit her. She had to be brave. If she wanted a chance at escaping, she needed to be smart.

"I don't know what you want with me." She said in a low, shaky voice.

She felt a hand slide up her inner thigh and her body tensed up. *Why is this happening to me?*

"She's got some muscles on her." The guy said, and she tried closing her legs but couldn't due to the ties shackling her ankles to the chair.

"Please stop." She whispered.

"What was that, honey? You want more?" He laughed, and she shook her head.

"Hey, hands off the merchandise. You know the rules."

"Oh, come on, man." He cupped her breast, and she reacted by jerking her head and ended up smashing the guy in the nose.

"Fuck!"

The others laughed at him.

"Dude, I think she broke your nose."

"Yeah, real fucking funny."

She wasn't prepared for the blow she took to the stomach, knocking the air out of her. Then a backhand landed across her face, and her cheek exploded with pain. Her chair wobbled slightly, then suddenly she was airborne. She and the wooden chair slammed into the floor, causing the wooden chair to splinter on impact. Her body felt numb, and she wondered if she had broken any bones. She was in too much pain to even try to move, so she just laid still. The blindfold she was wearing had slid down a smudge giving her a little visibility of where she was.

Three guys were huddled on the other side of the room. Two of them looked to be tending to the guy's nose she had broken. She lifted her head and saw an open window just above where she laid. No wonder the place was freezing.

She stole another glance at the guys who seemed oblivious to her presence. Maybe they thought she was knocked out. She weighed her options. Did she stay, or did she try to make it out of the window? Before she could decide, she heard footsteps approach, and she tensed, waiting for another round of punches, but it never came. Instead, a hand slid over her ass, and she tried to keep calm, but then his hands slipped between her legs, and she clamped her legs together, trapping the hand between her thighs. Her head was yanked back when the guy grabbed a handful of her hair. She swore a chunk had been ripped from her scalp.

"You know you broke my buddy's nose."

"Maybe next time he'll know to treat a lady with respect." Mia had no idea where her brazenness had come from, but it felt good to say that. She wanted to say a lot more but was interrupted.

"Bitch, respect is the last thing any lady deserves."

He hit her face several times, and she tasted the blood as her lip split open.

"Please, stop!" She screamed as he kicked her hip. She tried to curl herself into a ball on the floor, praying for the torture to end. He didn't stop as she took blows to her shoulder blades and other areas of her back. She bit her lip to prevent from crying out in pain. Tears leaked through the material covering her eyes as she lay there, helpless on the cold floor.

"Knock it off, asshole!" Someone shouted, and the man stopped, but not before giving her one last hard kick to the back of her thigh.

"Hey man, we were just following the boss's orders." The guy chuckled. "We may have gotten a little carried away, but we wanted to have a little fun. It would be a shame not to fuck the little beauty before we had to off her."

Mia heard a grunt.

"Why did you punch me?"

"Just shut the fuck up. The boss is not going to be happy with what you've done. Go load up the truck."

"What about the bitch? We can't just leave her."

The guy looked over where Mia laid motionless on the floor. "She ain't going anywhere. Come on, we've got a shit ton of materials to load, and I don't want to be here all night."

She heard a few mumbles, then footsteps followed by a door slamming.

She panted hard, and each breath was as painful as the previous one.

The material tied around her head had slid up a little more, and she saw there was no one around. She waited a little longer to listen for any sign that the men were still inside the building. She took another peek under the slit of her blindfold and confirmed the coast was clear, but there was no telling when they would return. If she had a chance to escape, now was her moment of opportunity. She couldn't hesitate. It was now or never.

She slowly rolled and tried sitting up, which was a hard task with her hands still tied together. It was a small movement, but so painful. She ached all over. She channeled a phrase her brother used to say to her when she needed a good push. *"If you want something bad enough, you'll do whatever is needed to succeed."*

Repeating those words to herself, she reached up with both hands and grabbed hold of the window sill above her, and pulled herself up. She didn't waste time as she slid the remainder of the window up. She shivered as the cold air hit her wet clothing. She wasn't sure which way would be easier on her body to get out. She didn't have a lot of options, nor did she have much time to debate it, knowing she could have company any second.

She pushed past the pain and slid onto the window ledge, then swung her legs over the side. She tried to push the blindfold off her head, but it was tied too tight. She was lucky she had a little bit of vision. When she looked down, she hadn't realized how high up she was. She estimated she was maybe ten to fifteen feet above the ground. She bit her lip, knowing the landing would hurt, and there was a high probability she could break something. The only thing she had going for her was the cluster of bushes below to help break the fall.

She didn't give herself any time to think about it as she held her breath and shoved off the ledge. She overshot her intended landing zone, and as soon as her feet hit the loose gravel, she toppled over onto the ground and cried out in pain, immediately grabbing her ankle. In the distance, she could hear the sound of water and realized she was near the river.

She heard the engine of a car, and her heart hammered in her chest. She needed to find cover. Just as she got herself up onto her knees, a set of headlights rounded the corner and were headed straight toward her.

"No, no, no." She whimpered as she tried to crawl across the gravel. The tiny chards of rocks dug into her skin.

The headlights grew brighter, then suddenly she was blinded by them when the person clicked on the high beams. She felt so weak and was in too much pain to continue, and she collapsed to the ground just as the vehicle skidded to a stop inches from her. The car door opened, followed by heavy footsteps that grew louder with each step. "Oh, dear god." She whispered.

A hand touched her cheek, and she flinched.

"Fuck!" A guy with a heavy English accent stated.

He was right next to her head. She could feel the warm puffs of air as he spoke in her ear.

"I promise I won't hurt you. I'm going to get you out of here."

The rope around her wrists loosened, sending her blood flowing to her numb hands and fingers. She couldn't see a damn thing because the material had slipped back down, covering her eyes.

"Please, help me." She rasped out as the man gathered her in his arms and started walking. A burst of warm air hit her skin. He lowered and placed her on what she assumed was the backseat of the vehicle before covering her with a blanket.

She reached up to slide the blindfold off, but he stopped her.

"Sorry, love. You need to leave that on," He told her, pulling her hands away from her face. She didn't understand. He had helped her. Why couldn't she see him? Her body went rigid. Unless he was part of the crew that had kidnapped her. Before she could fully panic, she felt the pinch to her neck, and within seconds she was fast asleep.

Mia slowly awoke. She felt groggy, her mouth felt like it was full of cotton, and her head pounded, making it painful to open her eyes. Fighting through the discomfort, she pried her eyes open enough to focus on her surroundings. Even though the room was dark, it had a familiarity to it. The blanket covering her was soft like butter, reminding her of the Vera Bradley throw blankets she kept around her apartment.

She laid there for a moment, trying to get her bearing. As she stared up at the ceiling, she focused on a large dark spot that resembled a similar water spot she had on her ceiling when a pipe in the apartment above hers busted and water leaked through. She suddenly realized why this place felt familiar—it was her apartment. Had everything that happened been a dream?

She shot up off the couch and cringed, feeling the pain all over her body. She fell back into the plush leather and moaned. She reached over and flipped on the lamp that sat on the table next to the couch.

She had so many questions—questions she knew she didn't have the answers to. The last thing she remembered was that a good Samaritan had found her, and being wrapped in warmth. How had she ended up back in her apartment?

The fear she had experienced before came roaring back. Could the person be in her apartment right now? Who were they, and how did they know where she lived? She had lost her cell phone when she was picked off the street, and she didn't have any identification on her. Her body trembled in a combination of fear and adrenalin.

With no landline and no cell phone, she had no way of calling anyone. She looked at her watch and saw it was three o'clock in the morning. She hadn't been too far from her building when she had been abducted. Not knowing the range of operation between her phone and smartwatch, she tried to send her brother a text through the watch. It just spun, indicating she was out of range. Then she spotted her laptop on the coffee table. She could send a message to him through his email and send a private message to Alex through Facebook.

She reached for the laptop and noticed there was a note taped to it. Handwritten was a warning for her to get out of town as fast as she could, that she was in danger.

Fighting through the pain, she stood up. Where was she supposed to go? Her flight wasn't due to leave until ten o'clock. Could she go to the police? Another option was to leave for the airport and just wait until her flight left. At least she would be in the public eye. Police were always stationed at the airport; she could seek help there.

Her ankle was bruised and swollen. She could hardly put any pressure on it, but she managed to limp to her bedroom. She needed to change out of the wet clothes and get shoes. And she needed to do it as quickly as possible. After what she went through, she wasn't taking the stranger's warning lightly. She didn't want to be in the apartment any longer than she had to be.

She tried to clean up her face the best she could, but she was a mess. Her eye, cheek, and lip were all swollen and bruised. She changed into a pair of sweats and a long-sleeved t-shirt. Her ankle was too swollen to wear regular shoes, so she opted for a pair of flip-flops. It would have to do for now. She pulled her suitcase into the living room. She also had a backpack that she used for work she would take with her and her purse.

She stepped wrong, and her ankle gave way, and she fell into the coffee table, causing some magazines and papers to fall off.

"Shit!" As she started to gather the items to place back onto the table, something shiny under the table caught her attention. She looked closer and realized it was a key. And not just any key; it was the key that Stitch had given her to his cabin. She grabbed it and threw it in her purse.

Suddenly, the heating system kicked on, and the popping sound made her jump. With every creak she heard, she became more terrified. Just as she went to stand, there was a knock on her door. She didn't move a muscle and stared at the door. When the doorknob jiggled, her heart rate sped up. Were they coming back for her?

She panicked. She grabbed what she could carry, her backpack and purse, and as fast as she could move, she headed toward the window in her bedroom. She unlocked it, pushed it open, and was hit by a cold burst of air, but she didn't let it slow her down. She crawled out onto the rickety metal fire escape, and slowly and carefully made her way down the eleven flights.

When she made it to the bottom, she started walking down the block and then flagged down the first cab she saw.

Once she was safe inside the vehicle, she told the driver to head to Newark Airport.

As the cab drove through the city's quieter streets, Mia leaned her head back against the seat and tried to process what in the hell was going on. She thought back to everything, but she just couldn't shake off a comment one of the guys made. The "boss" had sought her out.

A sickening feeling hit her gut. If she had been targeted, it was possible whoever was responsible for her abduction and beatdown could be tracking her. After all, someone close to the situation knew to warn her. Could they know her travel schedule and that she was going to visit her family? Tears hit her eyes. She couldn't put her friends and family in danger. She could never forgive herself if someone were injured or worse because of her. Her head hurt even to think, but she was facing a dire situation.

Nobody would expect her to take a bus. She could pay cash and probably get away using an old fake ID she still had from college. She dug through her purse to see how much cash she had on her. She counted two-hundred-twenty-seven dollars. Bus fares weren't that much. She could surely afford a one-way fare. As she folded the money and tucked it in her wallet, she noticed the silver key she had thrown into her purse. It had landed in one of the side pockets. But the way it was positioned and stood out is what had caught her eye. Any other time she threw something into her purse, it fell into the deep black hole at the bottom and would sit there until she cleaned her purse out. This particular key had landed in the smallest side pocket, standing straight up, so when you open the bag, you couldn't help but see it. She began to wonder if it was a sign. Could this key be the lifeline she needed to help her escape and ward off any danger to her family?

Stitch's cabin would be empty right now since he was spending Thanksgiving at Ace and Alex's. It'd be the perfect place to seek shelter until she could contact her brother. She'd look for one of those pay-as-you-go phones at the bus terminal.

With a plan in mind, she put it into motion. She tapped on the plexiglass, separating her from the cab driver.

"I changed my mind. Please take me to the Newark bus terminal instead?" She instructed the driver. With the nod of his head, he took the exit leading out of the city, and hopefully, taking Mia one step closer to safety.

CHAPTER SEVEN

Ace stared at his phone in shock as he read a text from his sister. Literally, his mouth gaped open in disbelief.

"Ran into trouble, may not make my flight. I'll call when I can".

What the fuck kind of message was that? He had heard his phone vibrate with a text around three-thirty in the morning, but at that precise moment, he was balls deep inside his fiancé, and when he saw it was Mia and not work calling him in, he decided it could wait knowing she was due to arrive this morning. But now, he wasn't sure.

The more times he read her words, the more pissed off he got. He dialed her number, and again it went straight to voicemail. He disconnected and threw the phone down onto the table, and ran his hands through his hair.

Alex looked over from the stove where she'd been all morning cooking. "What's wrong, honey?"

Ace looked up as Alex walked toward the table. "I don't understand Mia's message." He showed her the text message.

Alex's eyes widened, and she even looked confused. This was so not like his sister.

"When she says trouble, does she mean like real trouble?" Alex asked, and Ace could see the worry in her expression. Hell, he was concerned.

He shook his head. "I don't know. I've tried to call her a few times, but her call goes to voicemail, and texts I've sent go unanswered."

"What about your mom or sisters? Have they heard anything from her?"

"No, nothing."

"That's really strange. When Tenley and I talked to her the other night she seemed excited about coming down."

"Something is wrong. I just know it. Mia never misses a holiday. Plus, she's an explainer." Alex's look of confusion made him elaborate. "She likes to explain herself down to the very last detail, even though it annoys the hell out of me." He read the text to her again, and Alex drew her eyebrows in.

She reached out and touched his arm, and he knew it was a gesture of comfort. It was a quality that he loved about her.

"Maybe something came up with her job. She did say that she has been inundated at the clinic. From the sounds of it, she works from sunup to sundown. Maybe she was having second thoughts on coming down and wants to just chill by herself for a long weekend. I mean, it can get pretty crazy hanging with our little family," Ace gave her a sideways look, and Alex threw her hands in the air. "Hey, I don't know, I'm just thinking out loud." She got up from the table and walked over to the counter, and continued to cut up more vegetables. She looked over her shoulder, "Give Stitch a call; maybe she called him." Ace didn't miss the small smile on her face.

"Why would she call him?" He barked, causing her to turn around and raise an eyebrow at him, and she sighed.

"Maybe, because they talk on the phone and just maybe she mentioned something to him. We've talked about this, but I guess you just choose not to listen. You know, for someone who is so detailed-oriented in your day-to-day life, you sure are oblivious, or maybe just in denial to your surroundings here at home." His eyes widened at her smart-ass comment. He stared at her back while she continued to busy herself around the kitchen, getting things ready for dinner and for Irish and Bailey's small wedding ceremony that was taking place on their back patio before they all sat down for a Thanksgiving feast.

Damn, now that he thought about it, they'd held three weddings at the house within the past nine months. Shit, he should start charging a venue and catering fee, considering Alex orchestrated everything from decorating down to the food.

He shook his head, realizing he was getting off track. He wanted to focus a little more on this Mia and Stitch "thing." Was there an actual "thing" between the two of them, and he wasn't aware? No, surely, Stitch would have talked with him. At least he better had, if he knew what was good for him.

He gave Alex another look, this time giving her his best interrogator look. It was the one he used when he confronted an enemy who had valuable information he wanted. "How often do they talk?" And, damn, if her eyes just twinkled. He should have known better than to pull the SEAL routine with her. Alex was a born fighter and wouldn't back down from anyone or anything, including him. Before she could answer, the doorbell rang, bringing their discussion to a temporary halt. But he would get answers even if he had to play dirty to get them.

He pushed away from the table and stood, pointing his finger in her direction. "We are not done with this discussion."

"Whatever you say, Ace." She replied over her shoulder with a sassy smile as she watched him. He couldn't help but smile and shake his head. God damn, he loved her, sass and all.

CHAPTER EIGHT

Mia stepped off the bus and almost tumbled over when her ankle gave out. Thankfully, she was close enough to the bus to catch herself. The pain had gotten worse, and the ibuprofen she had taken a few hours ago had worn off. She had a couple of prescription pain pills left over from a dental procedure she had a few months ago, but she wasn't keen on taking prescription pain medicine. She and pain killers didn't mix well. They made her a little looney in her opinion before they'd knock her out for hours. That wouldn't bode well for her on a bus when she needed to make multiple transfers. Once she was at the cabin and behind locked doors, only then would she consider taking one.

At least she had made it to the small town, and it didn't appear that she'd been followed. She had watched people closely at each transfer station. Not that she would know what she'd do if someone had acted suspicious, but at least she was keeping aware of her surroundings.

She glanced around and saw through the window that there were some open chairs inside the small bus station. Her next obstacle was figuring out how she was going to get to the cabin from here. She assumed she could either uber or catch a cab. Neither one made her feel warm and fuzzy. She was skeptical of anyone right now. The problem was she still didn't have a phone. The two bus terminals with a small store inside them were out of pay-as-you-go phones. Hopefully, Stitch had a landline that she could call her brother from.

She hefted her backpack on her shoulders and hobbled inside. She ignored the stares from people. The bruising on her face had gotten worse. She had managed to make it all the way to the town using the excuse that she had been in an accident when people would ask what happened to her.

She carefully sat down and pulled her pant leg up to check on her ankle. It was twice the size it was when she left New York. She wasn't meant to even be walking on it. Once she made it to the cabin, she'd elevate it and ice it.

Thinking about the cabin, she fingered the key in her jacket pocket, making sure it was still there. That was all she needed, to get here and then lose the damn key.

She looked around, then noticed there was a taxi stand just outside the opposite set of doors. She was about to get up to head in that direction when Lena, the nice older lady she was seated next to on the bus, approached. Mia smiled, but that smile faded when she caught sight of the large man following Lena. Mia studied him as he neared. He was tall, about her brother's height, and with dark hair. He wore a pair of jeans with a button-down flannel shirt and coat. But when her eyes landed on the Sherriff's badge clipped to his shirt and the gun on his waist, she gulped.

She tried to put on her best smile as Lena stopped in front of her, but she couldn't keep her eyes off the Sherriff who stood beside Lena.

"Mia, I know you said that you were heading to your friend's place, but I was concerned about you taking a cab there. Not that this area is ridden with crime, but you are a pretty young lady, and well, I don't want to see anybody take advantage of you. And, it just so happens that our own Sherriff Prescott is here. Sherriff, this is Mia, the young lady that I was talking to you about that needed a ride to her friend's place."

Shit! Mia wanted to crawl into a hole and hide. The last thing she needed was the Sherriff all up in her business right now. She didn't miss the way the Sherriff studied her. He was more than curious. Of course he was; after all, she looked like she had been in a boxing ring with Rocky Balboa for a few rounds and came out on the losing end.

"Those are some nasty bruises." He said, not looking away, and reached out to touch her chin.

"She was in a car accident just the other day. Where did you say that happened again?" Lena asked.

Mia stared at the Sherriff and then nodded her head and took a step back. If she wanted to get out of this situation without the Sherriff wanting to ask more questions than she was willing to answer, then she needed to play along.

"New York."

"Hmm...that must have been a doozy of an accident." The Sherriff stated, and Mia felt bad for lying to him; after all, he was law enforcement. Then there was Lena, who had been nothing but nice and helpful since they met at the Maryland transfer station. But she couldn't trust anyone right now, and she certainly didn't need a nosey Sherriff getting all up into her business. Her brother would take care of things. That is once she was able to call him.

Mia forced a smile on her face. "Yes, sir, it was. But I'll be fine. As soon as I get to my friend's place, I plan on taking it easy for the next couple of days."

"Sherriff Prescott, do you think you could take Mia to her friend's place? If you're heading home, it's on the way."

Mia started to panic; she didn't want the Sherriff driving her anywhere, let alone knowing where she would be staying. She was hoping to just fly right under the radar.

"Oh, that's okay. I really don't mind grabbing a cab. I'm sure the Sherriff has better things to do than play taxi."

She looked up at the Sherriff, and he gave her a firm expression and squinted his eyes. There was no way in hell he had bought her story. Ace would get the same look when he thought someone was trying to pull the wool over his eyes. This guy was intense and fierce-looking, not to mention skeptical. Fuck a duck; she was screwed. If he was anything like Ace, there was going to be no arguing with him.

"Things don't operate the way they do in New York City, honey, and that includes getting a cab." The Sherriff said in a commanding tone as he turned his eyes on her, and she wished the floor would just open and swallow her. The conversation was turning into what her brother would call a clusterfuck. She shifted on her feet. As if sensing her unease, the Sherriff softened up a tad and stuck his hand out.

"Let's start over. I'm Sherriff Prescott, and I run this town. Well, I try to keep it civil." He smirked, and Mia couldn't help but smile as he was trying to be nice. She placed her hand into his rather large one.

"Mia." She responded, hoping that would be enough for the curious Sherriff.

"Hi, Mia. Welcome to Sugar Bend."

She swallowed hard as his eyes studied her face. There wasn't anything she could do to hide the bruises or the busted lip. Her throat seemed to dry right up like a summer day in the desert.

"Thank you, Sherriff." He looked at Lena and smiled. He had a great smile when he wasn't scowling.

"Lena, I'll make sure that Mia gets to her friend's house safe and sound."

She patted the Sherriff's arm, "Such a good man." She turned back to Mia. "You're in good, capable hands, dear. I hope to see you around town during your stay."

As soon as Lena was out of sight, the Sherriff turned his skeptical eyes back on her before he crossed his arms in front of his chest. Yep, exactly like Ace. She wondered if he ever served in the military.

"Honey, you are obviously in a lot of pain. First, what can I do to help you? Do you need a doctor?"

She felt the tears hit her eyes instantly. This guy didn't know a damn thing about her, and he was already offering to help her instead of interrogating.

She swallowed through the emotion. "No, sir. Like I told Lena, as soon as I can get to my friend's place, I'll be fine. But thank you for the offer."

"Who is this friend of yours, and where do they live?"

She contemplated giving him a false name, but he gave her the impression that he took care of his town and probably knew every person who lived here.

"Evan Watson."

The Sherriff raised his eyebrows and nodded his head. "Evan or Stitch, as most call him, is a good friend of mine. I didn't realize he was coming up here this weekend." He said inquisitively.

Oh, for crying out loud. Of course the Sherriff knew Stitch. "Oh, Evan's not coming." She replied, and the Sherriff's dark thick eyebrows went a notch higher. "I have a key to his place. He told me I could use the cabin." She pulled the key out of her jacket pocket and showed it to him. "See."

That seemed to appease the Sherriff because he nodded, but she still got a feeling he was going to press for more.

"Well, if you are ready, I'm ready. It's about a thirty-minute drive from here."

"Are you sure you really don't mind? I mean, it's Thanksgiving, and I don't want to keep you from your family."

He smirked. "I'm good, but thank you for your thoughtfulness. It's very kind of you."

She got her backpack situated on her shoulders again. "Do you mind if I use the restroom really quick before we leave?" She needed to give herself a few minutes before she got into the car with the Sherriff, because god knows what type of questioning she may up against. Plus she really did need to pee.

"Not at all. When you're finished, meet me outside. I'm going to pull the truck up closer to the door, so you don't have to walk as far."

"Thank you."

As soon as Mia disappeared into the restroom, the Sherriff pulled his cell phone from his pocket as he walked out to his patrol truck. Hitting the Stitch's number, he listened to it ring.

CHAPTER NINE

Memories were being made at Ace and Alex's house. After a short, simple, but beautiful wedding ceremony for Irish and Bailey, everyone had gathered around the three tables to enjoy the Thanksgiving feast that Alex had prepared.

Stitch looked around; he guessed there had to be close to fifty people in the house. How in the hell Alex managed to cook the amount of food she had was a wonder to him. But, then again, that was Alex. The woman could manage any task put in front of her.

All was quiet in the world, at least where he and the team were concerned, so that in itself was a blessing. Thanksgiving was his favorite holiday, so he was thrilled to be able to spend it with his family and friends who meant the world to him. The only downfall was Mia's absence. He had been looking forward to spending time with her in person.

Over the course of the year, he had fallen in love with Mia. Some people may say he jumped the gun, but he knew that Mia was meant for him deep in his heart. Ever since he found out she was spending the holiday with Ace, he'd been excited to sit down with her and cut through all the red tape keeping them apart, as well as discussing the best course of action in telling her brother. They were all adults, but Ace was very protective of Mia.

He grinned to himself as he watched everyone enjoying the food in the company of friends and family. A moment as such was what Thanksgiving was all about. Being able to celebrate with those you are thankful to have in your life.

"Honey, have you heard anything from Mia yet?" Charlotte, Ace's mom, asked her son, which got Stitch's attention. Anything about Mia these days got his attention.

Everyone was a little concerned about Mia's whereabouts. Stitch could also tell Ace was annoyed with the text she sent him. Ace wiped his mouth with a napkin and shook his head. "No, I haven't, and I don't know whether

I should be pissed off at her or concerned. The whole thing is just uncharacteristically, not like her."

"Is there anyone we can call and see if they could check on her? At least to put our worries at ease."

Ace turned his scrutinizing eyes on Stitch, and Stitch suddenly got a funny feeling in his gut, especially when he saw Alex's eyes widen as if she just had an "oh shit" moment. She almost pulled it off and tried to cover her expression when she picked up her glass of wine and took a drink.

"Have you heard anything from my sister?" Ace asked him, and suddenly Stitch found himself the center of attention as everyone paused mid-conversation to hear what he had to say. Christ, could this get any more awkward? He put his fork down and thought about how to respond.

"Why would you think I would know?" He replied, raising an eyebrow, wondering what was really behind Ace's line of questioning. Ace glanced at Alex, and Stitch swore he saw the corner of Ace's lip twitch, and he certainly didn't miss the twinkle in Alex's eye either.

"Well, you do talk to her, right?" Ace questioned.

There was no way Stitch could lie. It would be disrespectful, and Ace wasn't just a teammate; he was a close friend.

He licked his lower lip. "Occasionally," he answered vaguely.

"When was the last time you spoke with her?"

"When she was here last, right after the incident with Bailey." Stitch locked gazes with Bailey across the table from him. "Sorry, sweetheart, I didn't mean to bring that up."

The new bride smiled and winked at him. "That's okay, Stitch."

"That was weeks ago. Did she happen to mention anything to you then?" Alex asked, joining in on the interrogation, because it was beginning to feel a lot like it.

"No, but I could see she was stressed out. I asked her about it, and she vented a little. But you know Mia, she just smiled and said she'd get through it."

67

Alex touched Ace's hand. "Remember what I told you this morning, Ace. Maybe she really is burnt out and just needed some relaxation and not the craziness of being around all of us."

"Okay, I can understand that, but she could have at least called and told us that. But, no, she just sends a fucking cryptic text message then shuts her phone off."

Sienna, Irish's six-year-old niece giggled, and Ace looked at her and winked, "Sorry, sweetie, mark one down for me."

Irish looked between Ace and Sienna. "That's one, what?"

Ace grinned. "I was telling Sienna that was one for her swear jar."

Stitch couldn't help but smile either. Sienna had a swear jar, and for each swear word someone said, the person had to put a quarter in her jar. She had to have earned a few hundred dollars just in the short time she'd been living with Irish.

Sienna giggled again and looked at Irish with the most adorable face Stitch had ever seen. She was a beautiful little girl, and if you didn't know she was Irish's niece, you would think she really was Irish and Bailey's biological daughter. She had both Irish and Bailey's blonde hair and blue eyes. Stitch was so happy that Irish and Bailey had officially adopted Sienna.

"Uncle Ace gave me five bucks."

"For what?" Irish asked, looking back at Ace.

"For my swear jar, silly. I also got five bucks from Uncle Potter, Uncle Diego, Uncle Frost, Uncle Skittles, Uncle Stitch, and Uncle Dino." She said, gasping for breath at the end. Then she scrunched her little nose up and looked at Ace. "What did you call it again, Uncle Ace?"

Ace smiled. "An upfront payment."

She looked back at Irish and crossed her arms in front of her chest, appearing all sassy. "It's called an upfront payment."

The room erupted in laughter at the shocked expression on Irish's face. Apparently, he was unaware of his daughter's "savings" account.

Ace lifted his beer to his lips. "We all figured with the amount of cuss words spoken between us, five dollars each should suffice the swear jar, at least for tonight."

Irish looked between Sienna and the guys.

"How long has this been going on, and how often do you give her money?"

Stitch chuckled and slapped Irish on the back. "Pretty much every damn time we all get together and the kids are around."

"Holy shit! That's like every fucking week. Why am I just hearing about this?" Irish said, making eye contact with Bailey, and it made Sienna giggle again. She looked up at her daddy with hyer baby blue eyes.

"Daddy, you need to pay up." She told him as she held her little hand out.

"Fuck me…" He muttered under his breath as he tried to find a quarter in his pocket, but apparently, he said it too loud because Sienna's eyes lit up again, and Stitch knew what was coming. "Oh, screw this." Irish turned to Bailey. "Do you have five dollars?" He asked, and everyone in the room laughed as Irish handed over five one-dollar bills to Sienna, and she stuffed it into the little pocket on her dress.

Stitch was reaching for his drink when he felt his phone vibrate in his pocket. He was surprised to see Sherriff Prescott's name flashing on the screen. He was a good friend and a former Marine. Why the Sherriff was calling him now was a bit alarming. His first thought was something was wrong with his cabin as the Sherriff kept an eye on it for him.

Not wanting to be rude and take the call at the table, he excused himself and went out onto the back patio.

"Sherriff Prescott," Stitch said, answering the call.

"Hey, Stitch. Happy Thanksgiving."

"Happy Thanksgiving to you as well. What's going on?"

"Well, I have a little situation up here in Sugar Bend."

"And, you're calling me, why?" Stitch asked as he leaned against the deck's railing.

"Well, I just met an interesting friend of yours."

Stitch chuckled, thinking what friend of his could be in Sugar Bend, considering most of his good friends were inside Ace's house having dinner.

"Does this friend have a name?" He replied sarcastically because the only friend Stitch had in Sugar Bend was the person he was currently on the phone with. The name his buddy spoke next had him reeling back the laughter and going on instant alert.

"Does a Mia ring any bells? She claims you gave her a key to your cabin."

Stitch stood up straight and looked through the house's window where all of Mia's family and friends were enjoying the holiday. A million questions went through his mind. The main being, why in the hell would she be at his cabin when she was supposed to be here with her family? The hair on the back of his neck stood, alerting him that something was wrong. It was the same sensation he got when he was out in the field on missions right before things went to shit.

"Your silence tells me she is indeed a friend."

He licked his lower lip and pinched the bridge of his nose.

"She is, and yes, I did give her a key. But the funny thing is she's supposed to be here in Virginia Beach with her family. She sent her brother a very cryptic text early this morning saying she ran into trouble and might not make her flight. We've all been a little concerned, to say the least, considering she hasn't answered any of our calls or texts."

"Her brother?"

"Yeah, Ace is her older brother."

"Shit…" The Sherriff cursed in a tone that Stitch knew well. Whatever the hell was going on had the Sherriff upset.

"What's going on, Blake?" Stitch was already walking back toward the back door.

"Listen, I don't have a lot of time before Mia comes outside. I'm at the bus station here in town, and I just happened to run into one of the townsfolks who mentioned there was a young lady on her bus that possibly needed some assistance."

"Assistance? Damn it, Blake, what are you saying?"

"Look, I don't know all the details because she's not really talking, but she is claiming that she was involved in a car accident up in New York."

70

"A car accident?" Stitch noticed how the tone in the Sherriff's voice indicated he wasn't buying that story. "You don't believe her?"

"No, but I'll give her credit for trying. Her injuries are definitely not from a car accident."

The word injuries made Stitch stop his forward movement, and his body became rigid.

"What type of injuries are we talking about?" He asked in a low voice.

"In my opinion, it looks like she was involved in a fight."

Luckily Stitch was standing close to the house and grabbed onto the windowsill. Mia was one of the nicest, sweetest people in the world. Who in the hell would have hurt her?

"How bad is she, Blake?" He asked, gaining his composure back, although he was very concerned. Christ, Ace was going to bust a fucking gasket when he heard about this. Why hadn't she called someone if she was actually in trouble?

"Pretty bad. She's got bruising on her face, she's favoring her left side, and she's got a pretty bad limp, maybe an ankle injury. Not to sound mean, but she is a mess."

"Fuck!" Stitch yelled out, running his hand through his hair.

"I told her that I'd give her a ride up to the cabin. She was planning on catching a cab."

"Does she need a hospital?"

"She doesn't want to go. Personally, I think she needs to be checked out."

"Thanks for calling, man. Do me a favor, can you please let her know that you've spoken with me and that we are on our way? I'll give you a call when we get close. If her condition changes before we get there, take her to the hospital. Even if you have to drag her kicking and screaming."

"No problem. I'll hang around until you guys get here."

Stitch disconnected the call and stood there watching through the window as everyone sat around the table, smiling and laughing. It was exactly where Mia was supposed to be right now. He needed to talk to Ace. They needed to get to Mia quickly.

71

Suddenly, Alex's head popped up in the window; she was at the sink rinsing off dishes. Stitch tapped on the window and smiled when she jumped. It wasn't often you could scare or frighten a woman that went head-to-head with a terrorist. His smile died when he thought of Mia and the trouble she could be in.

He pointed at Ace, and she nodded her head in understanding. She walked over and whispered into Ace's ear. His eyes shot to the window, and Stitch motioned for him to come outside. Ace wiped his mouth with his napkin and set it aside on the table before giving Alex a quick kiss. He wanted that. He wanted a woman he could cater for and love. He wanted Mia.

Ace walked outside and closed the door behind him.

"It's fucking cold out here. What's up?"

"That was Sherriff Prescott on the phone."

"Blake from Sugar Bend?" Ace asked, and Stitch nodded his head as he bit the inside of his cheek. He was still pissed that someone hurt Mia and that she didn't call someone. "What did he want?"

"Apparently, your sister is on her way to my cabin."

"My sister, Mia?" Ace asked as he stood and crossed his arms in front of his chest. Stitch could see all of the questions forming in Ace's head.

"I don't have a lot of information, but she's in trouble, Ace."

"What do you mean she's in trouble?" He asked in a low voice but one that meant he wanted answers, like yesterday. Unfortunately, Stitch couldn't give him much, which he knew Ace wasn't going to be happy with.

"Blake thinks someone attacked her. She is injured. He doesn't know the extent of the injuries, although some are visible. She tried to tell him she was in a car accident."

"He didn't believe her?"

"No."

Ace paced the deck. His heavy footsteps against wood planks echoed in the quiet night. After a couple more paces, he stopped and stared at Stitch with his hands fisted at his sides.

"What are her injuries?"

72

"Blake said they're pretty bad. He thinks she needs to go to the hospital, but she's against it. He is taking her to the cabin."

"I don't understand. Why in the hell didn't she come here? Why didn't she call me? Or better yet, why didn't she go to the police?" He shook his head.

Stitch shrugged his shoulders. "I can't say what her reasoning was for not calling, but if you think about it, why would someone run and not contact anybody for help?"

Ace stared at Stitch. "You think someone may be after her? Shit, it's a three-hour drive to your cabin."

Just then, the back door opened, and the rest of the team walked out along with Derek and Tink. Tink was a former SEAL himself and one of Alex's uncles. Stitch and Ace explained to them what they knew.

"I can get you guys there sooner," Tink interjected into the conversation as he stood off to the side, listening. Tink owned an elite security business working black ops missions for the government.

"How?" Stitch asked.

"Did you forget my company owns two helicopters? I can call and have one fueled and ready by the time we get to the helipad."

"If someone is after my sister, then she could be a sitting duck up in the mountains all alone."

"Then let's go," Tink stated, pulling his phone out and making the call.

CHAPTER TEN

"Mia, are you sure I can't take you to the hospital to have a doctor examine you?" The Sherriff asked as he glanced over at her before returning his eyes to the road. Mia already had the same discussion with him before they even left the bus station's parking lot. He was very adamant about taking her to the hospital. She wouldn't have argued in any other situation, but it was too risky in her case. If she went to the hospital, her identity would be placed into the computer system, and any smart computer junkie could find her in a heartbeat. She couldn't have that. Stitch's cabin was the safest bet right now. The cabin had no connection to her family, so those looking for her would have to dig really deep to put the connection together to even think about heading this way.

When the Sherriff had told her he had spoken to Stitch and that they were on their way, she felt relieved. She was nervous as to how her brother and Stitch would react to seeing her injuries. Judging by the pain in her body, it could take weeks before returning to her normal self. Before she got into the truck, she had taken one of the pain pills. Hopefully, she'd make it up to the cabin before it took effect.

She looked in the Sherriff's direction. "I'll be fine once I get to the cabin and can lay down. But thank you."

She noticed the way his hands gripped the steering wheel, and he clenched his teeth. He wasn't happy, but it was her decision, so the remainder of the drive was in silence.

Her eyes had just started to close when she felt the truck pull off the smooth asphalt and onto a more rugged road. She became alarmed at how dark the area was. The only lights came from the headlights of the truck. It was creepy and eerie. She couldn't even see lights from any nearby houses. She wished she hadn't watched so many scary movies over the years because the imagery was like she was driving into one.

"Where are we?" She asked, trying to see through the darkness.

74

"This is a private road that leads to the cabin. Not many neighbors up this way. I'm sure that's why Stitch bought the place."

She looked back out the window into the darkness and was relieved that the Sherriff had been adamant about driving her. There was no way in hell she would have been comfortable here alone, especially with the circumstances surrounding her. Stitch's place was far from civilization. As if the Sherriff knew the crazy thoughts floating through her head, he said, "If you're not familiar with the area, it can get kind of creepy. Especially at night."

Yeah, no shit. She swallowed hard. Right before she answered, the truck came around a bend and merged onto a smooth, paved driveway that was lit up like a runway at a busy international airport. Her eyes followed the path of lights leading to a gorgeous two-story log cabin. She pressed her face against the glass as they pulled up and parked in front of the steps that led to the inviting wraparound porch complete with rocking chairs, potted plants, and even a porch swing. She hadn't even seen the inside and was already in awe. The porch swing had her name written all over it.

"This is beautiful. Are you sure we're at the right cabin? With all of the lights on, it looks as if someone is home."

The Sherriff put the truck in park and turned off the ignition. "Wait until you see it in the daytime. I'm jealous I didn't buy it when Old Man Larkin put it up for sale. Stitch has done a lot of work to the place to bring it back to its former glory. Starting with all the solar outdoor lighting he installed. Since he doesn't get up here as often as he would like, he wanted the property to appear as if someone lived here all year round."

She opened the door wanting to get a better look, but when she twisted to slide out of the truck, the pain that tore through her mid-section made her pause. She bit down on her lip to stop herself from crying out. How in the hell was she going to get out of this monstrosity of a truck? The damn thing was so high that the Sherriff had to lift her and set her in it. She tried to position herself differently, but the muscles still pulled and caused tremendous pain no matter what she did. She prayed she had no broken ribs.

However, she had heard that bruised ribs felt almost as bad as broken ones. If she wanted to get into the house, she would have to suck it up.

She held her breath and counted to three. When she got to three, she pushed off, but a set of hands on her thighs stopped her.

"Whoa, easy does it."

She glanced to her left and was met with a set of angry and concerned eyes of the Sherriff.

"Honey, let me help you out and into the house." She nodded, but then a thought hit her. And it was a crazy thought. She wondered if it was the medicine making her looney. But what did she know about this Sherriff? Sure, the townspeople seemed to fawn over him, but that could just be an act. She'd read in the news about individuals like him and how they use their power to manipulate people.

Once he helped her down, she stepped to the side, and in doing so, she tripped over her feet and almost fell. If it weren't for the Sherriff's quick reflexes, she probably would've ended up flat on her face. Not that it would matter because her face was already messed up.

She steadied herself before her gaze landed on his hard, penetrating stare with his hand resting on the butt of his gun attached to his hip. She swallowed hard.

"Are you okay?" He asked.

"Yes, I'm sorry." Oh geez, how could she explain to him what her thoughts were without either insulting him or pissing him off more than what he already seemed to be? He probably thought she was some nut case and wishing he hadn't offered to give her a lift. She took a painful breath.

"Let me start by saying I think my pain medicine is affecting my rational thinking. It's just that I don't really know you, and here I am getting into your truck and letting you drive me out into the boonies, in the dark. I'm mean, you could be a serial killer for all I know."

She was expecting some type of lecture, but instead, she was thrown for a loop when the big man threw his head back and roared with laughter.

"If it helps settle your nerves, I'm happily married to the love of my life, and we have two amazing little girls." He pulled a picture from his wallet and showed it to her.

"They're beautiful." She looked up at him and gave her shoulder a slight shrug. "I'm sorry. That was a ridiculous thought. Here you are being nice, and I'm acting ungrateful and so disrespectful."

"Don't be sorry. It's actually nice to see you are aware of your surroundings. Although it is a little late in the game, considering I already have you at the cabin." He raised an eyebrow at her, and she lowered her head. She felt so stupid.

She went to reach for her bags, but he waved her off, telling her he would get them. He followed, keeping his hand at her back as she walked up the steps to the porch. Jesus, just walking up five steps was like trying to climb a mountain. Her legs shook as they started to cramp. The Sherriff helped her with the last step. She inserted the key, unlocked the door, then disarmed the alarm with the code that Stitch had given her. She turned toward the Sherriff as he set her bag down next to the couch.

"Stitch and your brother should be here in about thirty minutes."

"I know it's Thanksgiving, and you probably want to spend it with your family, but would it be a terrible inconvenience if you stayed until they got here?"

"Not in the least," he nodded his head toward the couch. "Why don't you get yourself comfortable and get that leg up? I'll grab you some ice. Do you need anything else?"

"I think I'm good. Thank you again for everything."

"It was my pleasure. Go on and lie down."

She made herself comfortable and laid her head on one of the many throw pillows, then pulled a blanket draped over the back of the couch onto her. The chill she had was forgotten as soon as she got a whiff of the blanket's scent. It smelled like the cologne that Stitch wore. She inhaled the woodsy, spicy scent, and damn, did it smell good. She needed to find out what brand he wore and buy him a lifetime supply of it. Her eyeslids began

77

to droop, and within seconds she was overcome with darkness as sleep took over.

৵

Sherriff Prescott pulled an ice pack from the freezer and wrapped it in a dishtowel. He was angry. Actually, angry put it mildly. He was downright pissed off like no tomorrow. He wanted answers—to know the circumstances surrounding her injuries. Mia seemed like a sweet woman, and it upset him that someone had laid a hand on her. He knew Stitch and her brother well, and both were going to lose their shit when they saw the damage inflicted upon her. He almost went against her and drove her to the hospital. Granted, he wasn't a doctor, but anyone in their right mind could see she needed medical attention. His lips tilted upward. If she wouldn't go to the hospital, he'd have the hospital come to her. He pulled his cell phone out and sent a text to Doc O'Neal, the local town physician.

He walked back into the living room with the ice in hand and wasn't surprised to see she had fallen asleep. He couldn't help the small smile hearing her soft snores. The poor thing had to be exhausted. Traveling from New York by bus in the condition she was in was miraculous. He situated the ice pack on her ankle before fixing the blanket so it covered her whole body. His phone chimed with an incoming text from Stitch, letting him know they were fifteen minutes out. One of his deputies had met the group at the landing site and would bring them up to the cabin. He planned on sticking around because he wanted to hear Mia's story. Being the Sheriff, he was responsible for the town and its residents' safety, and if there could be trouble coming this way, he wanted to know so he could prepare.

While he waited for the cavalry to arrive, he made use of the time building a fire in the fireplace. After the fireplace glowed from the orange and purplish flame, he strode back into the kitchen and made a pot of coffee. He had a feeling they were going to need it. Once the coffee was brewed, he poured himself a cup, checked on Mia again, then went outside to wait. As he sat there on the porch, he scanned the darkness beyond Stitch's property for any sign of movement.

78

Stitch was a quiet guy, liked his space, so the Sherriff had to wonder just how important Mia was to Stitch. Stitch's cabin was his haven. He didn't allow just anyone up here. Granted, she was Ace's sister and probably knew him, but for him to hand over a key to her, she must mean something. Stitch was a hell of a guy. He was a loyal friend, respected SEAL, and shit, he deserved a good woman. He didn't know a lot about the woman currently sleeping inside, but he was a good judge of character. In his opinion, Mia seemed like a sweet, caring lady, maybe had a little stubborn streak in her, but obviously, she got caught up in a really bad situation. He hoped like hell that Stitch and the guys could get through to her.

Moments later, a set of headlights appeared in the distance. He stood and stepped down off the porch as the SUV came to a stop. Stitch was the first one out.

"Sheriff." Stitch said before glancing towards the house. The others got out, and everyone greeted each other. "She's inside?"

"Sound asleep on the couch. I texted Doc O'Neal. He should be here within the hour." The Sherriff could see the anxiousness in Stitch, and he couldn't blame him. "If you don't mind, I'd like to stick around until she wakes up and you guys talk to her. If there is a chance that trouble could be following her, I'd like to know and help where I can."

"Absolutely."

Ace then stepped forward, "I can't thank you enough for sensing she was feeding you a line of bullshit. Mia can be stubborn."

The Sherriff grinned, "No thanks needed. Your sister is a tough cookie. Exhausted, but to make it here in the condition she is in, she is tough. You guys can buy me a beer later."

Every step closer Stitch got to the front door, the more nervous he became. His body was practically shaking from the adrenalin surging through him. For the last hour, he had so many different thoughts and images of Mia running through his brain that it made his head spin.

He wiped his sweaty hands on his pants before opening the door. It was quiet except for the sound of the crackling fire. He looked over at Ace, who nodded his head for him to go first.

They made their way into the living room and came around the couch, and Stitch fell to his knees next to the sofa the moment his eyes landed on Mia's bruised face. Jesus, her eyes, cheek, and lip were all swollen and discolored. The blanket covered the rest of her frame, and quite frankly, he was afraid to see the rest of the damage to her body. Stitch took a couple of deep breaths to calm himself down. Ace, on the other hand, wasn't fairing too well. His eyes looked like they were about to pop out of his head, and his jaw appeared to tick.

"Jesus Christ." Ace spoke in a low voice, and Stitch could hear the pain and anguish. Stitch pushed a couple of stray hairs from her face. His fingers traced the bruising over her cheek. Whoever the fuck did this to her was a dead man.

"My God," Derek stated, followed by Tink's comment, "Car accident my ass. Those are fucking finger marks on her neck."

Stitch looked at the Sherriff, who stood behind the couch looking down at Mia.

"Were you able to get anything from her? Who may have done this?"

"No."

"She definitely needs to go to the hospital."

"I think so too, but she was very adamant about not going."

Stitch ran his hand through his hair. Mia was stubborn. She inherited that trait from her brother.

"Stitch, we need to wake her up." Ace told him, but part of Stitch didn't want to. She looked so peaceful lying there, but Ace was right; they needed answers, especially if there was a chance that someone could be looking for her. But more importantly to get a better understanding of what her injuries were.

Stitch gently rubbed her shoulder, and she moaned, causing him to pull his hand back. Christ, he was afraid to touch her. "Hey, Mia, come on, you need to wake up. It's me, Stitch. Ace is here too."

80

She started to stir a bit. "Stitch...Ace..." She said, and Stitch wasn't sure if her voice sounded froggy from her sleep or if her throat was injured.

Ace squatted down next to the couch, and Stitch gave him a little room. This had to be so difficult for Ace to see his sister battered and bruised.

Suddenly, Mia let out an earsplitting scream as her eyes popped open. She shot up off the couch and stumbled over the coffee table. Her unexpected movement had caught Ace off guard, and he fell backward. If it weren't for Derek standing nearby and able to steady her, she might have fallen into the fireplace.

"No! Let me go!" She shouted, trying to wriggler out of Derek's grasp.

She was stuck in a flashback or something, but before she hurt herself any further, Stitch called out to her in a loud, stern tone. "Mia, stop!"

Mia froze, and her teary eyes widened, then darted around the room. Nobody moved a muscle waiting to see what her next move would be. It wasn't until she locked gazes with Stitch that she realized her surroundings. She blinked rapidly then burst into tears as she sunk to her knees.

Stitch stepped over Ace and rushed to Mia's side. She grabbed onto him, clutching the front of his shirt.

"Your safe, baby. We're here now." He cooed to her as he rubbed her back. She buried her face in his chest, and he held her while her hot tears soaked through his shirt. He glanced around the room and met Ace's gaze. Stitch couldn't read his expression. He'd never talked to Ace about his feelings for Mia, and now was not the time to do so, but soon he would.

"Let's get you back on the couch." He said to her. She started to stand then yelped as her leg gave out, almost making them both fall. Thankfully, Stitch caught them both. He swung her up into his arms and walked to the couch.

Her body trembled as he held her. She had her eyes closed.

"It hurts too much to move." She cried, and his temper flared, seeing her like this. Knowing that some piece of shit with no respect for a human life did this to her pissed him off seven ways to Sunday.

❧

81

Not only was Mia in extreme pain, but she was embarrassed. She couldn't believe she had totally flipped out the way she had. But between the pain medicine and anxiety, the guys' presence had caught her off guard. She was on edge, and on the verge of passing out.

After several tense and silent moments, Mia's tears turned into hiccups as she tried to get herself under control. Now that her adrenalin rush had subsided, the pain seemed to spike to a level she could no longer tolerate. It made her sick to her stomach.

She laid her head against Stitch's shoulder.

"I don't feel well."

Stitch pulled her a little closer to him, and she wanted to melt into him. He caressed her back lightly, sending a feeling of warmth throughout her body.

He adjusted her on his lap, and the slight jostle caused enormous pain to hit her ribs, and she let out another yelp.

Stitch froze and looked down at her. "Jesus, Mia, where else are you hurt?"

All eyes were on her waiting for her to answer. She looked down at her hands that were clasped in her lap. Stitch lifted her chin, so she was looking at him. His eyes were so focused and intense, but beautiful at the same time.

"Be honest, Mia. Where else are you hurt?" He asked again.

The tears hit her eyes.

"Mia?" Ace started in on her.

"All over." She sniffled and tried to fight back the tears, but she couldn't. "They beat me all over."

Stitch hugged her to him, and she buried her face in the crook of his neck and cried. He slowly and gently caressed her back.

"I know this is hard for you, but we need to ask you a few questions." Stitch whispered into her hair.

She wiped her eyes and looked up at Stitch who brushed a stray hair off her bruised cheek. "I don't know who they were. They knocked me out once they threw me in the van."

"You don't know who they were? What did they look like?" Ace asked as he crossed his arms in front of his chest. Her brother was fired up.

"I don't. I was finishing up my run when two guys pulled me off the street. They were wearing masks, and when I woke up in the warehouse, I was blindfolded."

They asked her more questions, and she answered them as best she could. She explained how she managed to escape and then how someone, a stranger, came to her rescue, but at the same time offered her a warning.

She looked at her brother.

"I'm sorry, Ace. I tried to do what I thought was right. I didn't want to take the chance and put everyone in danger."

"I was so pissed off when I saw your text this morning."

Mia's head snapped up, and she looked at her brother with her eyebrows scrunched together.

"You got my text?"

"Yeah, it came through around three-thirty or so in the morning, but I didn't actually read it until later."

"That's interesting because I lost my phone during the scuffle with the men. I tried to send the text from my watch once I was back in my apartment, but it didn't go through because I wasn't in range."

"When you left and went to catch a cab, you must have been within the range of where you dropped it because I got it."

"Mia, can you describe the warehouse you were in? Or anything you can remember?" Derek asked.

"No, like I told you, the blindfold they had tied around my head was super tight and double-knotted. I was lucky it had slid up just a smidge so I could somewhat see what I was doing."

"What about the men? Anything descriptive about their voice, or build, maybe?"

"From what I could tell, there were three men. One of them came later, and he is the one who had stopped the one guy from beating me. I didn't catch any names, but again, they had drugged me with something, so my mind was a little slow and fuzzy. I did detect New York accents. The guy who grabbed me was really big; bulky, but not all muscle either. The other guy had a much smaller build. That's about it."

"What about the stranger you spoke of? The one who rescued you on the street. Anything descriptive about him?"

"He had an English accent. He was kind, but at the same time didn't want to reveal himself. I'm assuming he was the person who left the note."

Ace sat down on the coffee table in front of Mia. He took her hand.

"Do you have any idea what these guys wanted with you?"

She shook her head, and her emotions came flooding back, remembering they had plans to kill her.

"I don't know for sure, but I think I was targeted."

"You're positive you weren't just in the wrong place at the wrong time? That this wasn't a mugging or random assault gone bad?" Ace asked, and again she shook her head.

"I remember one of the guys mentioned that I was the one who their boss had his eyes on. He also said that it would be a shame to not fuck me before they had to off me."

The vein on the side of Ace's head pulsated, and his jaw became tense.

"They said they were going to kill you?"

"That's what they said."

Ace's eyes darkened, and his grip tightened on her hand. His nostrils flared, and she knew he was trying not to show his anger in front of her.

"Ace..."

He leaned forward and kissed her forehead. "All that matters is that you are safe now."

She was exhausted and in a lot of pain. She tried to relax her body against Stitch, but she couldn't fight the agony any longer. She hadn't even realized that tears were flowing down her cheeks until Stitch wiped them away. She felt so numb and confused. Why her?

"What is your pain level, on a scale of one to ten?" Stitch asked.

She closed her eyes and leaned against his muscular frame. "Twenty." She started to second guess her decision not to get checked out at the hospital. Before she could conjure another thought, Stitch stood with her in his arms and started walking. He said something to the guys, but she wasn't paying any attention. The only thing she wanted was another pain pill to knock her out.

≥

Stitch could feel how tense Mia was and knew she was in pain.

"Please don't let them find me again." She whispered. She was breathing heavily, and then her body started to tremble.

Stitch looked at Ace and could see the effect this situation was having on him. His eyes were glassy. There had been only one other time he'd seen his team leader come close to crying, and that was when they had found Alex beaten and shot in Afghanistan.

Stitch turned to the Sherriff. "When did Doc say he'd be here?"

"Should be here in about ten to fifteen minutes."

"Let's move her upstairs to the bedroom. At least there, she'd be more comfortable. I have some mild pain killers, but I would rather the doc check her out first."

Ace nodded his head and gave Stitch room as he started toward the staircase. Mia whimpered, burying her face in the crook of his neck and shoulder.

He felt terrible for causing her more pain, but it was important to get her comfortable, and it would give the doctor room to examine her.

Ace went up the stairs first.

"Which room?" He asked, and Stitch nodded to the left that led to his bedroom. It was the only room with a made bed, and the only room he wanted Mia staying in.

Ace opened the door and turned on the table lamp sitting on the dresser. He hurried over to the bed and pulled back the covers. Stitch then laid Mia down, but Mia wouldn't let go of him.

"Mia, drop your arms for me, please. We need to get your jacket off." She did as he asked, but she kept her eyes closed and turned her head. He looked at Ace.

"Help me get this off of her."

The two of them maneuvered the light jacket off of her.

85

"Oh, Jesus!" Stitch whispered as they raised her shirt to look at her midsection. She was bruised all over. Her beautiful olive skin was marred with black, blue, and reddish welts.

"Fuck! Do we take her to the hospital? This shit is bad." Ace admitted taking in the sight of Mia's immense bruising.

Stitch shook his head. "Let's see what doc says first. If he thinks she should go, then we'll work it out."

Ace looked on as Stitch cared for Mia. His heart was heavy, and he was full of emotions—sadness, anger, and helplessness. This was different from what he was used to dealing with. In his line of work, he rescued and protected people, but those individuals weren't his family. This ordeal brought back memories from when Alex had been kidnapped in Afghanistan. He never wanted to go through the worry of finding or protecting a loved one against the enemy again. Unfortunately, the world was filled with sick people who preyed on others, and there were no guarantees.

He knew Mia was scared, in pain, and he would move heaven and earth to take it all away from her.

He helped Stitch get Mia's foot propped up to try and help with the swelling.

"Ace, would you mind running down to get some ice, and then grab her bag on your way back?"

With a nod of his head, he exited the room and headed down the stairs. When he got to the bottom, Tink and Derek were still in the living room talking. When they saw him, Derek asked, "How is she?"

Ace blew out a deep breath and took a seat in the chair.

"I don't know how in the hell she functioned enough to make it here. If she doesn't have any broken ribs, it would be a fucking miracle."

"She was running on adrenalin."

"Where do we go from here? Do we contact the NYPD and file a report?"

"Actually, Tink and I were just discussing that. If what Mia said is true and she was targeted..." Derek paused and took a breath. "Ace, your sister could've been targeted for human trafficking."

"But Mia said one of the guys mentioned 'offing' her."

Tink shrugged his shoulders. "He could've been referring to as 'offing' her onto someone else."

"Shit!" Ace didn't even want to think about the possibility of Mia being pulled into a human trafficking ring.

"If she was picked out because of her looks like a specific order, it's possible these guys could still be looking for her. My company has worked many jobs taking down these types of people. They are sick individuals, but men and even women will pay top dollar to get what they want."

"She is tired, in pain, and on edge right now. My opinion is to let her get some sleep tonight. Maybe with some rest, she can think a little clearer and possibly remember any details she may have forgotten." Derek said.

Ace nodded his head. His commander was a hard man and took his job seriously, but Ace knew the older SEAL hated seeing one of the women close to the team put in danger.

"As much as I want to take her home with me and protect her, I think she made a wise decision in heading up here. This is a safe place for her for now. If these people are still looking for her and can connect her to her family, they could come to town looking around. I think the best course of action is to act as if we haven't seen her. Do either of you have any contacts at the NYPD?"

"I do," Tink said. "What do you have mind?"

"I think we should file a missing person's report." Both Tink and Derek gave him a questionable look. "Hear me out. By doing so, if someone is watching, they are going to see that and believe that we truly don't know where she is. This can also give the police some room to work. They'll have cause to interview people. Maybe, co-workers and others she hung out with. You never know, maybe it could lead us to the stranger who warned her."

Sherriff Prescott walked back into the room, and at the same time, Stitch made his way back downstairs.

Ace stood up and looked toward the stairs. "Shit, sorry. I got sidetracked talking with Derek and Tink. Is Mia okay?" He was paranoid about her being alone, even though they were all in the house with her.

"I think she passed out. I'll take up the ice in a minute." Stitch walked further into the room. "What were you guys talking about?"

"You got any beer?"

Stitch smirked. "Yeah, there should be a case in the fridge."

Ace nodded, and they all moved to the kitchen. Once the beers were passed around, the Sherriff started the conversation.

"I spoke with Doc O'Neal. He's about five minutes out. He apologized, but he got a call from the hospital and had to make a quick stop there first. I wanted to give him an update on the situation and how his assistance needed to be on the down-low."

"Her ankle is the size of a grapefruit. I didn't realize how swollen it was until Ace and I helped her get it elevated," Stitch said as he leaned against the counter with his arms crossed, looking worried and pissed off.

"I know, Stitch. I tried to convince her to let me take her to the hospital to get checked out, but she was very adamant about coming straight here. Hell, every time she moved, you could see the pain etched on her face." Sherriff Prescott stated.

Ace, Tink, and Derek explained to Stitch and Blake what the three of them talked about, and both men agreed that it was a good idea to keep Mia hidden at the cabin and treat her absence as a disappearance.

Ace ran his hand through his hair. "I don't understand why she won't just go to the hospital." Ace exclaimed and started pacing again. At the rate he was going, he was going to wear a hole in the floor.

"She didn't want her name entered in a computer system," Tink said.

Derek whistled and shook his head. "Smart girl. If someone is after her, that is the first place they're going to look considering they know she was injured."

"Dammit!" Ace shouted, slamming his fist down on the counter. "I can't believe this is happening. My mother is worried sick about her. I have to at least let her know that Mia is safe." He looked at Derek. "Do you mind calling the Colonel and giving him an update on the situation? Ask him not to give my mom any details about Mia's injuries yet. It will at least put her worry at ease."

"I can do that. We'll get to the bottom of this, Ace. Be thankful we know she's safe here." Derek turned his attention to Stitch. "You are officially assigned to Mia for the time being. She doesn't leave this cabin without you."

"What about the team?" Stitch asked.

"I'll handle your absence. Plus we can shift some teams around to facilitate any deployments should they arise. Your job is to keep Mia safe until we get a handle on the situation."

Stitch nodded his head and then looked at Ace. "Are you okay with this?"

"If I weren't, I wouldn't let it happen," Ace stated firmly. "Keep her safe."

"She won't leave my sight. I'm going to go get an ice pack on her ankle and let her know that the doc will be here soon."

Ace took a deep breath as Stitch walked out of the room. He did not doubt that Stitch would protect his sister to the fullest. Then a thought hit him, and he wondered why he didn't think to ask Stitch earlier. Why did Mia even have a key to the cabin?

Stitch made his way back up the stairs. He knocked on the door. He didn't want to barge in there like an overprotective caveman. He wanted to hold her and make her feel safe and protected. Though he wasn't happy with the circumstances, he couldn't deny that he loved how she curled up in his lap earlier.

Getting no response, he cracked the door, "Mia?"

He heard a sniffle before she answered. "You can come in."

He pushed the door open, and was surprised to find her sitting on the window seat, looking out toward the woods at the back of the property. It was one of the best views in the house during the day, and he sometimes found himself sitting in the spot just staring and thinking.

89

Her back was turned, and he noted she had managed to change into her pajamas. With her hair pulled off her neck and wearing a tight camisole type sleep shirt, he could see the dark bruising along her shoulder blades. Christ, was she bruised everywhere? He walked over and placed a hand on her back. She tensed up and pulled away as if his touch burned her.

"Mia?" He questioned.

She turned her head, and the tears that ran down her cheeks nearly brought him to his knees.

He sat down next to her and carefully pulled her into his side. She came willingly, and wrapped her arms around him, then buried her face in his shirt.

"Everything hurts so bad." She used her shirt to wipe her face. "I can't take the pain anymore; I feel so weak."

The dark circles under her eyes indicated she hadn't slept. She looked exhausted.

"You've been running on adrenalin, and now your body is coming down from that high. It's expected that you would feel worse." He kissed her forehead. Even with all of the bruises, she was still as beautiful as ever. They held each other's gaze, and as much as Stitch was trying to resist, he couldn't. With Mia still in his arms, he slowly lowered his head, and he knew when she realized he would kiss her because she closed her eyes. He pressed his lips lightly against the corner of her mouth, being careful not to press too hard. It was quick, although now that he had a tiny taste of her, he craved more.

Her eyes fluttered open, and he saw the sadness and hurt in those brown orbs. "Stitch…"

Before he could say anything, a knock sounded at the door, breaking the tension in the room. She jumped, and he gave her a serious look.

"That would be the doctor."

"Doctor?" She asked, looking a little unsure. "Aren't you pretty well trained in medicine and injuries? Can't you look over my injuries?" She asked him, her voice full of hope. He would have loved to look over her body, but for different reasons.

"Mia, you need real medical attention. I'm trained for combat injuries when we don't have the luxury of professional doctors and nurses at our sides. The Sherriff called the town doctor as a favor. Once he heard the situation, he came right over. Let him look at you, please. You can trust him."

He thought she would try and resist, but surprisingly she just nodded her head in acceptance or defeat. He wasn't exactly sure which one.

The doctor stepped in, and Stitch gave her an assuring hug before excusing himself and joining the others downstairs.

CHAPTER ELEVEN

Mia gasped as the doctor pressed on a tender spot near her hip, and the older man frowned. When the Sherriff had called him and explained Mia's situation, he was glad he had been on his way home and could make the trip over. Seeing her cringe in pain each time he touched her upset him.

"It hurts that bad, honey?"

"Well, when your ribs and back take a size thirteen boot beating, it is bound to be a little uncomfortable." She tried masking her agony with a little humor, but she failed miserably. He took a deep breath and exhaled, wondering how this woman managed to survive and escape the hands of such evil bastards. Mia was close in age to his own daughters, and imagining either of them in a predicament like Mia's angered him. He dug into his bag and pulled out an ace bandage, and began to wrap her ribs. She wasn't going to be doing much at all for the next couple of days except for resting. He wished she would let him take her to the hospital to get an x-ray. Whomever she was running from, she was extra careful not to make her whereabouts known.

He stepped back from the bed and surveyed her. "Well, my dear, you are going to be very sore for the next week or so. Don't be surprised if you feel worse over the next couple of days before you start to feel better. Your orders are to rest, rest, and more rest. No moving around if you don't have to. And, keep icing that ankle, the ribs, and your cheek. I'm going to leave some pain medicine to get you through tonight. I'll leave a prescription with Stitch for you to fill. Make sure you take them. It will help with your recovery. Let those men downstairs help you."

His eyes traveled to her legs, specifically the bruising on her inner thighs. He had noticed the discoloration when he arrived but avoided asking that question from the start, but it was something he needed to know.

"Mia, I need to ask you something, and I want you to be truthful."

"Okay."

"Honey, were you sexually assaulted?"

A tear slid down her cheek, and immediately he thought the worst. This poor young woman had been through hell and back. He couldn't help it as his fatherly instincts kicked in, and he leaned down to pull her into a gentle hug while she cried. Obviously, the frightened woman needed to vent her emotions, and he would certainly hold her while she did. Hell, he needed to calm himself down. After letting her cry for a bit, he asked, "Mia?" He pressed, needing an answer.

She looked up at him with those brown eyes that were now red and glassy from crying, and his heart broke. But seeing her shake her head no before she answered helped bring his temper down a notch, and he gave her a soft smile. He still had his arm around her and gave her another hug as he thanked the lord above.

He pulled away and stood. "Get some rest. I will leave both my office and cell number with Stitch. You call me at any time, okay?"

She gave him a small smile. "Thank you, Doctor O'Neal. I'm sorry that my situation pulled you away from your family."

"Oh, honey, with the houseful of people that followed me home from my brothers, your call couldn't have come at a better time, although I wish it would have been under different circumstances."

She painstakingly slid under the covers, and he helped tuck her in nice and tight.

She smiled up at him. "Could you please let the guys know I'm going to lie down? I'm really tired."

"I will, but take this first." He handed her one of the pain pills. "That will ensure you sleep. Something you need a lot of right now."

He couldn't resist. She needed all the love and comfort right now. He bent down and kissed her forehead, and she smiled up at him before closing her eyes.

Stitch sat on the arm of the sofa. His leg bounced in anticipation of hearing what the doctor had to say. Not much was said between the guys since Doc O'Neal had arrived, which was about 45 minutes ago. Tink and Derek sat talking amongst themselves about who they knew up in New York that could help. Ace, on the other hand, was back to pacing the living room. He knew this was hard for his friend. Hell, it was hard for himself. He cared for Mia so much.

Moments later, Doc finally emerged from the bedroom and walked downstairs.

"What's the verdict?" Stitch asked as the doc walked further into the room and took a seat in the empty chair. He gestured for everyone to sit. Stitch was reluctant to. He felt restless, and sitting would only make him fidget more.

The older man removed his glasses and rubbed his eyes. Obviously, this had been hard on him as well.

"She's in a rough state right now, but I expect her to make a full recovery. She has a lot of bruising, but I don't think anything is broken; however, I can't be a hundred percent without taking x-rays. Did she mention to you that she was drugged?"

From the blank expressions on everyone's face, it was apparent that this was new information.

"I'll take that as a no. I don't think she knew either. She told me that she was hit in the head pretty hard. As I was examining her, I noticed a red spot just above her shoulder. To me, it looks like an entry point of a needle. She said she felt really woozy. But that could have been because of the trauma to her head. Either way, to be safe, I took a blood sample and will see if it produces anything. Certain drugs can stay in the body for several days. I will drop it by the hospital on my way home and ask them to put a rush on it.

"Are you talking like a date rape drug?" Stitch asked, not liking where the conversation was heading.

Doc nodded his head. "That, amongst other drugs that can be used to incapacitate someone."

Stitch swallowed hard, and he thought about his next question. It was one he didn't want to ask, but it was inevitable. "Was she sexually assaulted?"

Ace raised his head, and Stitch could see the turmoil his friend was facing. Even Derek and Tink leaned slightly forward making sure they wouldn't miss the answer. They all waited on pins and needles for the doctor to answer.

"There was quite a bit of bruising on her inner thighs, but when I asked her, she said she wasn't."

"If she was drugged, and then knocked out at one point, could it be possible that she was and just doesn't remember it?" Stitch asked.

"Yes, that is possible, and I had the same revelations. However, the bruising stopped midway up her thigh. I honestly don't believe she was."

Stitch hadn't realized he was holding his breath until he started to see black spots from lack of oxygen.

Doctor O'Neal stood and looked at Stitch. "I left some pain medicine to get her through the night. She already took one. Here is a prescription for more. She will need them, and they will keep her sedated, which is best for her body to heal. Try to keep her hydrated, and as far as food goes, keep it light; soups, smoothies, protein shakes, that sort of thing. I hope to hell you find the sons of bitches who did this to her. No woman deserves what she went through."

"We will. Don't you worry," Ace stated firmly that left no room for argument.

Stitch turned toward the doctor. "What can we do to make her more comfortable?"

"Just rest and lots of it. She needs to stay off that ankle. She told me to let you know that she was going to lie down."

"Well, we all appreciate you taking time away from your family to help."

The doc chuckled. "I'll tell you the same thing I told Mia upstairs. You all actually did me a favor. My family can be a bit boisterous at times. Your call was perfect timing."

Stitch shook his hand. "Well, regardless, it was very much appreciated, and if you ever need anything, please don't hesitate to call."

"Thank you, son. And like I said, be sure that young lady gets plenty of rest."

"Yes, sir. She will be under our protection, and we will see to it she takes it easy and has plenty of rest."

The air was cold and crisp, but the twinkling stars' display coupled with the subtle glow of the moon was stunning to gaze at. In fact, it was one of the many reasons Stitch had purchased the cabin. There had been plenty of nights of just sitting outside, staring at the sky and using the peacefulness as a tool to help clear his mind and thoughts.

Stitch sat in one of the Adirondack chairs around the stone firepit. After he had bought the cabin, the first project he tackled was the huge deck wrapped around the entire house. Once the deck was in place, the firepit was installed along with the built-in deck lighting.

Before coming outside, he had gone upstairs to check on Mia. She was out cold and sleeping soundly. She looked tiny lying in the huge bed. It had taken willpower not to kick off his shoes and crawl in next to her.

He rubbed his hand over his jaw feeling his whiskers, and exhaled as he thought about what situation they would be facing if the Sherriff hadn't been at the bus station when he was. He was thankful Mia had befriended that woman on the bus, and she had been nice to introduce Mia to Blake. He would have to get that nice lady's address and send her a thank you gift.

He took a swig from his beer and heard one of the loose boards by the door creek, signaling someone had joined him. Seconds later, Ace appeared and took the chair across from him. He looked across the glowing fire and met Stitch's gaze.

"You okay, man?"

He nodded his head. "Just thinking how lucky we were that Blake was at the bus station tonight."

"I agree. It's pretty fucking scary. I still can't believe this. I mean, we train for this type of shit, but when it hits close to home, it's different in so many ways."

Stitch was getting tired of seeing the women close to him fall victim to the assholes of the world. First, Alex, with her ordeal with the terrorist who kidnapped and nearly killed her. Then there was Tenley. Damn, talk about an emotional rollercoaster for that woman. She gave Potter a run for his money. Her troubles started when she was caught in the middle of two drug cartels. Next was Autumn, Frost's wife. She had been stalked by her ex-sister-in-law but had also caught the eye of a shrewd businessman. She was kidnapped, and when she tried to escape from his yacht, she hit her head and fell into the ocean. Her son Cody was the true hero in her case. The damn kid paddled close to a mile and a half into the ocean on his surfboard to save his mom. Then last but not least, there was Bailey. Sweet Bailey, Irish's new wife. She put herself in harm's way after she too was kidnapped by a greedy guy who was after her money. Her parents were in on the set-up as well. When the asshole tried to shoot at the team, Bailey had wrestled him for the gun and ended up being shot. Her situation had been touch and go for a while, but as the weeks went by, she recovered. Except for the fact that she may never be able to carry a child. Now, here they sat, trying to figure out what type of mess Mia had found herself in.

"Did Derek get a hold of the Colonel?"

"Yeah, and according to him, my mother is a basket case right now and is demanding to see Mia."

"Shit..."

"Yep, my thoughts exactly. You know my mom, there is no stopping her when she puts her mind to something, and I know she'll find a way to manipulate the Colonel. Then before you know it, she'll have him driving her up here." He took a drink of his beer and grinned. "You think I'm joking?"

Stitch didn't doubt that at all. Charlotte Chambers was a force to be reckoned with. A few years ago, having lost her husband, the spunky and determined woman took on the task of running a ranch and succeeded. That woman could bust balls like there was no tomorrow.

"Maybe if Mia's feeling up to it tomorrow or the next day, we could arrange a Skype or Facetime call between the two of them."

"That might work."

For the next couple of minutes, they both sat there staring at the fire as it crackled and flickered in the darkness. They both were trying to process the situation. Now would be a perfect time for Stitch to speak with Ace about Mia and the feelings he had for her. After today's drama, there was no way in hell he was taking a backseat. Either Ace accepted it, or he didn't. If he didn't, Stitch would deal with it, even if it meant parting ways with the team he trusted and loved, but he would to avoid any conflict with Ace.

Just as he sat up straighter and was ready to talk, Ace cleared his throat. "So, you and my sister, huh?"

Okay, apparently, Ace was thinking along the same lines. Since Ace was allowing him to come clean, he needed to not fuck it up. Ace was a straight-forward guy. No bullshit, just the god's honest truth was what he wanted and expected, and Stitch respected him for that. Both as a friend and his team leader.

He looked Ace in the eye from across the fire pit. "I'm not gonna lie, man. I'm in love with Mia, and I have been for a while. Before you ask, no, there has been nothing between us. But I can't hold back any longer. Though she and I never talked about it, I tried keeping my distance out of respect for you. And yes, she and I have been in contact a lot over the last year, but that was the extent of it. Do I wish I had acted on my feelings before now? Abso-fucking-lutely, because if I had, we wouldn't be sitting here right now while the woman that we both love is lying upstairs beaten to hell." His nostrils flared. He was fired up, and holy shit, did it feel good to say all of that out loud finally.

Ace stared at him, and Stitch wasn't sure if Ace had heard him or if he was silently plotting his death.

After a few eerily silent moments, Ace said, "I appreciate your honesty. It is quite obvious you care for her a lot. From the way she latched herself onto you earlier, I can see she reciprocates the same feelings for you." Ace took a moment as if gathering his thoughts. Stitch knew this had to be challenging for him. Hell, if he himself had a sister and one of the guys made a move on her, he'd probably feel the same way. Then Ace pulled a total one-eighty and grinned as he leaned forward, perching his elbows on his knees. He clasped his fingers together and rested his chin on his fists. "This is probably going to shock you, but I am happy as fuck to hear that."

Stitch's eyes widened with that shared information. And, definitely not what he was expecting. From the conversations that Stitch had with Mia, Mia and Ace were very close, not to mention how protective Ace was of her, especially when it came to men. She had told Stitch that when Ace first joined the teams, he had given her a lecture about not getting close to any of his teammates because he knew firsthand how most of the guys operated around women.

"But, since you're being honest, I feel I should do the same. I think I've known for a while. The signs were there, people talked, but I chose to ignore it. Looking back, her face always lit up when you walked into the room or whenever your name came up in conversation; there was more excitement to her voice."

"I don't know when it happened, and I am sorry for not coming to you sooner. All that I can say is that she makes me happy."

"All I want is for her to be happy, and I can tell that you do that. Just promise me you will love and treat her with respect. As I know, she will do the same for you."

"I wouldn't have it any other way. She is my number one priority. I'm just glad I gave her that key when I last saw her or god knows what we would be dealing with."

"Yeah, I've been wondering how in the hell she got a key to this place." Stitch explained how that came about, and Ace closed his eyes. "Damn, I feel like I've failed her. I've tried to watch out for her since she was the youngest. I've been so preoccupied with other things that I didn't even notice."

"You're too hard on yourself, man. You live a busy life, and so does Mia. I almost didn't see her struggles at first, either."

"Well, maybe now you can help us convince her to move to Virginia Beach."

Stitch grinned and took a drink from his bottle. "That was the second discussion I planned on having with her."

Ace gave him a sideways look. "What is the first?"

"Telling her that I love her. Especially now that I got her big brother's stamp of approval."

Ace laughed. "You are such an ass."

The two shook hands and guzzled down the rest of their beers before calling it a night. Tomorrow they would put plans in motion to hunt down the individuals responsible for Mia's assault.

CHAPTER TWELVE

The next morning, Stitch sat in the recliner chair he and Ace had moved upstairs and into his room last night. He was serious when he said he would be there for Mia no matter what. With how serious her injuries were, she wasn't going to be able to move much on her own. Doctor O'Neal hadn't been lying when he said that she would feel a lot worse before she felt better.

Overall, she seemed to have had a pretty good night. She only woke up twice. Once because of a nightmare, and the second because of the pain. The latter had been just three hours ago, and he had given her another pain pill so he was anticipating she would sleep for another couple of hours.

Ace, Tink, and Derek were downstairs making plans. Ace had called Alex last night and explained what was going on, but she had been sworn to secrecy as they didn't want everyone to know in case someone did come snooping around. The fewer people who knew, for the time being, the better and safer.

Stitch had felt bad for Ace because, at the crack of dawn, Ace received a phone call from a very irate Charlotte Chambers. Apparently, the Colonel's little chat with her last night hadn't gone over too well, and she was demanding to see her daughter. Ace explained to her that for the sake of Mia's safety, this was the way it had to be for a little while, but that he would set something up for Mia and her to speak. That had seemed to cool her britches for the time being.

He looked at his watch. Alex would be arriving in about thirty minutes or so. She had offered to drive his Jeep up to the cabin so he and Mia would have transportation once everyone left later in the day. She was also stopping at a store to pick up some clothes for Mia, considering she only had what was in her backpack, which Stitch thought was only two or three outfits. He didn't have a timeframe on how long they'd be staying, but he figured it would be more than two days. She would especially need warmer clothes, considering snow was in the forecast.

Once they knew the cabin was secure, Ace, Alex, Derek, and Tink would fly back to Virginia Beach. Ace wasn't thrilled about leaving his sister and even tried to come up with excuses, but in the end, he knew it had to be done to smoke out whoever was after her. At least Ace knew he could count on Stitch to look after her and keep her safe.

Alex was a bundle of nerves as she drove up the long driveway to Stitch's cabin. Any other time she would be smiling and happy to get away for a few days in the mountains. Stitch always let the team stay at his place when he wasn't using it. It was a nice retreat away from the bustle of daily life.

Unfortunately, this trip wasn't about pleasantries and fun times. Based on what Ace had told her last night, her friend and future sister-in-law was in some serious trouble. As the team would call it, it was FUBAR.

She parked the Jeep right in front of the steps to the front porch and turned the engine off. She hopped out and started gathering the bags of clothing and other items she picked up for Mia. As she was bent over, trying to consolidate some of the bags, a set of strong arms came around her waist and pulled her backward. She squeaked in surprise but didn't even have to turn to know it was Ace, as he lowered his head and kissed her neck.

"Hey, sweetheart." He said in his deep raspy voice of his that still to this day turned her into a big pile of goo. Turning in his arms, she snuggled into his chest and hugged him. She felt how tense his body was, and all she wanted to do was to help ease his pain. When they spoke last night, he had opened up to her about him having a hard time dealing with Mia's injuries. From Ace's description, it sounded pretty bad. Alex knew Ace was beating himself up and felt somewhat responsible because he hadn't been in touch with Mia recently. She had to remind him that it wouldn't have mattered if he had spoken with her or not because nobody could have predicted what had happened to her.

She pulled back and looked up at him; he was staring right back at her. His blue eyes held so much emotion. It wasn't often she saw this side of him. The side that was hurting and needing comfort. When he did, she made sure she was there to support him with whatever he needed, and she always would.

"How's Mia?" She asked, sliding her hands up his chest to his broad shoulders. He squeezed her tighter around the waist.

"Stitch said she woke up a few hours ago and was in a lot of pain. He gave her another pain pill, and she fell back asleep." He took a deep breath and released it before continuing. "She's in bad shape, Alex. I mean, no woman or man, for that matter, should have to go through something so horrific."

From the expression on his face as he stared at her, Alex knew his thoughts were heading back to Afghanistan. She slid her hand down his side and pinched him through his shirt.

"Stop!" She demanded.

"Stop what?"

"I'm not stupid, Ace. I know what's you're thinking about. Remember we talked about that, and we both agreed to put that time behind us. Now, Mia is your sister. You've looked after her, her entire life, well, when your career permitted. You were the big brother that probably every little sister wanted to have. Someone they could count on protecting them and guiding them through life."

He ran his hand through his hair. "Yeah, and look how that ended up for her."

"Ace, Mia is a grown woman with a good head on her shoulders. You can't always be there, nor will you ever be. Life happens, and unfortunately, not all of life's experiences are warm and fuzzy moments. You of all people know how cruel people in this world can be."

With his silence, she took that moment to hug him, resting her cheek against his chest, listening to the sound of his heart beating. "I needed that," he said softly into her hair, rubbing his hand up and down her back. She savored moments like this and wished she could stay in his arms forever.

"You needed what? I didn't do anything?"

He gently gripped her chin, tilting her face towards his, and gave her a soft smile.

"That hug, and for you being the rock of our family, the team, hell the world. I feel like I don't tell you that enough. Thank you for being here and helping. I know you sacrificed your Black Friday shopping to be here."

She pressed her hand against his cheek. "Ace, I wouldn't want to be anywhere else. Mia is like family to me already and a wonderful friend. I'm here for both of you." He bent his head and kissed her.

"I love you so much."

"I love you too." She said with a grin. But she was starting to freeze her ass off standing outside, although Ace's large muscular body infused some heat into her. It was colder up in the mountains compared to the beach.

"As much as I would love to stand here and stay in your arms, do you think we could possibly move this indoors? I'm kinda getting colds" she said as her teeth started to chatter.

He chuckled and grabbed the bags from the back of the Jeep while she closed it up and locked it. When she turned and started walking, Ace slapped her hard on the ass, making her yelp. She rubbed her butt cheek and glared at him. That made him laugh harder, and all she could do was smile. Hearing him laugh and seeing a smile on his face meant she had done her job.

∽

Stitch stood in the kitchen with Alex while Ace spent some time upstairs with Mia. He pulled a beer from the refrigerator and held one up for Alex, but she refused.

"I have a feeling I'm going to need to be the sober one once we get back home. Ace already mentioned he wanted to swing by Bayside on the way home. Plus, isn't it a little early to be drinking?"

He shook his head as he popped the top to the bottle of beer and took a nice long slug of it.

"I still can't believe that Mia could've possibly been pulled into a human trafficking ring," Alex said as she took a seat at the kitchen table and sipped her coffee. She had gotten to see Mia for a few minutes when she got to the cabin, but Mia was still sleeping. "I mean, you hear of that happening, but you never expect for it to happen to someone you know. It is crazy scary."

Stitch brought his beer over to the table and took a seat across from her.

"Tink and Derek have been talking to some big shot Detective in New York that Tink knows. The hope is they can get some leads after the missing persons report is filed. According to the detective, they have some leads on some possible groups who they believe are connected to human trafficking. They haven't ruled out other organizations or gangs either who could've had beef with one of Mia's friends, and they were using her to set an example or make a point."

"Well, hopefully, they can find out something, and fast. How are you holding up?" She asked, holding his gaze, and he shrugged his shoulders as he traced the rim of the beer bottle with his finger. He wasn't really in the mood to talk about himself and his feelings right now. Just like Ace, he felt guilty and somewhat responsible for what happened to Mia. He had thought about it last night while he watched her sleep. He did the one thing he never did: he played the "what if" mind game, and it had totally fucked with his head.

"Stitch, I'll tell you the same thing I told Ace earlier; you can't blame yourself. You don't know who she hung with up in the City and who may have had their eye on her. You have to live in the moment. Just be there for her and help her heal. Hey, at least she was smart enough to know your cabin was a safe house. Be thankful that she at least got away and is here with you now."

Stitch ran his hand over his unshaven face. "She means so much to me, Alex. It killed me to sit there last night and listen to her moan in her sleep as if she was reliving the beating she took, and then when she woke up in the middle of a nightmare, she clung to me, and I felt so helpless because there wasn't a damn thing I could do but just talk to her until she fell back asleep."

She reached across the table and took his hand. "Sometimes just having someone to hold us and letting us know that everything will be okay is all we need."

"Are you sharing your experience?"

She smiled softly and squeezed his hand. "I don't think I could've made it through my recovery if it weren't for Ace being my rock. Believe me when

105

I say having the right person by your side makes all the difference." He thought through her words, and she was right. He'd seen it not just with Alex, but also when Tenley, Autumn, and Bailey all found themselves recovering from their bad experiences. Hell, he'd seen it in combat.

"I understand what you're saying, but this time around feels so different with Mia."

"You're in love with her, aren't you?"

One hundred percent, he was in love with her. A day never went by that he didn't think about her. Even when they were out on missions and had some downtime, he thought of her. Even decisions he'd made within the last year, he'd found himself wondering if Mia would be happy or approve. Like when he was looking for a house after Frost and Autumn moved in together. He found one he liked, but he wasn't sure if Mia would like it, so he passed on it. He looked at Alex. It was no use trying to hide his feelings.

"I am. I told Ace last night."

Alex raised one of her manicured eyebrows in his direction, completely surprised by his statement, but he didn't miss the sly smile playing on her lips.

"Maybe I do need that beer after all. This is a major development in the romance saga of Stitch and Mia," she said with a laugh, also making Stitch chuckle. "And, I am dying to know the reaction of my husband to be."

Stitch was still laughing. Alex could be such a wise-ass, and he loved her for it too. "He was happy for the both of us, and he's fine with it."

She smiled. "Really? It was that easy?"

Now Stitch smiled. "It was. And believe me, it was easier than I thought."

"Well, I'm sure he is thrilled. You're a great guy and he knows you'll take good care of her."

He studied Alex's reaction. He thought she would be more surprised. "Why don't you seem so surprised?"

"Well…."

"Alex…" He loved his best friend to death, but damn she could sometimes meddle in shit, though her heart had good intentions.

106

She raised her hands up. "Okay…I probably shouldn't tell you this, but since you are one of my best friends and Mia means a lot to me, and I want to see you both happy, I'm going to let you in on a little secret. Back when Tenley got in trouble, and you guys were getting ready to deploy, Ace and I had a conversation. Ace had been a little worried about that guy Mia was seeing."

"The Green Beret?" Nobody knew the guy's name, but Stitch hated the man for how he had treated Mia. Any man who was unfaithful to his woman was just a douche bag, and clearly the asshole didn't deserve Mia.

"Yeah, him. Anyway, Ace noticed that Mia hadn't been her happy-go-lucky self. He wasn't sure what to do or how to approach her on the subject. I suggested that he ask you to see if you had any insights."

Stitch pointed to himself. "Me? Why would you tell him to talk to me?"

She grinned, then took a sip of water. "Because I knew that even though Mia was dating that guy that you and her had been talking. A lot."

"How did you know?"

"Because Mia told me. You know us girls like to gossip." Oh yes, he knew very well how the women liked to gossip. Especially the group of women that included Alex, Tenley, Autumn, Bailey, and now Mia. "And, you want to know what Ace told me?"

"One could only guess," he said, lifting his beer and taking a swig.

"He said that he wished it was you who was dating his sister."

Stitch coughed as he choked on his beer, which made Alex giggle.

"Surprised ya, didn't I?"

All Stitch could do was nod his head because that was a pretty big news flash.

"Ace said that if the both of you were dating, he would at least know she was in good hands. He respects you."

"And, you never thought to clue me in, knowing that was the main reason why I stood back and didn't make a move sooner? Especially after that dick cheated on her?"

She gave him a devilish smile. "Hey, I've been told not to meddle in other people's relationships."

He balled up a napkin and threw it at her, and she laughed. If it weren't for her meddling, there was no telling if Potter, Frost, or Irish would be happily married now. He could only wonder what she had told Ace.

CHAPTER THIRTEEN

Elijah paced the length of his living room in his penthouse. The heels of his Armani dress shoes clicked against the marble floors with every step he took. He was pissed. Two of his employees had fucked up big time, and because of their stupidity, he had some major covering up to do.

"You okay, boss?"

Elijah whipped his head around to see Claus standing in the doorway. Ignoring his question, he asked, "Did you take care of the situation?"

"It is being done as we speak."

"Good. I don't want anything traced back to me. Where are Oscar and Jules?"

"Down at the docks working on installing those new cages on that cargo ship so everything will ready for the shipment scheduled for next week." Claus walked a little more into the room, and Elijah saw him holding a shopping bag.

"What is that?" He asked.

"The items from the girl that were left at the warehouse. Vargas bagged it up. He is also taking care of the clean-up."

Claus handed over the bag, and Elijah took a peek inside. It was just a pair of socks, running shoes, and a black zip-up hoodie. A smell tickled his nose. It was a familiar scent. He removed the hoodie from the bag and brought it to his nose, and inhaled again. It was sweet, not too strong, but enticing. It was Mia. The scent from the hoodie was the same perfume that Mia wore, and instantly the vision from the night at the gala fluttered through his mind. He damned himself for telling her to take a few extra days to visit with her brother. She wasn't due back to the office until Wednesday. With the situation he was currently dealing with, it could turn out to be a good thing since he'd be preoccupied making sure Oscar and Jules' fuck up was concealed.

"Are Oscar and Jules sure she didn't get a look at them?"

"No, they said she was blindfolded the entire time. They are aware of how bad they fucked up."

"They both are lucky they aren't floating in the Hudson River right now."

"I can still make that happen."

"No. We have enough to deal with right now. I don't need another reason for the cops to start sniffing around. We need to find out who that woman was that escaped and deal with her. Press Oscar and Jules for more information. I want to know where they picked her up from, and have them give you a better description than a 'hot raven-haired woman with a fuckable body'."

"I'll talk with them. I'm supposed to meet up with Vargas later next week to go over plans for the next shipment. He said he knew of a more concealed place outside the city to hold the dogs until they were adopted. Since he was at the warehouse, I'll see if he can provide any other information. However, he got there just before she escaped."

Elijah let out a frustrated sigh and sunk down into the chair.

"What are we doing about the Willow situation, now?"

Willow was the woman Oscar and Jules were supposed to nab off the street. Now he was faced with two problems.

"There is no situation with Willow."

Elijah quirked his eyebrow, and Claus grinned, then looked at his watch. "Willow should be on her way to her new home."

"New home?"

Claus shrugged his shoulders. "I don't have an exact location, but Chen Pham was more than willing to take her off your hands. I was surprised at the price he offered for her." He gloated.

"You sold her to Pham?" Elijah ran his hand through his hair. "Jesus, she probably would have been better off if you just killed her. I've heard stories about Pham. Not many women last more than a month with him."

Claus, again gave a shoulder shrug. "Do you really care?"

"No. As long as she can't open her mouth around here, I don't give a fuck what happens to her."

"She was an easy target. I picked her up this morning as she was out walking in Central Park. Not sure anyone taught the stupid girl not to walk alone in the park while it was dark."

Claus gathered his coat and car keys. "I have the crew meeting me at the warehouse. I'm concerned with the amount of close calls we've had the last few weeks. Ones that could have been prevented if those responsible had been paying attention. I'm going to let them know that if there are any more screw-ups, heads will roll. Literally."

Elijah nodded his head as Claus showed himself out the door. Elijah grabbed his glass and walked over to the windows overlooking Central Park; it was a magnificent view as the windows pan floor to ceiling. He lifted the glass of whiskey to his lips and took a long sip. In his other hand, he still clutched the jacket belonging to the woman who could potentially bring down his empire. He swallowed hard. Finding her in the city was going to be like looking for a needle in a haystack. His only hope was that she was too out of it to remember where she was.

CHAPTER FOURTEEN

Mia started to stir. She felt as if her body and mind were playing a game. Her mind said it was time to wake, but her body seemed to disagree. At the moment, she felt secured and at peace. Her mind might have been a little fuzzy, but she recognized right away that she wasn't in her bed. Her mattress was nowhere near as comfortable as the one she was curled up in.

She let her eyes adjust to the little bit of sunlight peeking through the slats in the wood blinds. The first thing that caught her attention was a picture on the table next to the bed. She couldn't help the small smile that formed. It was a picture of Stitch in uniform standing with what she assumed were his parents. Stitch carried both his mom and dad's features.

Her eyes slowly moved about the room. It was very homey—calm and peaceful, just like Stitch. The contrast of the dark logs that made up the house's interior and exterior, along with the wildlife photos blended with the military pictures and decor, made her smile because it was what she would expect from Stitch. Even the wood frame of the bed matched the color of the logs. She may live in the city, but her blood ran country, and the look and feel of the room made her feel right at home.

She snuggled further into the down pillow that smelled like Stitch, but that teensiest movement set off a chain reaction of pain throughout her entire body, bringing tears to her eyes. Parts of last night started to come back to her. She remembered meeting the Sherriff, and he had driven her to the cabin. Her brother and Stitch had shown up with a few other people. She recalled talking to them—about what she couldn't remember, because she had been out of it. Her mind wasn't firing on all cylinders between the pain, adrenalin crash, and pain medicine. She did recall a doctor had examined her.

Suddenly she let out a gasp and touched her lips. Had Stitch really kissed her last night?

Before she could put any more thought into it, she groaned, feeling the need to use the restroom. She was content and didn't want to move, but her bladder was going to burst if she didn't relieve herself soon. She could see the bathroom door just a short distance away, but with the way her body felt, it may as well have been a mile away. She wasn't even sure if she could walk. But if she didn't find a way to get her ass out of bed, she would have a messy and embarrassing situation on her hands.

Slowly, and with a lot of small movements, along with a few expletives, she was able to get her legs over the edge of the bed. Trying to use her core muscles to sit up was another story. She tried to channel happy thoughts while battling through the pain and agony until she was in an upright position. She even gave herself a weak fist pump for the little feat, though it felt as if she just conquered the world. The impromptu celebration quickly faded to a thing of the past when she realized the bed was so high off the ground. Her feet didn't even reach the floor. She hadn't remembered the bed being this high when she got in it, but then again, last night had been a complete blur.

Her mouth dropped open when her eyes landed on the clock sitting on the nightstand. She had slept almost the entire day. In the next hour or two, it would be getting dark and time for bed again. Not that she would complain, because she still felt exhausted.

Scooting her butt closer to the edge of the bed, she damned her bladder. She just wanted to curl back up in the warmth of the fluffy comforter and go back to sleep. Once she got far enough off the edge and her toes touched the hardwood floor, she pushed off. She had no chance of standing as her legs felt numb and gave right out from under. She crumpled to the floor with a hard thud. "Sweet baby Jesus," she whimpered when the pain erupted through her body. Tears filled her eyes.

She wasn't sure how long she had laid on the floor, trying to calm her breathing and racing heart, but she gasped when a set of strong arms lifted her. She was cradled against a warm, broad chest. Without opening her eyes, she knew it was Stitch. His scent gave it away.

Stitch and Blake were putting away the groceries that Stitch had ran out and picked up. Ace and the others had left around noon to head home, and

113

since Mia had still been asleep, he decided to make a quick run to the store to pick up some food and fill the prescription that Doctor O'Neal had left for Mia. Sherriff Prescott had stopped by to see how Mia was doing, and since he was there and wasn't on call per se, he offered to stay at the cabin while Stitch ran out to the store.

"I told Tink to let his Detective friend in New York know that if I can be of any assistance to reach out," Blake said to Stitch.

Stitch stopped what he was doing and turned toward him. "I appreciate that. I just want to find out who was responsible and make them pay. They need to be caught."

"I agree."

Suddenly, there was a loud thump from upstairs. Stitch dropped the box of noodles he had in his hand, and both he and Blake took off running, taking the stairs two at a time. When Stitch got to his bedroom, Mia's sobs from inside the room ripped through him. When he pushed the door open and found her on the floor, he rushed to her side.

"Mia?" He questioned as he lifted her into his arms and sat on the edge of the bed. Her low gasp and tense body signaled to Stitch that she was in tremendous pain. He felt bad for making her hurt worse, but dammit, what had she been thinking trying to get out of bed by herself. Doctor O'Neal told her she needed to take it easy and let others help her.

"Mia." He said, brushing her hair from her face. "Talk to me, Mia. What happened?"

She opened her eyes and met his gaze. The agony that filled her showed in her eyes. He adjusted her body as she leaned against him.

"Ow, ow, ow." She whispered in a raspy voice.

"How can I help?" Stitch asked.

"I don't know. Everything hurts." Her body was tense, and he could feel her holding her breath. When he looked down, her face was all scrunched up, and she had closed her eyes again.

He pulled her close to his chest, and soon he felt her body start to relax as her warm puffs of air could be felt through his shirt. When he brushed her hair off her face, her cheeks felt a little warm, and he wondered if she could be running a low fever.

"I'm so sorry that you're hurting," he told her as he looked into her brown eyes.

"I can't move a muscle without something hurting."

Blake cleared his throat, and when Stitch looked up, he was standing in the doorway. Stitch didn't miss the slight twitch of the former Marine's lips before the man nodded his head and left them alone. Blake was the one person who Stitch had confided in about his attraction to a certain woman, though he never revealed who the woman was. They had been out having a few beers when the subject was brought up about Stitch settling down. Apparently, the alcohol that night had been truth serum.

He turned his attention back to the beauty in his arms. When their eyes met again, the rope around his heart tightened even more. He hadn't lied to Ace when he told him that he was in love with Mia. What started as a crush quickly morphed into love the more time he spent with her. He wanted to tell her how much he loved her, but she wasn't in the mindset for that proclamation. He gently wiped the tears from her red-stained cheeks, and she flinched. He had to bite the inside of his cheek to keep his anger at bay. He didn't want her to think he was angry with her.

"I can't believe that I slept all day." She said in a husky but sexy voice that totally turned him on.

"You need the rest."

She nodded again, then laid her head against his shoulder. One of the many things he was taught during his lengthy combat medic training was to keep the injured calm, even during the midst of a battle. And, Christ all mighty was this a battle.

So many emotions filtered through Mia's head, making it hard for her to think straight. Her brain didn't want to cooperate. That was probably from the drugs the doc gave her. Being in Stitch's arms grounded her. He was full of warmth, and his presence gave her the sense of protection she was seeking. She moved just slightly and felt the ache in her ribs, then as if right

115

on cue, the pressure on her bladder increased. She looked up at the handsome man embracing her, and she felt her cheeks flush. *Jesus, woman, get your shit together. You need to pee.*

Stitch chuckled, and she saw the amusement dancing in his warm eyes. He smiled and kissed her forehead. "Before you ask, yes, you said that out loud."

She ducked her head in complete embarrassment. Her brother used to make fun of her when they were kids because she would talk to herself, or 'think out loud,' as she liked to call it.

"I really need to use the restroom, but I don't think my legs want to work."

"No worries, sweetheart." As if she weighed nothing at all, he stood with her and walked to the bathroom. He set her feet down on the cool tile floor in front of the toilet and held her hips to help steady her. "Can you handle this by yourself?" He asked, nodding his head toward the toilet. She should have been embarrassed by the situation, but right now, she couldn't care less. All that mattered was emptying her bladder.

"I think I can handle it—alone." She watched him as he studied her, probably asking himself if she was telling the truth. Once he seemed satisfied, he nodded his head. And, thank god, because she really didn't want to tinkle with him watching and listening. Before he left, he told her to holler when she was finished, and he'd help her back to the bed.

Once he closed the door, she exhaled. He was so intense, and though he smiled here and there, she sensed his edginess, but she knew it wasn't directed at her. Turning toward the mirror above the sink, she gasped at the reflection staring back at her. Her face looked like a big discolored blueberry with all the bruising and swelling. Her arms were covered with black and blue finger marks. She was sure she would find the same types of marks and colors on her legs and torso. No wonder Stitch wouldn't stop staring at her. She looked like someone's science project.

She grabbed the edge of the vanity and lowered herself to the toilet. It was a painful process. As she did her business, her eyes spotted the jacuzzi tub sitting in the corner. It was as if a spotlight shined down on it. It was surrounded by windows, and even had candles around the edge of it. Oh man, she'd do anything to be able to soak her body in that thing. The candles gave it an intimate setting, and she couldn't help but wonder if Stitch had brought women up here before. Not that she thought he was a saint, but the vision of him with another woman caused a slight ache in her chest. An ache that she didn't need to have right now because she had enough bumps and bruises to deal with for the time being.

She used the vanity to help her stand. She couldn't pull her eyes from the tub. She could fill that monstrous bathtub with piping hot water and soak her aching body until she shriveled up like a prune. The only problem she saw with that idea was how she planned to get herself in and out of it. She could hardly walk, much less maneuver herself in and out of that thing.

She felt so emotional. She was completely helpless and vulnerable right now. Those feelings didn't sit well with her because all her life, she was taught to be strong, confident, and independent.

She wasn't sure how long she stood there in a complete daze when she felt those familiar arms come around her waist. She looked at her reflection again in the mirror and saw Stitch looking at her as he stood towering behind her, and she met his eyes. "Look at me. I look awful."

He pressed his body closer against her backside and moved her hair off her right shoulder. Ever so gentle, he pressed his lips against her bare shoulder. She closed her eyes from the intimate and tender gesture and relished in the feeling of his firm lips pressed against her skin.

"You are the most beautiful woman I know, even with the bruises, and those'll fade over time." His words brought a slight smile to her face and made her heart beat a little faster. His fingers brushed against her sides where her shirt had lifted. His touch added to the sexual sensation flowing through her.

"How can I help you?" He whispered in her ear.

She looked at him then glanced over her shoulder at the bathtub. "I'd love to soak in the bath. But I don't think I can get in and out of it on my own."

Stitch had already been thinking that a nice warm bath with some Epsom salts would be good for her body and help her relax. Now, whether she was up for his idea was a different story. But he wasn't leaving her alone in the tub when she could hardly hold herself up.

"How about if I sit with you in the tub? You can lean on me instead of the hard porcelain." He wanted to laugh at the look she gave him. Even with the bruising on her face, he could see the blush running through her cheeks. "Hear me out. So, for neither of us to feel awkward, I'll wear a pair of shorts, and you can wear one of my t-shirts." He knew his shirt would probably come down to her knees, so she would feel comfortable and be covered." When she agreed so easily, he wanted to pump his fist in the air.

Stitch started the bath then helped Mia into one of his shirts. Seeing her bruises again along her ribs and back made him angry. He stepped quickly out of the bathroom and stripped down to his boxers, and pulled on a pair of his PT shorts. He was seriously rethinking his genius idea now. Now he would have to bear the punishment of having her body wedged between his legs and pressed against him. He ran his hand down his face. Keeping his hands to himself wasn't going to be easy.

She called out, letting him know that the tub was getting full. He shook all the naughty thoughts whirling through his mind and got his game face on. He needed to be a professional about this. Yeah, that was it. He would treat this like it was any other mission. This was about Mia's recovery. So quickly, he sighed in defeat. Yeah, try telling his dick that, because right now it wasn't cooperating, and the last thing he wanted to do was embarrass himself or scare her off.

He walked into the bathroom, and she stood there, holding onto the vanity for support. She looked sexy as hell in his clothes. She tried pulling it down even lower though it already came to her knees. He swallowed hard. Fuck being professional.

"Are you okay?" She asked him as she nibbled her bottom lip, pulling him from his inner thoughts.

"Yeah, I'm good. You ready?" She nodded her head.

"Put your arms around my neck. That's it."

He lifted her, stepped into the large tub, and sank in the water. Once he got Mia positioned and comfortable in between his legs, she relaxed back against him. She let out a soft hiss, then moaned, and dammit, his cock stirred, and there was not one fucking thing he could do about it. It had a mind of its own when it came to Mia.

"Comfortable?" He asked through his gritted teeth.

"Perfect, this is just what I needed." She replied, leaning her head back against his shoulder. Her arms were perched on his bent knees that were caging her in. The feel of her dainty fingers on his skin was seriously testing his patience. He didn't know where to put his hands, so he rested them along the side of the tub and made himself relax as well. She was right; it was perfect.

After about a good thirty or so minutes soaking in complete silence, the water started to cool, and he ran his hands up her arms and gently squeezed her shoulders.

"How about we get you out of here and into some warm clothes, then I'll make us some soup for dinner. You need to get something in your belly."

"Okay." She sleepily agreed, and he smiled as he carried her from the tub to the bedroom.

He set her feet down on a towel and told her to hold onto the chair to steady herself and avoid putting any pressure on her bad ankle. He noticed it was pretty swollen, but she hadn't iced it at all since she had been sleeping most of the day. He would need to remember when they got downstairs to get an ice pack for her.

He stepped away for just a second to grab a dry towel for her, and when he returned, she was breathing heavy, and her lips were quivering as if she were fighting back the tears. Concerned, he rushed to her side.

"What's wrong?"

A tear slipped out of her eye, and she shook her head.

"In the bath, I felt so relaxed, but now I ache so bad. I just want it to go away, dammit!"

"Aww, baby." As gently as he could, he wrapped her up in his arms and pressed her close against him. He kissed the top of her head. "If I could take the pain away from you, I would."

She sniffled, then shivered, and he realized she was still standing there soaking wet. The cabin's temperature was kept around seventy degrees, so he knew it had to be chilly for her.

"Let's get you out of this wet shirt and in some warm clothes, yeah?"

"You're going to have to help me wrap my ribs again. Doctor O'Neal did it for me last night, and there is no way I can do it myself."

He smiled softly, trying to mask his worry, knowing the pain she was in. He pushed a strand of hair off her face and tucked it behind her ear. Despite what she went through and the injuries she sustained, she was a trooper. He promised Ace he would take care of her, and by god he would even if it killed him to see her perfect body and not touch it intimately. At least not until she healed.

"Whatever you need, I'm here to help," Stitch told Mia as he released her. She felt the loss of his touch and wanted to scream for him to come back. She wasn't usually a needy person, but she felt safe and content wrapped in the comfort of his arms. She watched him disappear into his closet, then reappear seconds later dressed in a pair of black sweatpants, and she swore her tongue rolled out of her mouth like those cartoon characters.

He said he would help with whatever she needed, and she wondered if that included helping with the ache she had between her legs. Him standing there with his upper body full of muscles on display made her pussy ache just about as bad as her ribs felt. Her body temperature skyrocketed, and she damned her libido at a time like this. Being with Stitch in the bathtub felt so good and so right. Thank god he sat in silence and didn't want to talk, because she wasn't sure she would be able to concentrate on what he was saying when all that she could focus on was his erection pressing into her back.

Stitch walked over and picked up some shopping bags she hadn't seen by the door, and she wondered where they came from.

"Alex picked up a few things for you. She wasn't sure what you needed, so I told her to get you whatever she thought you'd need between clothes and personal items." He dumped the contents of the bags onto the bed then looked at her.

"Why do you look flushed?" He asked her, and she damned her traitorous body.

Probably because of the naughty thoughts she was thinking. Not that she was going to tell him that. She looked at the items on the bed and noticed a couple of pairs of sexy thong panties laying right on the top of the pile of stuff he had just dumped out. He must have noticed because he looked down at the panties, then looked back at her and gave her a devilish smile. "Nice." She swore her face must have turned fifty freaking shades of red.

He picked up the black lace undergarment lying on top, walked over to her, and squatted down. "Put your hands on my shoulders." The tone of voice was deep and sexy sounding. She focused on his handsome face, and then her eyes traveled to his shoulders that he wanted her to hold on to. Was he out of his mind? If she touched those muscles of his, she wasn't going to want to stop at his shoulders. She heard him chuckle and looked back into his eyes that were twinkling and full of mischief.

"I would love to know what you were just thinking about because your cheeks are so rosy right now that it is downright sexy and cute."

She cleared her throat and rolled her eyes, trying to act unaffected while gripping his shoulders. "Let's just get this over with." When he laughed, she could feel the muscles jump under her fingertips, and she bit her lip to keep from moaning as he slid the panties up her legs and under the towel, letting his fingertips glide over her skin. It was intimate and oh so stimulating. She was going to kill Alex when she saw her. Well, she may thank her first before she killed her.

She jerked when his hands patted her ass before he stood up, towering over her short frame. She wasn't sure what to think right now. She was frazzled and sexually aroused that she wanted to pop a pain pill, wait long enough for it to kick in and throw him onto the bed and ride him into the sunset or until the pill knocked her out. Holy shit balls, being isolated with him for who knows how long was going to be agony if she couldn't get her hands on him.

"Now, the shirt." He told her as he carefully and skillfully maneuvered the wet shirt over her head while she clutched the towel to her body. Standing in just a towel and a thong, she should be cold, but considering how turned on she was, the heat flowing through her veins was enough warmth to ward off the chill.

"What do you want to wear to bed?" He held up some tops that Alex had gotten, but they were camisoles, similar to what she wore last night. They were fitted, which meant they would cling to her body. She was going to have her ribs wrapped, so she wanted something loose. But nothing in the pile of clothes on the bed looked to be loose-fitting. She looked at Stitch and shook her head. "Can I wear one of your t-shirts?"

He grinned, then walked into the closet again and came back with a dark green t-shirt. He helped her put it on, and once the soft, well-worn shirt was in place, he stepped back, and she watched as his smile grew.

"Fucking perfect," he said, staring at her chest. Okay, she had boobs, but they were nothing to hit home about—at least in her book—but when she looked down and read what the shirt said, she couldn't help but smirk.

"Watson's Property"

She looked back toward him and raised an eyebrow. "Nice, Stitch. Do you have a stockpile of these you give to all of your women?"

He frowned as if she had hurt his feelings. "I only have one of those, and you're wearing it."

She felt bad for insulting him. She was just trying to be funny. "Stitch, I'm sorry."

He kissed her forehead. "I'm not mad."

"No, but you're upset, and that wasn't my intention."

"Mia, I swear I'm not mad or upset." He winked at her. "You look good as my property." She grinned, and he walked back over to the bed and grabbed a pair of loose-fitting pajama pants and held them up. "How about these?"

"Perfect."

"Yes, you are." He replied, then bent down to help her as she stepped into them, again making her blush.

Dinner was a quiet affair, and Stitch was glad for the silence. Again, he was forced to hide his anger. Before they had come downstairs, he had wrapped her ribs, and the discoloration along her mid-section infuriated him. He had broken ribs before, and seeing the damage to Mia's skin and thinking that Doc said he didn't think any were broken was a fucking miracle. He was disturbed at the sight of her injuries. The bruising on her skin looked so angry. The red, blue, and purple marks covered most of her upper body, front and back, including her shoulder blades. He hoped that Tink and Derek's detective friend got a lead soon because the fucker responsible was going to pay.

Mia put her spoon down and yawned, and he knew the pain pill he had given her before dinner was working its way through her system. Not only because he could see her getting sleepy, but she also seemed less tense, as if the pain wasn't as bad as when he first brought her downstairs. She patted her belly.

"That was the best tomato rice soup I've had. Is that your recipe?" She asked him as she wiped her mouth with the napkin.

He nodded. "Well, it's my mom's. She used to make it for me when I would come inside from playing outside in the cold as a kid. It goes along great with a grilled cheese sandwich."

She smiled. "You have to love a mom's home cooking. I miss my mom's cooking. She tried to teach me, but cooking was one of those things I wasn't interested in learning. Now I kinda regret it. Most of my cooking either comes in a box—frozen or dry with instructions." She lifted her glass of water to her lips. "But I will say when it comes to macaroni and cheese or mashed potatoes; I am the master at making those from scratch."

"Well, you will have to make them for me one night."

Mia giggled. "That would be the dinner of champions. A starch and carbs fest."

"Who cares. I love them both, and now you've piqued my interest, so you'll have to make them. Once you're better, that is." He said, giving her the eye saying she better not push it.

They talked a little longer while he cleaned up the kitchen. She argued with him when she tried to tidy up the table and wipe it down. She didn't win that battle. He explained that Tink's contact at the NYPD was looking into her abduction and assault and filing a missing person's report to see if that produced any leads. He really wanted to press her to see if she remembered anything she hadn't mentioned last night, but her eyes were already getting droopy. When she yawned again and wobbled in the chair, he knew it was time to get her back upstairs and into bed.

He removed the ice pack from her ankle, set it on the table, then bent over, ready to scoop her up. "Grab on," he said to her and smiled when she did without any hesitation. Once he had her cradled in his arms, she laid her head on his shoulder. From the time it took to walk from the kitchen up to the bedroom, her eyes were already starting to close. He leaned down and kissed her forehead.

"Sleep tight, sweetheart."

He was just inches from her face, and her eyelids fluttered open, just enough to peek at him.

"Where are you sleeping?" She asked in a whisper, and he glanced at the chair next to the bed.

"This is your bed," she told him.

He grinned. "And you belong in it."

"Stitch, it's big enough for both of us to share."

Jesus, she was really testing his patience tonight. The thought of sharing his bed with her made his dick harden. "The chair is fine. For now."

Thankfully she didn't argue. He stood there and waited as she tried to fight the sleepiness, but eventually, her eyes slowly closed, and within minutes, her breathing evened out, indicating she was fast asleep and would be for hours. He had some paperwork he needed to catch up on. He was heading up part of a new training the base was conducting. He'd work on that for a couple of hours before he'd try and get some sleep himself.

124

CHAPTER FIFTEEN

Elijah sat behind his desk, staring at Detective Russ McDonnell from the NYPD as he tried to come to terms with what the detective just explained to him. He had to have misunderstood the detective, because there was no way Mia—his Mia—was considered a missing person. He cleared his throat before leaning forward in his chair.

"Detective, are you certain we're talking about the same Mia Chambers? A doctor with this clinic."

"I'm afraid so. She was due at her brother's place Thanksgiving morning but never arrived on her scheduled flight. He and other family members tried contacting her but to no avail. After twenty-four hours of no contact, they contacted the NYPD, and officers were sent to her apartment, which they found empty. Because of the holiday, it's been hard to contact her neighbors, friends, and coworkers. That is why I'm here so early today."

He suddenly felt as if he could be considered a suspect. In Willow's case, yes, but he honestly had no idea where Mia could be. It was upsetting.

"If she never arrived at her brother's, that means she's been missing for five days now."

"That is why the police and her family are very concerned about her well-being."

"Well, how can I help?"

"I am hoping I can ask you a few questions."

Elijah knew he had to be careful. As much as he was concerned about Mia, he also had to be cautious while providing any information in case the detective would be looking to lure him into a trap. On the other hand, he also couldn't blow the police off, as that would surely send a red flag up and make them take a closer look at him.

"Sure."

"When was the last time you saw or spoke with Dr. Chambers?"

Elijah explained about seeing her at the Fur Ball, then at work the following day. He omitted the part about her showing up at the clinic after the gala because his cousin was an irresponsible idiot.

"So, you two were on a date?" The detective questioned with a raised eyebrow.

"No, I wouldn't consider it a date. It was a work function. I had an extra ticket to the event, and I thought that with Mia being new to the practice that it would be a great networking opportunity for her to meet some clients and other City officials."

"Did the two of you ride together to this work function?"

"To the event, yes. I hired a car service. I left before she did; however, after the car dropped me off, it was sent back to the hotel to pick her up and take her home." He would need to confirm that Claus contacted his friend at the car service to make sure that was the story they used if they were ever questioned.

The detective scribbled notes in his notepad before asking, "Anyone, in particular, she was *networking* with who paid extra attention to her during the evening?"

Elijah shrugged his shoulders. "I'll admit, detective, Dr. Chambers is a beautiful woman. She caught the eye of a lot of men that evening." Including himself, but the detective didn't need to know that. "I was around her most of the evening, but I can't say that I noticed anything out of the ordinary."

"I see. What time did she leave the office the next day? Did you have any contact with her that day?"

"I'm not sure I'm following Detective. Am I being investigated?"

Detective McDonnell smirked. "No, we're just trying to create a timeline of Mia's known whereabouts. Are you aware of any clients or other staff members from the clinic who may have had a problem with Dr. Chambers?"

"None that I'm aware of. Dr. Chambers is well-liked amongst the staff."

"Would you mind if I questioned a couple of members of your staff?" He flipped a page in notepad then looked back at Elijah. "Specifically, a

Danny Nichols and Willow Marshall. They are known friends of Dr. Chambers."

Elijah instantly felt sick. He had already informed the staff that Willow had resigned over the holiday and wouldn't be returning. He was preparing to tell the detective the same thing, but a knock at the door interrupted him.

Before he could get up out of the chair to see who it was, the door opened, and his cousin Marlon appeared, along with Oscar and Jules. He bit the inside of his cheek, trying not to reveal his displeasure, but these three were the last people he needed in this office right now while the NYPD was questioning him.

Marlon's eyes landed on the gold badge hanging around the detective's neck, and his eyes widened before he looked at Elijah.

"Sorry, we thought you were free. We'll come back later," Marlon told Elijah, but it was too late as Detective McDonnel stood, folded his notepad, and slid it into his pocket.

"Oscar Torres," the detective called out and Elijah watched in horror as all the blood drained from his face. Could he look any more guilty?

Detective McDonnell eyed Oscar with a questionable look while resting his hand on the butt of his gun.

"Funny meeting you here. That nose injury looks painful. Who'd you piss off to get that?"

Shit! Elijah had heard all about how the missing woman who had escaped had headbutted Oscar breaking his nose. Oscar wasn't the sharpest tool in the shed. The way he just stood there staring at the detective wasn't doing him any justice. His behavior screamed guilt.

Thinking quickly, Elijah stepped forward, "Marlon, this is Detective McDonnell. Detective McDonnell, these three men are employees of the clinic. They help with our clients who have larger animals that require house calls, like horses and such." He chuckled, putting on an acting job that would have won him a bloody Oscar. "Oscar, unfortunately, met his match with a young colt he was helping move last week and caught a hoof to the face."

The detective nodded his head, but his unreadable expression was what worried Elijah. He wasn't confident that the detective bought it.

Detective McDonnell glanced back at Oscar. "You should be more careful, but then again, I've heard that animals have good instincts." He turned back toward Elijah, and Elijah swallowed hard.

"Thank you for your time, Dr. Walters. If I have any other questions, I'll give you a call."

"Thank you, Detective. And, again, anything I can help with, please let me know. Dr. Chambers is a valued member of this clinic, and in any way we can assist, we will."

"Your cooperation is appreciated."

Elijah watched as the Detective showed himself out.

"What in the hell was that all about?" Marlon asked, and Elijah explained Mia being missing.

"Shit, are you being looked at as a suspect?"

Elijah sat down and leaned back in his chair. "No, they're just building a timeline of when she was last seen."

"What did you tell them?"

"The truth. That she and I were at the gala together, then I saw her briefly in the office the next day. I have no fucking idea where she is."

Elijah couldn't help the odd feeling he got in the pit of his stomach. It wasn't a good feeling either. He needed to watch his back. He'd put a call into Vargas, his informant he had inside the NYPD, and ask him to keep an ear out for anything related to Mia's case. He'd also have Claus ask around town if anyone had heard or seen anything. Jesus, he didn't need this shit right now.

Once Marlon and the others left to take care of some business, Elijah tried to occupy his mind with a backlog of paperwork, but it wasn't working. He couldn't come to grasps that Mia was missing. Knowing the type of criminal activities that took place around the city, he couldn't help but be worried. Mia may be independent, but she was no match for the thugs that ruled the streets.

He threw down his pen and stood up. Maybe some caffeine would help him concentrate. He picked up his coffee mug and headed to the breakroom. On the way down the hallway, he saw Danny.

"Dr. Walters, is it true that Mia is missing?"

Elijah nodded his head. "I'm afraid so Danny. Did the detective speak with you?"

"Yeah."

"Have you had any contact with her since work last Wednesday?"

Danny shook his head. "No, but I told the detective to talk to Willow. She and Mia were supposed to go out for drinks that evening. Willow said that there was something she wanted to talk to her about, but she didn't want to do it here at the office."

"Really?" Elijah suddenly wondered if his instincts were right. Had Willow caught on to his underground business? Has she planned on telling Mia? He then realized he was glad that Willow had been silenced.

"Mia and I were just talking about this last week, but have you noticed a change in Willow the last few weeks?" Danny asked Elijah.

Elijah lied, not wanting to draw any attention to himself for Willow's sudden resignation or disappearance.

"No, but I haven't really had much interaction with her. I will say that her sudden resignation caught me off guard over the weekend. She was a great employee."

"Mia noticed a change in her too. Actually, now that I think of it, Willow had given Mia an envelope but instructed her not to open it until they spoke that night."

Elijah's hairs stood on end, and he wondered what had been in that envelope that was so important that Willow had to discuss it with Mia outside the office. Could the mystery envelope still be at Mia's apartment?

Elijah played it off. "Who knows."

"Well, maybe Willow can give the detective more information. I gave the detective her phone number since she no longer works here. He wanted to speak with her."

He could only cover up Willow's disappearance for so long before someone started questioning her whereabouts as well. At least where Willow was concerned, she didn't have any family.

Elijah nodded his head. "Let's hope for the best and that we hear some positive news about Mia."

Once Elijah got back to his office, he closed the door, then picked up his phone and dialed Claus' number. He needed to make sure that there was no way anyone could trace Willow's disappearance back to him, and he needed to know what was in that envelope Willow gave to Mia.

"Hello."

"We may have a situation. I need you to do some investigating."

CHAPTER SIXTEEN

Mia was curled up on the couch in front of the toasty fire Stitch had started earlier that morning. She laid the tablet down next to her. Thank goodness, Alex had thought to get her a couple of items like the tablet and some magazines that would keep her occupied, considering Stitch didn't have a TV at the cabin. She was finally starting to feel a little better and had more mobility than she had six days ago. Her primary source of pain was her rib area and shoulder blades. Overall she'd been a good patient and had followed Doctor O'Neal's orders. It didn't hurt to have Stitch looking after her to ensure she followed the doctor's directives. He still insisted on carrying her around wherever she needed to go. As much as she wanted to try to walk more independently, she also cherished being held in his arms.

What had been bothering her, though, was his avoidance of the attraction between them. Yes, he had flirted and made comments, and had even kissed her that first night, but over the last day or two, he'd been a little more distant when it came to them. For her, every time Stitch walked into the room, she could feel the atmosphere change. Maybe it was her that needed to initiate things.

"Hey," Stitch greeted her as he walked into the living room, and again his appearance created an energy that felt like a power surge had struck her. The connection between them was so strong.

She wondered where he might be off to, considering he was dressed, had his boots on, and carried his coat. She couldn't help the jealousy swirling around in her. She would kill to go somewhere, even if it was just a trip to the store. Hell, she'd settle for just a car ride. She just wanted to get out.

"Hey yourself," she replied, flashing him a smile.

He walked over and sat on the coffee table in front of her. She stared at his thighs and the way his jeans molded to the muscles flexing against the material.

"How are you feeling today?"

She sat up a little straighter. "Not as sore as yesterday. I might feel a little better if I could get out of the house for a bit, even if I just sat outside on the porch. I need some fresh air." The closest she'd come to fresh air was when the front or back door opened, and she caught a breeze. "Don't get me wrong. I appreciate everything you have done for me, but I'm feeling antsy, especially now that I'm not sleeping most of the day. I've always been an active person, and I have to say, out of all my body parts, I'm sure my eyes are in the best shape right now considering I do over three hundred eye rolls a day."

Stitch laughed. "I kinda figured. I thought maybe we could go a little further than the porch, though."

He had her attention. "What did you have in mind?" She asked, sounding overly hopeful to her own ears.

"Maybe a drive along Skyline Drive, stopping at a few of the overlooks so you can get some fresh air, then grab an early dinner in town on the way back."

If she could bolt upstairs to grab her shoes, she would, but instead, she opted for a big smile. "I would love that. When do we leave?" She asked, starting to lift herself from the couch. She was already dressed in a pair of black leggings and a white long-sleeved tunic. All she needed were shoes and a coat.

Once she was steady on her feet, Stitch stood up. She knew he was observing her. She surprised him when she got up on her tiptoes, putting most of her weight on her good ankle, and kissed his cheek. His skin felt smooth and warm against her lips.

"Thank you for everything, Stitch."

He placed a hand on her hip. "I would do anything for you, Mia. Anything." They stared at one another for several seconds before Stitch said, "I already brought your shoes down, and Alex left a coat for you. Do you need any help getting them on?" Ordinarily, she would have been appalled by him asking her that, but considering that bending over was still a difficult task with her ribs, all she could do was smile up at him because he was sincerely only trying to help her.

"Alex made sure that I had shoes I could easily get my feet in and out of." She opened the box and showed Stitch the light gray slip-on tennis shoes, and he smiled.

"Alex thinks of everything."

Oh, how his statement was true. Little Miss Alex didn't miss a beat. Mia still couldn't believe the sexy panties and bras Alex bought her during her shopping trip.

Stitch held her jacket open for her, and she slid her arms in. He was so gentle it warmed her heart.

"We can also stop at any stores you want along the way. There are a couple of really cool antique shops. I know you like to browse through those."

"That sounds great. I would love to stop and look around if you don't mind."

"As long as you're feeling up to it."

"Trust me; if I'm not, I'll let you know. If we don't make it to them, I can always come back." She glanced over her shoulder and found Stitch staring at her. She looked down at her hands that were clasped together. "Well, that is if I'm welcomed back considering all the trouble I've caused."

He placed his hand against her cheek, and his thumb caressed her bottom lip. She couldn't resist the pull, and she leaned into his touch.

"You're welcome here anytime. In fact, I hope you decide to spend more time here with me." He looked so serious as he told her, and Mia could only hope he was telling the truth because she would absolutely love to spend more time at the cabin with him. She just needed to get to the bottom of the mess she was currently in currently.

The drive along the scenic route was the perfect distraction that Mia had needed. The beauty and calmness the mountains had to offer were breathtaking and tranquil. They had driven a few hours, stopping along the way at various points to view the mountain landscape as well as the many historical spots. She never realized how rich the locale was in Civil War history. She was bummed she didn't have her phone to take pictures, but

Stitch had taken some. She would definitely be returning when she was healed to tour the nearby caverns, maybe get a little snow skiing in, and exploring more of the mountains and communities surrounding it.

On their way back home, they stopped at a little Mom and Pop diner that Stitch regularly frequented when he was up this way.

Finding a table near the back, Mia looked over the menu. She couldn't stop thinking about the last few hours and how Stitch's attentiveness was so different today than the last few days.

Around the cabin, he operated in a work mode mentality. Every now and then, he would sneak a little innuendo in, but today was different. It felt like a turning point in their relationship. That power surge feeling she got had been with her all day. His attentiveness had been off the charts. When they stopped at Hogback Lookout, her favorite lookout stop of the day, Stitch had held her hand the entire time. When they stood together gazing out over the valley below them, he'd hugged her close to him. She savored every moment of the closeness. Neither one had much to say during the drive, though she did want to ask him if he'd heard anything about her case, but it had been too special of a day to ruin it with that ugliness.

Since that first night, she found it frustrating that he had yet to try and kiss her again. She had wondered if she needed to make the next move and show that she was all in for them being together. They definitely needed to talk because the biggest obstacle facing their future together was her brother.

"You're not hurting, are you?" Stitch asked, getting her attention and pulling her from her thoughts.

She shook her head and gave him a soft smile. "No, what made you ask that?"

"You got quiet, and your eyebrows were drawn in." He reached over and brushed his thumb across her forehead. The move sent little tingles through her body. She hadn't realized she was that deep in thought.

"Your expressions are one of the qualities I love so much about you. The way you express yourself, whether you're talking, or like just now as you were thinking."

"Unlike you and my brother, who are tough people to read, but that doesn't mean I don't try to decipher whatever y'all got going through those thick skulls of yours."

He chuckled. "Well, we have had some practice. Believe me, that practice has saved our lives on numerous occasions."

An older lady with graying hair approached the table, and a huge smile crossed her face when her eyes landed on Stitch.

"Stitch! I thought that was you. It is nice to see you again. It's been a while." The lady looked at Mia and smiled. "And I see you brought some company with you."

Stitch smiled. "Hi, Fran. It has been a while."

"Well, it's always a pleasure to see your face around here."

"Fran, I'd like you to meet Mia. Mia, this is Fran. She and her husband, Theo, own this place."

Mia shook Fran's hand. "It's nice to meet you, Fran."

"Likewise, honey. What can I get you two? The special today is pot roast with green beans, mashed potatoes, and a corn muffin."

At the mention of food, Mia's belly decided to alert the entire mountain population that she was hungry.

Stitch laughed. "I guess I should have fed you earlier."

"The special sounds yummy, and obviously, my stomach already approved. I'll take that and a sweet tea, please."

Stitched loved that Mia wasn't a self-conscious eater. He'd seen her put away some food.

Apparently, it had surprised Fran too, because Fran smirked at Mia. "I like you, sugar. A beautiful woman with an appetite." Then she looked at Stitch. "Do I need to ask you what you want?"

"Nope."

"I'll add another special in for you. It'll be out shortly."

Stitch looked across the table and found Mia staring at him. She leaned back in the chair, and her brown eyes sparkled as she spoke.

"This is a perfect ending to our day. I know I've said it several times today, but thank you. I really needed this."

135

He reached across the table and took her hand, stroking the top with his thumb. "It's perfect when you have the right company."

She didn't try to pull away. Instead, she relaxed.

"Can I ask you a question?" She asked.

"Shoot."

"What made you buy a cabin in the mountains? With your job, do you get a chance to come here often?"

Fran set their drinks on the table, and Stitch pulled his hand back to grab his glass and took a sip. He looked back at Mia.

"That's just it. It's because of the job. I wanted another place besides my apartment in town. I wanted a place I could escape to find peace and just take in what the world and nature offered. It's nice to come up here for a couple of days and tune everything out."

She understood what he was saying. She'd heard Ace say when he would come home for a few days to the ranch in Oklahoma. When he wasn't out helping on the land, she'd always find him sitting out on the back porch, taking in the peacefulness. Living in New York City and coming to a town like this gave her an understanding of what her brother and Stitch meant.

"I get it, and I can't disagree with you. It is nice to be able to just relax and not have to worry about life for a few days."

"I feel like I don't get up here enough."

"Well, you should definitely take advantage of it more often. It's a gorgeous town, and the views from your place are breathtaking."

Stitch grinned. "The view is what sold me on the place. Before we head back to the beach, there is something I want to show you that I've never shared with anybody."

They talked more about the town and the people that Stitch knew, then before long, Fran delivered their dinner, and they ate while enjoying one another's company.

When they arrived back at the cabin, Mia wasn't quite ready to go back inside, so she had asked Stitch if she could sit outside for a little bit. The temperature had dropped as the sun made its descent behind the mountains, and the moon made its appearance. Stitch had some work he needed to handle, so he made a fire in the firepit and then got Mia set up on the deck in one of the lounge chairs he pulled over.

After a quick run-through of his emails to make sure that the world wasn't falling apart, he sent off a few emails to the base training staff; he then grabbed another blanket off the couch and walked to the back door. He stood in the doorway, watching Mia take in the sights of what his little slice of heaven offered. Watching the day transition into night, Stitch himself got lost in the picturesque view, and in a matter of seconds, the glow of the sun was gone and replaced by the silhouettes of the mountain tops basking in the moonlight.

The nature and scenery fascinated him. His life as a SEAL hardened him over the years. Seeing the darkness and evil workings throughout the world took a toll on a person. But Mia managed to light up his life and remind him he was also a human being, and that there was so much good to see.

He continued to observe her as she watched the doe and fawn making their way through his back yard. The way the moonlight shined down on her as she stood against the railing was a magical sight. It was like heaven shined a spotlight on a true angel. Her face glowed as she took in the movements of the mama deer and her baby. The moment was priceless. Her humbled expression and the way she took in everything around her, as if not wanting to miss out on something, made his heart grow even more. She was a perfect mixture of every quality he imagined his future wife would have. She was sweet, caring, loving, brilliant, and a spitfire when she wanted to be.

He hadn't mentioned to her yet about speaking to Ace last week, but he planned on doing it tonight because he couldn't hold back his desire to not show her how much he loved and cherished her.

The fire crackled loudly, and Mia glanced over her shoulder, and her eyes fell upon him. He smiled and moved out onto the deck, taking her hand and leading her to the large lounge chair. Once he settled himself, he patted his lap, and her eyes widened.

"Please, Mia. Sit with me?"

137

Without saying a word, she lowered herself, and he scooted over a little. She turned and snuggled into his side, making him sigh in contentment.

"Did you get what you needed to do done?" She asked in a low voice.

"I did. What were you thinking about before I came out here?"

Her head tipped back, and she looked up at him with her brown eyes. "You."

His lips curled slightly. "Me? Really?"

She nodded her head yes, but then laid it back down on his chest, and he sensed that something was off.

"Mia…" She moved again, and the glow from the firelight shined on her cheek where the bruising was the worst. He ran his fingertips lightly down the soft skin. "I don't like seeing you hurting, emotionally, or physically. You don't deserve any of this."

She sighed. "I just want it to be over. I don't like the unknown and being afraid of what could be around the next corner." She looked up at him again and he saw the fearfulness in her eyes. It was a look he never wanted to see. But he sensed there was something else bothering her.

"What else?"

Her eyes widened, and he wanted to laugh because that move alone ratted her out. "What do you mean?"

"What else is bothering you? You mentioned you were thinking about me. Have I done something to upset you?" Stitch asked, hoping he hadn't. He admitted to himself that he'd been a little bossy over the last couple of days, but that was for her own good to help her heal.

"I'm afraid of losing you. I know we're both attracted to each other and we've been playing this cat and mouse game ever since the holidays last year, but I'm tired of running and hiding. I'm afraid that when this whole thing going on with me is all said and done with, you're going to realize that I'm too much trouble and you'll walk away."

Stitch was not only shocked, but he was pissed off that she would think he would be that insensitive to turn his back on her because of something she had absolutely no control over.

138

"Oh baby, let's get something straight right now. I should be insulted that you would even think I could be that shallow of a person." When she went to protest, he stopped her. "Let me finish. I can understand your way of thinking. You've really never had a serious relationship." When she looked surprised at his statement, he couldn't help but grin. "Just because I never acted on my feelings didn't mean I wasn't keeping tabs on you, sweetheart." When he saw the dawning light in her expression, he gave her a gentle squeeze and grinned. "I've had my eye on you for a while. It just took some time for my brain and heart to connect. I've wasted almost a better part of a year thinking about what others would think of us dating when I could've enjoyed that time with you. Yeah, you were still going to school, but still, we could've made it work. I kick myself in the ass every day."

"We both made that mistake. I knew after the first month of dating Terek that he wasn't right for me. I think I avoided you because of my brother. God knows what he would think of us dating."

"What would you say if your brother gave us his blessing?"

"I would say that would be a miracle. He doesn't have much patience when it comes to men and me."

He rubbed her back, "Mia, Ace, and I spoke the night you got here."

Her eyes snapped up, looking directly into his. "What exactly did the two of you talk about?"

"You and me, and what we have between us."

"And…"

He reached his hand under her hair, cupping the back of her neck, drawing her closer until they were nose to nose. He pressed his lips gently against hers, testing the waters. He wanted so badly to show her how he really felt and kiss her deeply. He wanted to taste every inch of her, but he was afraid he wouldn't want to stop, and her body wasn't ready for that yet. He released her lips and stared into her eyes that glistened.

"That should answer your question."

Her smile was so big, and her brown eyes sparkled. She kissed his cheek, then rested her head against his shoulder. She didn't say anything for a few moments, and he wondered what was running through her head.

"You okay?"

She nuzzled her face against the side of his neck.

"It's just a lot to take in. I mean, what if—"

He put his pointer finger against her lips to quiet her.

"Don't play the what-if game. Believe me. It's not worth the mind-fucking. Let's just enjoy the time now."

She smiled, then covered a big yawn.

He kissed the top of her head. "You've had a busy day. How about I take you up to bed?"

"Okay." She said without an argument, and he grinned.

He got her upstairs and into the bathroom so she could change into her pajamas. He took that time to change into something more comfortable. Pulling on a pair of lounge pants, he thought back to earlier in the day and how much he enjoyed spending it with Mia. She was definitely special.

She walked out, and he noticed she was favoring her ankle a little more than earlier.

He held out a pain pill and a glass of water to her. Surprisingly, she took it with no argument, then crawled in bed. He pulled the covers up over her, and she reached for his hand.

"Stay with me tonight?" She asked him as her brown eyes gazed into his.

"I haven't left you alone yet at night."

She looked over at the chair sitting next to the bed. "I don't mean just sitting here in the room with me. I want you to lay in bed with me and hold me. Please?"

How could he say no to that pout? Without a word, he walked over to the main light switch and flipped it, sending the room into darkness. Seconds later, the moonlight filtered through the window, bringing just enough light for him to make his way back to the bed. Not that he needed the light. He had a knack for finding his way in the dark. He pulled the covers down and slid into bed behind Mia. He pressed up against her back. When she tried to turn, he held her still.

"No, stay just like this. This is perfect."

They lay there in silence. It was what he'd dreamed of and something he'd wanted to do every night.

"Stitch?"

"Yeah."

"I have a confession." He could hear the sleepiness in her voice. She was ready to fall asleep any minute.

"What is it?" He asked, loving the way her body fit against his. Then she wiggled her little ass against his dick, and damn did he have the patience of a saint because he wanted to roll her over and bury himself in her. Then she said the three words that blocked everything his mind was processing, and his heart grew.

"I love you," she whispered before her breathing evened out. He grinned and snuggled closer against her body, then kissed her head.

"I love you too, Mia."

His phone buzzed, and he pulled it off the nightstand and smiled, seeing the message from Ace. It was going to be nice to surprise Mia tomorrow morning when he told her that Ace, Alex, and her mom were coming up for a visit.

❧

The next morning Stitch walked into the bedroom and smiled. He couldn't remember the last time sleep had come so easy for him. A lot of nights, he was met with demons from his past missions. Having Mia next to him had been comforting. She was a snuggler, but he didn't mind one bit. He loved having her close and in his arms.

He walked toward the bed, and she popped her head up. Her hair was all tousled, but she still looked sexy. She stretched like a kitten just waking from a nap.

"Hey, sleepyhead. How did you sleep last night?"

She smiled and curled herself around his pillow. "Well, considering I had a very comfortable pillow, I slept like a log." She turned her nose into the air and sniffed. "What smells so delicious?"

"That would be breakfast. Your brother and Alex will be here any minute, and they have a surprise for you, so you better get up and get ready."

He smiled when he saw her face light up. It was nice to see her smiling more.

"Ace is coming?!" She asked excitingly and tried getting out of the bed too fast and then winced as she grabbed her side. "Damn ribs are becoming a royal pain in my ass, I tell you."

He wanted to laugh but thought better of it. Instead, he lowered to a knee in front of her. She reached out and cupped his cheek. He turned his head and kissed her palm.

"You need to be careful. We did a lot of walking yesterday. Maybe too much, now that I think about it."

She smiled at him. "Stitch, yesterday was perfect. I'm just a little achy."

Her recovery was priority number one, and he didn't need her reinjuring herself and causing a set-back.

He stood up and took a step back.

"Stitch?"

"Yeah, babe?"

He watched her closely as she slowly got herself up out of bed and padded in her bare feet over to him. The good news was she seemed to be able to put more pressure on her ankle. He thought with all the walking they did yesterday, she would be feeling some soreness this morning. Once she was in front of him, she placed her hand on his chest. Her touch alone sent warmth through his body. When she looked up at him with those big brown eyes of hers full of so many emotions, he knew he was a goner. There would never be anyone else who stood by his side.

She nibbled her lip and appeared to have something on her mind. He placed one hand over hers that rested against his chest, and the other he wrapped around her gently as not to pester her injuries.

"What is it, Mia? You can be honest with me."

"I wanted you to know that I meant what I said last night when I told you that I loved you. You probably thought I was asleep, but I wasn't, and I heard you say it back but…" Her words trailed off, and he knew what was coming, but he was done pussyfooting around.

Once he finally swallowed the huge mass that suddenly formed in his dry throat, he was able to speak.

"Mia, I'm gonna lay it out for you. I've been in love with you since you showed up at Ace and Alex's last Christmas. I know we've been around each other different times before then, and I don't know....maybe it was because during those encounters, we really didn't get to spend a lot of time around each other, alone. I think I've always been attracted to you, but there were complications that we spoke about yesterday that I think prevented that attraction from growing. But getting to really spend time with you over this past year, I fell head over heels in love with you. And that's the honest-to-god's truth. I love you, and if I could marry you tomorrow, I would."

He loved seeing that big bright smile he knew she had. It was a part of her that he loved. She was always a people person and friendly. Unless you pissed her off, and then the gloves were off. He'd witnessed it.

"Now, I'll let you get ready since our guests should be arriving in the next twenty minutes or so, but if I know your brother, he'll probably be walking in any minute. He is anxious to see you." She grinned, and that look warmed his heart. He gave her another quick kiss. "When you're ready to come downstairs, holler, and I'll come and get you."

"Stitch, I told you, I need to start walking on my own, and that includes walking down the stairs. Even you've mentioned how I need to build back my strength."

Ignoring her comment, he said, "I'm sure the hot shower will feel good on those sore muscles."

"Actually, a hot shower sounds really nice."

"Just remember to sit on the bench. I don't need you falling down and hurting your pretty little self any more than you already are."

"Yes, Sir." She said as she gave him a mock salute then giggled when he gave her that stern look.

He pointed to the bathroom. "Go!" She chuckled again, and the sound went straight to heart.

"Love ya!" She called out.

"Love you too," he responded as he walked out of the room, feeling a little lighter on his feet. He shook his head. Damn, it felt good to be able to express his love to her finally. Now, he just needed to make sure her overprotective brother was really on board. He may have already talked to Ace about him dating Mia, but now it was time to clue him in that she was it and he wanted to marry her.

৩

Mia sat out on the deck with her mom. Alex was there, but then she had gone inside to give them some time alone.

Her mom reached out and pulled her into another hug, and Mia fought off the tears. She knew her mom had been worried and wanted to come sooner, but it hadn't been safe. It still wasn't, considering the police were still yet to obtain any leads on her kidnapping.

"Oh, baby girl, we were all so worried. Your brother knew something wasn't right when he read that text you sent."

"I hope he's not blaming himself for this."

"You know your brother. You were always his favorite. Since the day we brought you home from the hospital, he was always by your side. As you grew older, he was also the first in line to be the one to teach you things. And to this day, I think he still needs that connection with you. But you both are adults now, and I think he feels like he let you down."

"Why would he think that? He didn't know this was going to happen to me. Nobody did." Mia shook her head and took a deep breath before exhaling. "Mom. I don't even remember enough to give the police any information. I feel like I forgot something."

"Don't worry, honey. Traumatic events affect people differently. If there's something of importance, it will come to you, eventually. I'm sure. But for now, you need to put all that effort into healing."

"Tell me, how is Stitch doing? Is he taking good care of you?"

"Of course. I think he has gone above and beyond his call of duty. He's been super patient and very attentive. Yesterday he got me out of the house, and we drove up Skyline Drive and even stopped in town for dinner."

"Well, if my instincts are correct, I think that young man has had a thing for you since he first laid eyes on you."

"I don't know about that," she said and then looked out beyond the tree line behind the house. She needed to be honest with her mon.

"I was so afraid of what Ace would think. Stitch said he talked with him that first night, but I'm still not sold."

"I think you might want to have a chat with your brother." Mia looked at her mom. "Oh, sweetie, your brother knows you and Stitch are attracted to one another. Alex had to help him out a little. But you know your brother if it bothered him, don't you think he would have spoken to one of you by now?"

"I feel complete with him. I'm happy around him."

The amused expression her mother had on her face blossomed into a full-on smile. Charlotte pressed her palm against Mia's cheek. It was such a motherly gesture. "Honey, I have only wanted the best for you in your life, including a man. And I must say that Stitch is a man of honor, one who I know will have the best intentions for my baby girl. The two of you are perfect for each other."

Mia sniffled. Damn, she really didn't want to cry, but this was a happy moment. She lived for the day she could tell her mom about a man that she loved. She was always the one in her family that had sat back and watched her two sisters find love and get married. Then Ace met Alex, and even her mom was dating someone now. She felt the waterworks getting ready to start.

"I love him so much, mom."

"I know you do, sweetie."

Mia hugged her mom, then pulled away and picked up her mug of coffee. "So, now that you have the scoop on my love life how about yours? How is that hottie Colonel of yours?"

Her mom and Colonel Johnson, who ironically was the base commander in Afghanistan where Ace and Alex had met, were introduced to one another at Ace and Alex's place last year during Christmas. They immediately hit it off and started dating, currently running almost six months. Her mom had even moved from the ranch in Oklahoma to Virginia Beach.

Mia watched as a bright smile took over her mom's face.

"He is wonderful. Things are great between us. There is something that I wanted to talk to you and your brother about."

"What's that?"

"Mike asked me to marry him."

"Oh my god! Mom, that's wonderful. You said yes, right? Oh wait, does Ace know yet?"

"Yes, Mike actually asked him. Your sisters know too. Are you sure you're okay with it?"

"Why wouldn't I be?"

"Well, I just thought…"

"Because of dad?"

"Yeah, your father will always have a place in my heart."

"I know, mom, but you deserve to be happy too. And if Mike is the man that makes you happy, then go for it. Daddy would want you to live your life and be happy."

Apparently, love was in the air for most of the Chambers clan.

Ace couldn't stop laughing at a story Mia was telling. Talk about embarrassing to get caught with your pants down, literally.

"So, you see, Ronnie, one of the kids who lived down the road from us dared Ace to run down our street butt-naked."

Alex's eyes widened, and she covered her mouth. She looked at Ace. "You didn't?"

Ace laughed. "Damn right, I did. That kid was a punk, and damn if I was going to back down from a dare, especially from him."

"Yeah, but Sherriff Grate had perfect timing. I remember mom and dad getting that phone call telling them to come and pick up their son down the road and to bring clothes," Mia said laughingly.

"Maybe, but at least I had the attention from all the girls at school the following week."

Alex slapped Ace in the chest. "That is so wrong." Ace couldn't help but laugh. He put his arm around Alex and hugged her, then she reached over and squeezed his thigh. He looked down into her green eyes and couldn't believe how lucky he was to have found her. She was his heart and soul and another reason to give that extra percent when on a mission to make damn sure that he came back home to her.

"You know I love you."

She smiled. "I love you, too."

He turned his eyes back onto his sister. Oh, she wasn't getting out of this without her own little story. Yeah, little miss perfect wasn't the little saint everyone portrayed her to be. He took a drink from his glass before clearing his throat.

"I think it's only fair that we expose the skeletons from your closet, sis."

She tilted her head at him and gave him a look as if she had no clue what he was talking about. Ace grinned maniacally. *Let me refresh your memory.*

"Everyone always called her an angel. But you didn't fool mom." He glanced over at his mom and winked, making her smile. "Mom always said that you were the little devil, and she was right."

"I was not," Mia stated, her voice pitching high. "I've got that halo over my head."

Ace shrugged his shoulders. "Maybe, but what people don't see are the retractable horns that can sprout out of her head at any given time."

"What are you talking about? I was the good sibling growing up." She looked at her mom, who tried to stay out of the bantering, but all she could do was shrug her shoulders.

"Really?" Ace replied as he raised his eyebrows. "Let's see if you can recall the only time you ever got a spanking in your life." He didn't know what was funnier; how red Mia's face turned, or his mom who looked mortified as if she just had a flashback of that day twenty-one years ago. He gave Mia a wicked grin. "By the look on your face, I am guessing you know exactly what I'm talking about."

147

"Ace…" Mia warned. But Ace just smiled. What Mia had done was a classic. It was the day the entire town got to see a glimpse of the "real" Mia Chambers.

"Oh, well, now you have to share, considering how red Mia's cheeks are," Stitch said and kissed the side of Mia's head, making Ace smile. Stitch was a good man and good for Mia. He wished them both nothing but happiness.

He was shocked when his mom interrupted and continued telling the story. He didn't miss the slight twitch in her lips. Yeah, she was pissed all to hell the day it happened, but looking back now, it was funny as shit, and apparently, his mom thought so too.

"Well, my baby girl here, thought it would be funny to put an Alka seltzer in her mouth right before her baptism ceremony. Ace, Mikayla, and Maxie were all baptized when they were babies. Mia on the other hand, we had waited." Charlotte covered her face as if she was reliving it. "Oh my god, it was so awful. Here we were in front of the entire congregation because we decided to do it on a Sunday during church. Mia had taken a sip of water while Reverend Shay was talking, when all of a sudden, in the middle of his spiel, Mia started foaming at the mouth and growling like a rabid animal." Ace couldn't hold it anymore as he roared with laughter.

"How old were you?" Stitch asked Mia laughing.

"I was six," Mia said with a pout on her face.

Ace nodded his head. "See six as in the number of the devil." Mia flipped him the bird, and he threw his back and laughed harder, which made everyone chuckle.

He missed those times, but prayed when he and Alex had kids that they wouldn't pull a stunt like that. But considering Alex was a professional prankster, he wouldn't be surprised if his kids followed in their momma's footsteps. He looked over at his fiancé, and she was beaming. It hit him square in the chest. He was one lucky bastard. She was a woman of integrity, courage, beauty, intelligence, and pure badass. She moved her hand, and her diamond engagement ring sparkled in the light, and his chest tightened. He needed to put that matching wedding band on her finger. They'd talked in passing about setting a new date. But they needed to have a full sit-down conversation and talk it over. And with both their schedules, it almost made it impossible.

After dinner, while Mia, Charlotte, and Alex cleaned up the kitchen and spent more time together, Stitch and Ace sat on the patio by the fire.

Ace shook his head. "I still can't believe you and my sister are dating. I mean, I'm happy for you guys, and I'm fine with it, but it's just weird."

"There is something I wanted to talk to you about. I know the relationship between Mia and I is new, but having the last year to really get to know her on a friendship level, I know that she is the one for me. Once we get things settled with her case, I want her and I to discuss our next steps. I'd like to know more about her career path and where that takes her in terms of where she'll live, though my hope is she'll join all of us in Virginia Beach. After we get a clearer picture of those and settle down, I'd like to ask Mia to marry me, with your permission. I also plan on talking to your mom, as well. I love her, Ace."

Ace's eyebrows rose before he brought his beer to his lips, and Stitch waited.

"Christ, man, can you at least let me get used to you two dating first?"

Stitch chuckled, but then Ace sobered, "I couldn't ask for a better person to marry Mia. I know you'll take care of her just as she will do the same for you. Of course, you have my permission."

Stitch exhaled the big breath he had been holding in.

"Just don't beat me down the aisle, or I'll never hear the end of it from my mother or Alex," Ace followed up with.

"Well, you and Alex better start planning because I don't intend to wait too long. I've already wasted almost an entire year. I don't have that much patience."

Ace leaned back into the chair and got comfortable, stretching his legs out. The forecast called for a light dusting of snow in the area.

"Alex and I can't seem to get on the same page in terms of a new date. I know she wants that wedding just as bad as I do, but we can't ever find an open date. Shit is just non-stop right now. Between work and her Foundation that has taken off to extraordinary levels, we hardly see each other as it is. I just hate it hanging over our heads. More so for her. She had worked so hard getting our original date planned, and then you saw how that went to shit."

Stitch took a drink of his beer. "Sorry, man. I know Alex has been itching to get married. You both deserve it."

Ace smiled. "She deserves the wedding she wants. I mean, after all, you only get one, and if she wants the big dream wedding she planned, then that's what she's going to get."

Stitch chuckled. "But you have to have a date first."

Ace pointed at him. "Exactly."

"Well, you have a three-hour ride home. Maybe bring it up in the car."

Ace nodded his head, and Stitch could only wish his friends the best.

They sat in silence for a minute or two. The only sound was the fire crackling between them. Finally, Ace broke the silence.

"Derek said you had to report to base for that new training you've been helping to design."

"Yeah, it's this weekend. I thought I'd take Mia down with me. It could be good for her to get together with the others and have some normalcy. Maybe even make plans for Saturday night dinner at Bayside. Derek said things have been quiet, and nothing or nobody seemed out of the ordinary hanging around."

Ace thought about it, then shrugged his shoulders. "I don't see what it can hurt. Are you staying at your place?"

"No, I talked to my dad last night and explained everything to him. Mia and I are going to stay with him and mom."

"You know you guys can always stay with Alex and me. Shit, we have plenty of room."

Wasn't that the truth. The house had been bought initially by Alex when she moved back to Virginia Beach. Why she had decided to buy a five-bedroom home still puzzled Stitch and everyone else for that matter.

"Thanks. Mom and dad are excited to meet Mia. Have you heard any news out of New York?"

"Tink spoke with the detective yesterday. They're following up on a few possible leads, but whatever those are, he isn't sharing. Yet. Alex and I are taking a trip up there on Wednesday. Some of Tink's guys are going to go along."

"Why is that?"

Ace shrugged his shoulders. "Call it intuition. I just want to have a look around her apartment. Tink set it up with the detective. It'll be a quick trip up and back in the same day."

Ace leaned back in the chair.

"How is Mia really doing? I know my sister, and she isn't one to sit around on her ass. She doesn't know the meaning of taking it easy."

"She has been taking Dr. O'Neal's orders seriously. She is down to only one pain pill a day, and that's at night. If she has some discomfort during the day, she opts for something over the counter that won't make her tired.

"Is she getting the rest she needs?"

"Yes, yesterday was the first day I even let her out of the house. We took a drive along Skyline, stopped at a couple of the lookouts, then finished up with an early dinner in town. She even passed on stopping in some of the antique shops along the way."

At that news, Ace raised his eyebrows, clearly shocked. "My sister actually said no to going into an antique shop?"

Stitch laughed and took another slug of beer. "Yeah, that's how I knew she'd had enough for one day. After dinner, we came home and just relaxed. Well, I finished up that presentation I have to give this weekend on that new medic kit the government wants us to transition to."

"Well, everyone will be happy to see you back this weekend."

"Likewise," Stitch replied, clinking bottles with Ace.

An hour later, after Stitch and Mia had said their good-byes to everyone, Stitch turned to her.

"Are you okay?" He asked.

Stitch's voice grabbed her attention, and she looked up to see him standing in front of her with a concerned expression. When had he gotten there? She blinked her eyes.

"Mia..."

"Yeah, I'm okay; why?"

"Well, I called your name a couple of times, but you were staring at that fire like you were in a trance."

She noticed he had put a sweatshirt on. He smiled.

"I saw how you enjoyed sitting outside last night and again earlier today with your mom, so I thought we could sit out on the deck again and get some fresh air next to the fire."

God, could he get any sexier. Two qualities she loved about Stitch were his calmness and patience. Even though she had never seen him in action on the battlefield, nor would she like to for several reasons, she sensed that those traits followed him while deployed. Being a medic, he had to be able to keep his shit together in the heat of the moment.

Realizing she had zoned out again, she looked up again and smiled. "That sounds nice. As much as I love sitting here in front of the fire relaxing, Bambi up there is starting to freak me out a little. I feel like it's staring at me." She pointed to the stuffed, fake deer head mounted above the fireplace. Stitch laughed, then walked over and placed a jacket around her shoulders. He told her to hang on to the blanket, then he leaned down and scooped her up into his arms. She looped her arms around his neck and held on. As he made his way to the back door, she looked up at him. As much as she loved being carried all over by Stitch, she really needed to start walking and getting stronger.

"You know I could've walked the few feet myself. I believe we had this conversation this morning. My ankle is much better."

He shrugged his shoulders and gave her the cutest boyish grin, and she swore she saw his cheeks turn a light shade of pink. The expression took a couple of years off him. It was rare to witness, as men like Stitch and her brother were hardened trained killers but to be able to see and know the real men under the façade was a treasure.

"I figured I wouldn't have many more opportunities, so I'll take them while I can," he admitted, and she smiled and kissed his cheek. He sat down on the oversized chair, brought her down on his lap, and then fixed the blanket covering them both. She burrowed closer to him. According to the thermometer nailed to the banister, it was close to freezing. The temperature may have been cold, but being snuggled up with a human heater and the man she loved was hot.

For a few minutes, they sat enjoying each other's company and the peacefulness the scenery provided. Moments like this were what she wanted to come home to every night. At least when her man wasn't flying off somewhere to serve and protect.

Stitch's deep voice broke the quietness. "You mentioned your ankle is feeling better. How do the ribs feel?"

"It's bearable, but I won't lie; sometimes it hurts when I forget and make a sudden move. Like this morning."

"Do you think you feel good enough to head to the beach for the weekend?"

She looked up at him and wondered if he was just messing with her. If he were, that would be mean because she would love to see all her friends. Then she thought about the conversation she and Ace had earlier. With no news on her case, would they really take the chance of her being found?

"Really?" She found herself asking a little cautiously.

He pushed a strand of hair from her face. "Ace and I talked about it today. I have a meeting at the base that I need to be at, and he and I thought it would be good for you to get some socializing time in, even though I love having you all to myself."

She grinned. "I've enjoyed it here as well. It was needed, although I could've gone without the drama. But, I agree, it would be nice to see everyone. How long will we stay?"

"It'll be just for the weekend. We don't want to push it. There is a possibility that I may have to ship out for a day or two. It's for training purposes. If that's the case, I'd like you to stay with my parents until I return. Are you okay with that?"

"If you think that is best, then that's what I'll do. But why can't I stay with my mom and the Colonel? Or even Alex?"

"Because your brother and I both feel it would be safer to stay at my parent's house."

"Are we going to stay at your apartment, though? For the weekend, that is?"

"No, we're staying with my parents. I'd feel safer having the extra layer of protection."

Mia gave him an odd look. "What could be safer than having a SEAL as my protector?"

He grinned, showing off his cuteness. "Having two SEALs looking over you." He tapped her on the nose.

"Two? Which one of the guys is going to be staying at your parents with us?"

"Something you don't know but were bound to find out eventually, my dad was a former SEAL. He served the same time as Alex's uncles, just on a different team. Actually, Frost's dad served with my dad on the same team. It's how Alex, Tenley, Frost, and me all knew one another."

Mia was confused. "I get you, Frost and Alex, but how did Tenley fit in there? I thought she didn't have a dad growing up."

"She didn't. Her mom worked on base, and all the guys knew her. Plus, she went to the same elementary school as the rest of us."

"I think it is pretty awesome that you all have stayed best friends through the years."

"It was hard when Frost and I enlisted, and then Alex left for college before being recruited by the government."

She nuzzled his neck. "Well, I'm glad everything worked out for everyone."

He kissed her forehead as she lay against him. "Me too. So, are you good with the plan?"

"MmmHmm," she murmured. Inside she was doing a happy dance. It was going to be a fabulous weekend.

He gave her a hip a light tap. "Seriously? Darn, I was all pumped up for an impending argument."

"Oh, stop. Trust me; I think my ego can take a backseat where my safety is concerned. I will gladly take any and all advice from skilled professionals such as yourself and my brother. Or any other member of your team."

He pulled back and gave her a strange look. "Okay, where is the actual Mia, and what have you done with her?"

"This is the new and wiser Mia," she said as she stared into his eyes.

He cupped her cheek. "I don't want the 'new' Mia as you put it. I fell in love with the same person you are now. I fell in love with who you are on the inside. None of that has changed, and I don't want it to either. Now, do you want to tell me what had you so zoned out in front of the fire a little while ago that you didn't even notice me standing right in front of you?"

She laid her head back against his shoulder and looked up at the sky.

In the mountains, the stars seemed so much closer and appeared bigger and brighter. It was like thousands of diamonds sparkling against the ink-black sky.

"I was thinking about home, more specifically, where home is for me. I always considered the ranch in Oklahoma as my true home, but I haven't lived at the ranch in years. With my mom moving to Virginia Beach, the ranch really wouldn't feel like home anymore. I mean, my sister and her family will be living there, but it would feel weird since that's their home now to make new memories in."

"Aw, baby, you'll still have all of your memories to fall back on. Look at the brighter side of things. At least the ranch will still be in the family. I've met your sister and her family, and I know that she will carry on traditions you all shared when you were kids growing up."

"Yeah, you're probably right. But then I think about where my temporary home is now."

"Your temporary home?"

She sighed, "New York. I mean, I have a job that pays very well. When I say very well, I mean way above what the average vet is normally entitled to right out of school. But, honestly, the money doesn't make me happy. I

155

put in full days every day of the week. Some nights I don't even leave the clinic until around eight or so. I've only just begun my career, and I feel burned out already."

He shifted in the seat, where he could see her face better. "What are you saying, Mia?"

"I'm saying that I don't want to go back to New York. I want to be near my family and friends. I want to find a job in my field of work that I'll enjoy but still be able to have a social life." Stitch could tell she wasn't finished, so he waited while she found her words.

She pulled back and looked up at him, placing her hands against his cheeks. "I want home to be with you. I know that probably sounds crazy, considering we literally just confessed our love for one another a day ago, but I'm being totally transparent with you right now. I love you so much. I want our relationship to grow and prosper. I want us to start making memories of our own. I just want you."

When Mia finally finished, Stitch couldn't hide his excitement. Hell, he knew his smile was probably a mile wide. But damn if her words hadn't squeezed his chest a little tighter.

He held her chin and kissed her. "Your words undo me. I love you so much and want those exact things with you. When all this is over, I'm going with you to New York and helping you pack. I'm sure your partners in crime will be ecstatic to have you living nearby. But nobody will be any happier than me. Well, I take that back. Your brother is going to be damn happy. But, Mia, your home will be with me in my home until we find something we both want and are happy with."

"I wouldn't want it any other way."

She leaned forward and kissed him. When she went to pull back, he cupped the back of her head and drew her back in. He had been patient long enough. He wanted to taste her. He flicked his tongue against her wet lips, indicating he wanted in. She obliged, and he slid in, intertwining his tongue with hers. His hand slid to the nape of her neck, and he caressed her skin as he made love to her mouth. She shifted, and he felt her flinch before she pulled back. He licked his lips, savoring her unique taste, but when her eyes met his, he saw the agony and became immediately worried.

"What's wrong?"

"I just moved the wrong way, and my ribs didn't like it. I'll be okay in just a minute," she said, biting down on her lip and trying to hide her pain, but she was doing a terrible job and she knew it because Stitch narrowed his eyes at her.

"The last thing I wanted to do was cause you more pain."

"You didn't!" She pleaded with him. "I've waited over a year for you to kiss me like that. Pain or no pain, I wasn't letting it ruin the moment. Believe me; I want so much more of you."

Well, hell….how could he argue with that. He couldn't, but her pouty face made him chuckle.

"Babe, I enjoyed that kiss just as much as you, but you are in pain. Come on, pill time."

"Nooo…." She whined.

"Yes, remember no setbacks in your recovery." She looked up at him and stuck her bottom lip out, and batted those damn puppy dog eyes that would get her whatever she wanted. He gave her a quick kiss. "Don't look so sad; I'm joining you. Believe it or not, having you next to me helps me sleep better as well."

He stood, lifting her, and she snuggled into his chest.

After making another sweep through the house, double-checking the locks, and setting the alarm, Stitch stripped down to his boxers and crawled into bed. He wasn't surprised to find Mia already fast asleep. As soon as he cozied up behind her, she turned over and snuggled into his side, making him smile. He hoped like hell they would soon get a lead on the New York situation because he was ready to begin his life with her. He embraced her while her soft snores lulled him to sleep.

CHAPTER SEVENTEEN

"Detective McDonnell, it's nice to meet you," Ace said as he shook the detective's hand. "This is my fiancé, Alex."

The detective smiled. "It's nice to meet both of you. Follow me, and we can talk in my office. Would either of you like anything to drink?" He offered as they entered a small, bare-bones office. The only things that made it resemble an office space were the desk, a computer that looked like it belonged in a museum, and two chairs.

"No, thank you." Ace answered.

The detective motioned to the chairs. "Please, have a seat."

Once Ace and Alex were seated, the detective started to give them an update on Mia's case.

"I'll be honest with you. When Tink first called me and explained what happened to your sister, I thought we were dealing with a crime that we deal with daily. I know that sounds awful, but this is a dangerous city.

"But you don't think that way, now?"

"No. There's more to this case than meets the eye. I just haven't found that missing link yet, but I'm feeling optimistic that I'm close."

"Can you give us any update?"

"Right now, my focus is on Mia's place of employment."

Ace sat forward in the chair. "You think someone at her office was behind her abduction?"

"I don't know if they were behind it, but I have a hunch there is definitely something off about that place, and someone knows something."

Ace listened as Detective McDonnell explained the facts they had to go on. He hadn't been lying; there wasn't a ton of evidence. There were no witnesses to her abduction, and they looked into street cameras but only caught the side of the van they believed was used. Unfortunately, it was just a white delivery van with no distinguished markings. They interviewed her neighbors to see if they had seen or heard anything. The focus there was on the good Samaritan who dropped Mia off at her apartment. The detective was baffled by the mystery person's involvement in the ordeal. Whoever it had benn knew the placement of the cameras around her apartment building. He had been able to avoid every single one of them. All they had to go on was Mia's recollection from that night, which wasn't a lot.

The detective told them about visiting her workplace, and what Danny—Mia's friend and co-worker—had told him about Willow and how they couldn't locate her.

"So, this Willow girl is missing now, too?" Alex asked.

"We don't know for sure. According to Dr. Walters, he received her resignation via email during the Thanksgiving weekend."

"Can't you contact her family?"

"It appears she doesn't have any family. From records we were able to locate, she was an only child. Her dad died when she was young, and her mom passed away a little over a year ago. After her mom died, she moved to the city. It seems she's a loner, doesn't have many friends. In fact, Mia and Danny were who she would hang out with outside of work.

"You mentioned that Danny said Willow wanted to talk to Mia the night she disappeared."

The detective nodded his head. "Danny said that both he and Mia had noticed a change in Willow's behavior. He said it had started about a month ago. Danny also mentioned that Willow gave Mia an envelope and told her not to open it until they spoke."

"Have you been able to locate that envelope?"

"No. With your permission, we looked through Mia's apartment but couldn't find that or anything that could be a clue in her case. I was planning on calling Tink to see if he could ask Mia about it."

"I'll see her tomorrow, so I can ask her, if you'd like. I know you have other cases besides hers."

"If you could, I'd appreciate it."

"Would it be okay if Alex and I went by Mia's apartment to have a look around?"

159

"No, not at all. Would you care if I tagged along? Maybe we missed something when we were there. Since you're her brother, you may see something out of place that we didn't."

"Fine by me."

Ace pulled up to the curb by Mia's apartment. He handed Alex the key to the apartment.

"I'll let you off here, then go park the car in the off-site lot the detective told us to use."

Alex could tell that Ace was uptight and frustrated with the lack of information on Mia's case. She was frustrated as well, but she knew the police were doing everything they could.

She took the key from Ace, then leaned over, putting her hand against his cheek, and smiled.

"Ace, you need to relax a little."

He blew out a long breath. "I can't. Not until whoever is responsible for my sister's assault is caught."

"I understand. I'm not saying this will happen, but what are you going to do if you get called up, and there are still no answers? You can't let this consume you. If you let it, then you are putting yourself in danger and your team. Ace, look at the positive; Mia's safe. We have to give the police some time to put the puzzle together. If this puzzle is anything compared to the ones I've worked on, that missing piece will show up."

From the look in his eyes, Alex could tell she had gotten her message across.

Ace pulled her closer, fisted her ponytail in his hand, and tugged until her head tilted back. "Thank you," he said before he took her mouth hard in a crushing kiss that sent her heart racing. Damn, the man's kisses alone made her head spin.

When he released her, she felt flushed, but so loved.

He winked. "Go on; I'll be up in a bit."

She smiled, then exited the car and made her way into the building. Finding Mia's apartment was easy, and in no time at all, Alex found herself standing just inside. She moved further inside and closed the door but left it unlocked for Ace and Detective McDonnell. She walked through the living room, noting that the place was neat and tidy. Just the way Mia kept her place. As Alex went to walk down the hallway toward the two bedrooms, she stopped at the console table in the hallway and smiled at all the pictures Mia had displayed. There were pictures of everyone—her family, her brother's team, and even some of Alex and Tenley. But the one picture that stood out was the one of Mia and Stitch. Alex remembered taking the picture. It had been on Christmas, and they weren't even looking at the camera. The way they both gazed into each other's eyes, you could see the chemistry was there. It was a special moment between them.

Moving along, Alex pushed open the door to Mia's room. Mia had asked her to pick up a few things since they were coming. As Alex made her way toward the closet, the hairs on the back of her neck stood up. She knew that feeling well and knew she wasn't alone. There was someone in the room with her. The only spaces large enough for someone to hide were the bathroom or the closet. Her heart started to race as she thought about how she should play this out. She saw a large duffle bag next to the bed. She grabbed it and went to Mia's dresser and acted like she was pulling some clothes out to pack, but really she was texting Ace from inside the drawer.

Before she got a reply from him, the atmosphere in the room changed in a flash. Trusting her intuition, she took the bag and retreated from the room. She was midway down the hall when she heard the floor creak behind her. As she turned, all she got a glimpse of was a large hand coming at her. Grateful for her quick reflexes, she ducked just in time. She tripped on the bag she had dropped, which gave the guy an opportunity, and he took it. Wrapping his arms around her from behind, he lifted her feet off the floor. He was huge; about Ace's size. Using the wall in front of her as leverage, she pushed her feet against it and sent both of them backward and onto the floor.

The guy lost his grip, and she turned the tables on him and pounced like the fearless lioness she was. She couldn't claim a victory as he rolled them across the floor until he had her pinned under him. She wrapped her legs around his ribs and squeezed with all her might. He was breathing heavily, and his face had turned red. She managed to get her right arm free and swung, hitting him in the jaw, stunning him. Taking the opening, she scrambled to her feet and got into a fighting position. Hopefully, Ace could hear what was going on and would barge in any second.

"Who the fuck are you?" He asked, breathing heavily as he too rose to his feet. She would have ran for the door, but he stood between her and it. She didn't miss the heavy English accent.

"I should be asking you the same question." She wiped the blood from her lip when something on the floor where they were wrestling caught her attention. She realized it was a police badge at a closer examination, though she couldn't make out what it said. She looked up at the hulking of a guy. "You're a cop?"

He started to speak when the door burst open as the cavalry arrived led by Ace, although they were a little late to the party. Ace took one look at her, and his expression went from concern to rage in two seconds.

Ace and Detective McDonnell had just entered the lobby of Mia's apartment building when he received a cryptic text from Alex that read, "I'm not alone." He cursed and showed the message to the detective, and they took off up the stairs taking two steps at a time. As they rounded one of the landings, his phone rang with a call from Alex. He answered, putting it on speaker as he continued to climb the stairs. Instead of hearing her voice, the sounds of a scuffle was heard, followed by glass breaking.

Ace's adrenaline was pumping as he pounded up the remaining two flights of stairs. The entire time he could hear her putting up a fight. He was going to kill whoever laid their hands on her. As soon as they made it to Mia's apartment, he didn't waste a second as he kicked the door in.

"You're a cop?" Alex asked as Ace and Detective McDonnell filled the doorway. The guy, who was a pretty big dude and physically fit, turned and raised a gun, stopping Ace in his tracks.

"FBI, freeze!"

Ace slowly raised his hands, showing he wasn't armed. At least it appeared that way. His gun was tucked in the waistband of his jeans, concealed by his shirt and he had a second one strapped to his ankle.

He took a quick glimpse at Alex to make sure she was okay and became enraged when he saw the blood oozing from her lip.

"NYPD!" Detective McDonnell shouted from beside Ace with his weapon drawn and aimed at the stranger inside the apartment.

Nobody moved a muscle as the tension in the apartment escalated.

"Identify yourself," McDonnell ordered to the stranger.

"Terek Larkin, FBI. My shield is on the floor, and my identification is in my back pocket."

Ace saw the shield on the floor.

The so-called FBI guy lowered his weapon, and Ace heard the click of the safety being engaged and felt a little less apprehensive. He took Alex's hand and tugged her towards him. He stood in between her and Larkin, acting as a shield just in case. His hand went to her lip, where the blood continued to seep from the laceration, and he used his thumb to wipe away what he could.

"You okay?" Ace asked while putting some pressure on the cut to stop the bleeding.

He hadn't realized how bad he was shaking until she covered his hand. It was weird because as soon as her hand made contact with his, a sudden calmness overcame him. "I'm okay," she told him as he continued to stare into her emerald eyes. She repeated the words. This time a little slower, trying to get her point across. "I'm okay."

"You scared the shit out of me. When I heard…" She cut him off by getting up on her tiptoes and kissing him, hurt lip and all. He pulled her close and hugged her as their lips stayed pressed together. She gave his waist a little squeeze and pulled away, and he stared down at her. Her eyes glistened, but he recognized the look and her expression and knew she was telling the truth.

The FBI guy reached into his pocket and pulled out his identification, and handed it to McDonnell. Once he confirmed it was a legit ID, he lowered his weapon and holstered it.

"What is your business in this residence, Agent Larkin?" McDonnell questioned.

"I'm checking up on a friend."

"Mia Chambers is a friend of yours?"

"You could say that."

"What the fuck does that mean?" Ace interjected into the questioning, which drew a scowl from Detective McDonnell.

"Maybe I should be asking you three what you're doing here?" The agent countered, and that just pissed Ace off.

Ace went to reply to the pompous ass, but McDonnell beat him to it.

"Spare me the sarcasm, agent."

"Wait, did the bureau contact you?"

"Bureau? No, why would the bureau contact me?" McDonnell asked.

"About Mia."

"What about Mia?"

Ace folded his arms across his chest. He slowly started to get frustrated as they were getting nowhere with this guy.

"Look, all we're doing here is spinning our wheels. Why in the hell would the bureau contact the NYPD regarding my missing sister?" Ace asked the agent. Instead of another sarcastic response that he was expecting, the guy surprised him when his demeanor took on a whole different approach.

"You're Mia's brother? Wait…She's missing?" He then turned toward McDonnell. "I thought the bureau had contacted the NYPD about what happened to Mia last week." His eyes moved back to Ace. "I thought for sure she would go to you. I warned her to leave."

"You know what happened to her?"

The agent ran his hand down his face and genuinely looked upset.

"Okay, I think we all need to take a breath and maybe have a seat and discuss this," McDonnell stated and motioned to the kitchen table.

Agent Larkin turned to walk into the kitchen but clutched his side and moaned.

"Fuck!" He popped his head up, looking towards Alex. "Where in the hell did you learn to fight? I think you broke a few of my ribs."

Alex grinned, and Ace couldn't help the proudness he felt.

"I had some good teachers growing up," she replied.

"Okay, now that we've established that you got your ass kicked by a girl, let's get back to the subject at hand. Everyone have a seat," McDonnell ordered.

Once they were all seated, McDonnell started the discussion.

"Agent Larkin, this is Marcus Chambers, Mia's brother. Obviously, we are somewhat here for the same purpose, but it seems there is a lot more to Mia's case that's not being disclosed."

McDonnell looked at Agent Larkin. "Let's start with a basic question. How do you know Mia?"

Ace watched him, and for a second, he thought the agent was going to feed them a line of bullshit, and he had been prepared to call him out on it.

Larkin tilted his head and cracked his neck. "Mia and have a past."

"Oh shit!" Ace heard Alex whisper next to him, and he looked over at her.

"What?" He asked, and Alex grabbed his hand and gave him a warning look. It was a look he was familiar with; she was about to drop a bombshell.

Alex looked at Larkin. "You're Mia's ex?"

As the guy nodded his head, Ace's nostrils flared. Son-of-a-bitch! Mia didn't mention him by name much. When Ace found out he was a Green Beret, he nicknamed him the Green Beret, and when Mia would talk about him, she referred to him as the Green Beret to be sarcastic.

He looked over at the guy and glared at him. So this was the asshole who had disrespected his sister. The fucking Green Beret. He felt even better now that Alex gave him a good beat down, although he now wanted a crack at him.

As if sensing his anger, Alex squeezed his hand and reigned him in. "Ace, now is not the time to deal with that. Let's focus on the real reason we're here."

Alex turned toward Agent Larkin. "Agent Larkin, I'm confused. Mia said you worked as a Director of Security for some Fortune 500 company."

Ace thought the guy would want to play games, but he surprised him.

"That's my cover. Mia had no clue I worked for the FBI. Look, I can't go into a lot of detail due to the assignment I'm working on, but I'm concerned about Mia."

"Why?" Ace asked.

"Because I was there last week and saw the whole thing unfold. I witnessed Mia get pulled off the street."

Ace felt as if he'd been punched in the gut as all the air left his body. His head felt like it was literally spinning.

"Agent Larkin, can you tell us what you know or saw? Why didn't you help her, or call for help when it happened."

"I did. I mean, I called the bureau." Larkin raked his hand down his face in frustration. "Because of my current assignment, I couldn't just call the police, so I called my supervisor at the bureau and explained to him what was happening."

"What the fuck actually happened? Why didn't you help her when she was attacked?" Ace raised his voice.

"I was too far away. I couldn't have made it to her in time. Look, let me start at the beginning with what I know. At the gala that Mia attended last week, she and I ran into each other. It was awkward since that was the first time we were seeing each other since we had broken up. But what made it even more uncomfortable was that I acted like she was a complete stranger. The people I was with that night are criminals. And if they knew that Mia and I had a connection, they would start asking questions, and it could have led to my cover being blown, and put Mia's safety in jeopardy."

"Wait, she was with her boss all night. Are you saying that her boss is one of the criminals you're talking about?" Ace asked.

"She was with him, but as far as him being a criminal…he hasn't ever been charged with anything, but he is under investigation which I'll get to in a minute."

McDonnell agreed. "I was suspicious of him when I interviewed him. More so when three of his supposed employees showed up while I was there."

"Who were they?" Agent Larkin asked.

"Marlon Zurek, Oscar Torres and Jules Gudotti."

Ace saw the tick in Larkin's jaw. "I know of all three of them. Oscar and Jules do 'side work' for several employers around the area, if you know what I mean. It is all about the money for them. Marlon, on the other hand, prefers to reap the benefits from his cousin's work, without putting in too much work."

"I saw him talking to Mia right before she left the gala. When I questioned her afterward outside, she mentioned that Marlon wanted her to give Dr. Walters an envelope, and he was adamant that she get it to him that night. I knew something was up. I told her to watch her back.

"I was concerned, so I called a buddy of mine back in Washington and asked him to dig a little deeper into Dr. Elijah Walters. It didn't take long for him to get back to me. For the last year and a half, Dr. Walters and his clinic have been under investigation for smuggling."

"Ace, Tink was right. Mia was targeted for human trafficking," Alex said to him.

But Larkin interrupted. "No, Alex. Dr. Walters isn't dealing in human trafficking. But he is under investigation for puppy trafficking."

Alex covered her mouth as if shocked. Ace was aware of people smuggling dogs, but he didn't realize how big an operation it was until Larkin started explaining. He was shocked to learn how much money is made from an operation as such.

Larkin continued, "After finding out that information, I wanted to talk to Mia. I couldn't tell her anything because it's an ongoing investigation."

"So why are you telling us?" McDonnell interrupted, and Larkin gave him a serious look.

"Because I care about Mia, and I want to find those responsible for hurting her. And I trust you to keep this on the down-low."

With the nod of the detective's head, Larkin continued, "The next day, I tried calling and texting Mia to talk to her again, but she never responded. I was concerned and knew she normally goes for a run in the park between six and seven, so I waited to see if she would show. I watched her from afar."

Ace saw the pain etched in Larkin's face as he continued.

"I was a couple of blocks away standing next to my car when I saw it all go down. The dude snatched her so fast before he dragged her into an alley. I jumped into my car. I got to about a block away and the van peeled out of the alley. I followed them across the bridge into Jersey. The driver took the exit leading to the docks area. By the time I exited, I had lost them. I kept driving up and down each street, searching for a glimpse of the van. Along the way, I ran into a few individuals who I know from those streets. One of them said he had seen one at the far end within the last hour, so I headed in that direction. That was when I made the call to my supervisor. He warned me to back off before I blew my cover and assured me he would escalate the incident to the NYPD."

"But you didn't back off?" McDonnell stated more than he asked.

Larkin looked right into Ace's eyes as he answered, "No, I couldn't turn my back on her. On the north end, I made a turn and realized it was a dead end. As I was putting the car in reverse, something moving in the road caught my eye. At first, I thought it was an animal. I flicked the high beams on and moved a little closer, then realized it was a person. She was in bad shape when I got to her. I quickly picked her up and put her into my car."

Larkin paused and looked as if he was battling with himself.

"I couldn't take the risk of her knowing it was me. I spoke to her using an English accent, and then I gave her a drug to make her sleep. I feel awful about it, but it was the best for the both of us."

"Were you the one who left her the note?" Alex asked.

"Yeah. I honestly thought she would head to her family." He looked at Ace. "I came back later after I took care of a few things, and she was gone. I thought she would head to you. But now you're here saying she's missing."

Ace could sense the concern in both Larkin's expression and body language. Although he was very grateful for Larkin being concerned for Mia's safety and diligence in finding her, it still didn't mean he was letting the douche off easy.

Ace spoke up and looked at Larkin. "Before we go any further with this discussion, I need to know something. Why did you feel you needed to be concerned for Mia when you were unfaithful to her?"

"There are some things I need to explain to her about the night…."

"The night she caught you with your pants down, literally."

"Ace…" Alex warned him.

Larkin shook his head. "It's not what she thought." He blew out a breath. "It was a set-up to look like I was cheating on her so she would break up with me."

"Oh, please." Ace stated and rolled his eyes.

"Seriously. If my cover ever got blown, I didn't want to put Mia in some evil people's crosshairs because she was dating me. I swear to you, I didn't cheat on her. Yes, it looked that way. The woman with me that night is a colleague of mine, and she was in on it."

"Why didn't you just tell her you didn't want to be with her anymore instead of making her feel like she wasn't good enough? Although, she was at your place to dump your ass."

Larkin appeared taken back by that little tidbit. "What?"

"She went to your place to break things off with you. She knew there wasn't a future for the two of you."

"Well, that explains the distance she'd been putting between us."

Ace nodded in agreement as if the guy was a true dumbass.

Larkin gave Ace an odd look. "If you don't know where Mia is, then I'm very concerned for her safety. Criminals are connected in this city, and if Mia was targeted, she could be in grave danger."

Ace looked at McDonnell for guidance on the subject. He wasn't going to jeopardize Mia's case by opening his mouth.

McDonnell's eyes traveled to Larkin, and he pinned him with a stare, "What is said in this apartment, stays inside this apartment."

"Understood," Larkin stated. "And before you ask, I've already checked the place for bugs. It's clean."

McDonnell nodded. "Mia is safe." Both McDonnell and Ace explained the series of events leading to where they now were in the investigation. McDonnell also made it known that the bureau had never notified the NYPD.

Larkin looked at Ace for confirmation, and Ace nodded his head.

"Do you have any leads?"

"There are several directions we are looking, one being she could've been a target of human trafficking considering what Mia heard about "their" boss having an eye on her."

Larkin appeared to suddenly take on a sickly look, and Ace wondered what had brought that on.

"Man, are you okay? You look like you are going to vomit."

Larkin took a couple of deep breaths.

"I'm assuming you haven't checked the dock area in Jersey where I found Mia."

The detective shook his head. "We haven't had reason to look over that way. Since she was abducted in the city, our focus has been on warehouses near the water here."

Larkin looked Detective McDonnell in the eye. "You may want to expand that to include the docks and warehouses across the river. Lots of activity taking place over that way."

Larkin turned his attention to Ace. "Where is Mia now?"

"As Ace mentioned, she is safe, with her boyfriend, far from here," Alex stated, and Ace wanted to laugh at Alex getting a dig in at Larkin. She hadn't liked the guy since the night Mia called and told her what he had done. But the question Larkin asked next had Ace wanting to ask a few questions himself.

"Boyfriend?"

Ace smirked. "Yeah, boyfriend."

"Well, as long as it isn't her boss, then I'm happy she's happy."

"She's very happy, but why would you think she would date her boss?" Ace asked, looking confused and a little disgusted.

"Oh, shit…." Alex mumbled next to him, and for the second time within the same conversation, he looked down at her wide eyes and knew there was something that she and Mia had been keeping a secret. All he did was quirk an eyebrow, and she started spilling.

"The night of the gala," she gave Larkin a look as if she was asking him for confirmation, and from the expression on his face, Alex had hit the nail on the head. Now they just needed to clue him in.

"What happened the night of the gala?" Ace questioned.

"She came with Dr. Walters. All night he was glued to her as if he was staking a claim to her. I'll admit it pissed me off."

"That isn't all," Alex spoke up, and Ace could see she was battling something internally when she let out a frustrated sigh. "I promised Mia I wouldn't tell anyone."

"Alex, whatever it is, you need to tell us."

"She called me the next morning on her way to work. After the gala, she stopped by the clinic to drop some papers off to Elijah, which I'm now guessing is whatever Marlon gave to her."

"Hold up," Ace said, shaking his head. "I don't understand. She was with her boss all fucking night. Why didn't she just give him the papers then?" Detective McDonnell agreed with Ace.

"Fuck!" Larkin shouted.

"What?"

"Marlon." Alex nodded her head, but Ace's head was starting to spin with all of these new developments.

"Right, but according to Mia, Marlon was adamant she drop it off at the clinic that night on her way home. That's when…" Alex paused and bit down on her lip. It was a stall tactic.

"When what?" Ace pushed.

"He kissed her."

171

Several "whats" echoed in the room, and Ace had even more questions. Most he would save for his sister. Did she have a thing for her boss? What about Stitch? Fuck!

Alex spoke quickly, "It was unwanted. Mia pushed him off and told him he shouldn't have done that. He told her that it was bound to happen and that he'd wanted to kiss her since the day he first saw her."

Ace was thanking the Lord for the anger management skills he'd learned because he was ready to punch something. He was boiling. From the sound of it, Mia's boss had preyed on her from the start of her career. Now that he thought about it, he had a conversation with Mia right after she had accepted the job, and she had mentioned how her salary was way above the normal pay grade of someone just out of school. Did he pad her pay so she couldn't say no? He fucking manipulated his baby sister.

"Why didn't you tell me?" Ace looked at Alex for an answer.

"Because she told me not to tell anyone," Alex snapped back at him.

Ace looked at Larkin. "Look, as you go about your undercover assignment, can you at least give Detective McDonnell a call if you run across anything you may hear?"

"Absolutely. And I really meant it. I never intended to hurt Mia."

Ace smirked. "You didn't hurt her; you gave her that final push in the direction we were all hoping for."

Alex snorted a laugh and Ace smiled down at her, and winked.

Ace glanced around the apartment. It was clean and neat, just like Mia. She was always the organized one of the family. His eyes stopped on a vase of yellow roses on the breakfast bar. They looked fresh.

"Who sent her flowers?" He asked, and he didn't miss the annoyed looked that passed on Larkin's face.

"Dr. Walters."

Ace glanced at Alex. "I think I'd like to meet this Dr. Walters before we head home." He looked at Detective McDonnell. "Would you have a problem if Alex and I stopped in to meet Dr. Walters? After all, I am the concerned brother of his missing sister."

The detective shook his head and grinned. "No, I think it would be fine. Just don't go beating on the guy."

Ace took another look at Alex and winked. "It never crossed my mind."

Ace sat across the desk from Dr. Walters, trying to figure out if this guy was sincere, or just a good actor. His concern for Mia was more along the lines of a significant other, than an actual colleague, and that pissed him off now that he had a good idea of what the doctor's intentions really were.

"As I told the detective the other day, if there is anything I can do, please don't hesitate to contact me. Mia is a great asset to the clinic, and we are all very concerned."

"I appreciate your concern. My family and I are all shaken by her disappearance." Ace stood and motioned to Alex that it was time to go. She had seemed preoccupied since they had sat down, which wasn't like her. She usually was all into the details. "Well, we won't keep you any longer. We just wanted to stop in and be sure that you were aware of the situation."

"I appreciate that. And, again, anything I can do, please let me know. Mia is special."

Ace had to bite the inside of his cheek to not lash out at the guy. He and Mia needed to have a conversation about this guy. There was no way in hell she would still work for this character after all of this was over. He hoped that now she and Stitch were dating, she would decide to stay in Virginia Beach.

Dr. Walters walked them out to the reception area. As they parted ways, Alex almost ran into a gentleman coming in thru the door.

"Oh, I'm sorry. I wasn't paying attention to where I was going," she said to the man, and he just smiled.

"No harm," he replied and held the door for both her and Ace as they exited. When Ace looked back over his shoulder, the guy was checking out Alex's backside. Typically actions like that brought out the caveman in him and pissed him off, but lately, he'd been trying not to let a guy admiring his fiancé bother him. Instead, he took it as a compliment. That is unless he was acting like an ass about it and blatantly gawking, then he'd make it known that she was his.

Ace snuck a peek over at Alex noticing she had remained quiet as they pulled out of the parking lot and headed toward the airport. She was staring out the window. Ace recognized the look on her face. Something was on her mind, and she was thinking through her thoughts. About mid-way through their visit with Dr. Walters, she had sort of just shut down and sat there with a blank look on her face. It was odd because, in a situation as such, Alex liked to interrogate just as much as he did.

He was about to ask her what was wrong when she turned to face him.

"We need to call Detective McDonnell."

Ace raised an eyebrow at her. "Why?"

"Just pull the car over. Right there, pull into that parking lot on the left." She demanded in a serious tone that concerned Ace. He did as she said and pulled into a bank parking lot. He put the car in park then shifted in his seat to hear what she had to say.

"Remember when Mia was telling us about the night she was abducted?" Ace nodded his head; how could he forget. "Well, she mentioned when she went running, she was wearing a black zip-up hoodie, but when she was abducted, someone had removed it."

"Yeah?" He wondered where she was going with this.

"Ace, Mia's hoodie was in Dr. Walters' office."

He studied her for a few seconds. He saw the seriousness in her expression and knew she wasn't joking.

"I know it was hers because I bought it for her. It has the red "M" embroidered on the left sleeve." She took his hand, and her emerald green eyes bore into his. "Ace, Dr. Walter's had a hand in Mia's abduction."

Elijah was caught off guard when Vargas, his main informant in the NYPD, entered the clinic's front door. He was alarmed because Vargas never showed his face at the clinic during office hours.

Curious about the detective's spontaneous visit, he quickly finished up his conversation with the owner of one of his patients. Giving the Shepard a scratch on the back of his neck, he waved to Mr. Hines as he exited.

He made eye contact with Vargas and nodded for him to follow him.

Once they were in his office with the door closed, he turned on the detective.

"I thought I told you to keep your distance from the clinic. I don't need anyone getting ideas because they saw you here. It'd be different if you had an animal, but seeing you don't, it really doesn't make any sense for you to be here."

Vargas took a seat on the sofa and immediately reached for the lady's black hoodie recovered from the warehouse and brought it up to his nose. Elijah thought that seemed a little weird. When he made eye contact, Elijah raised his eyebrows.

"I don't think I will ever get that sweet scent out of my nose."

Elijah couldn't disagree. It was sweet, just like Mia, who wore the same aroma. She was both sweet and beautiful. He was worried about her. Hell, he knew the city wasn't a safe place to live, much less for a beautiful woman like Mia. He had been both shocked and startled by her brother's visit. His authoritative demeanor was on display while he and his fiancé met with him. Now, Alex, she was knockout herself. With those green eyes and tight little body, Demitri could fetch a fortune for her.

"Now that you've had your fix, do you want to tell me why in the hell you risked being seen by coming here?"

Vargas held up the hoodie.

"I thought you might be interested in knowing its owner."

Well, now that was a revelation he wasn't expecting.

"You've piqued my curiosity. Do tell."

"I don't have a name; however, I do have a picture."

"What? How?"

Vargas held up his phone, and as soon as the picture came into view on the screen, Elijah felt the blood drain from his face.

"Christ Elijah, you look like you just saw a ghost."

"That's Mia!"

Vargas gave him an odd look, and then he too looked taken back. "The doctor chick that works for you that Marlon talks about all the time?"

Vargas had never seen Mia, so he didn't know what she had looked like.

"Oh fuck…this isn't good."

The squeezing sensation inside his chest was almost too much handle. He closed his eyes. This could destroy him.

"Where did you get this? Who knows about this? Her?"

"From Jules' phone. The stupid fuck snapped a picture while she was unconscious. He left it in the warehouse, and I found it while I was wiping it down. He doesn't know I have it."

"How? How did this fucking happen?"

"They said that was the chick you had instructed them to get rid of."

"Not her!" Elijah shouted. "Willow. Willow was the one."

"I swear, Elijah, I didn't know who she was. They already had her at the warehouse when I arrived to facilitate the equipment and crates' movement. When I walked in, and they were touching her, I told them to leave her alone. I assumed she was one that you had told them to take care of."

"Then what the fuck happened to her?" Elijah asked, pointing to Mia's injuries.

Vargas grinned. "She broke Oscar's nose."

"Mia was responsible for that?"

"That's what set him off," he pointed to the picture of Mia battered and bruised. "That was the outcome. He just lost it. He threw both her and the chair. The problem was he didn't realize that when the chair broke, it left her arms and legs free. We, myself included, thought she was out cold. Unbeknown to us, she wasn't. She climbed out the fucking window while I had them help me move the crates. I drove all around the docks looking for her but she was no where to be found."

"Well, where the fuck could she be? Her own family doesn't even know where she is."

"What?"

"That big hulking guy and gorgeous brunette you passed coming in was her brother and his fiancé."

"No shit. What are they saying?"

"Nothing, because they haven't heard from her since that night. That's why they were in town. They were meeting with that Detective McDonnell, the one that questioned me the other day. If she escaped and isn't around town and hasn't contacted her family, where could she be?"

"Hard to say. She may have gotten scared and fled. Or, she could've run into some trouble around the area. You know the trash that hangs out around the docks. Especially at that time of the night. A woman as beautiful as Mia wouldn't want to be caught dead around those streets."

Elijah couldn't peel his eyes from the picture displayed across the phone screen. She was out there somewhere, and what scared Elijah was how much she knew and if it was enough to bring him and his operation down. As much as he would love to have her as his own, his priority was his business. If that meant sending Mia to the same fate as Willow or worse, then it was what would be done.

"I need to find her, Vargas."

Vargas grinned. "Marlon mentioned you had your eye on her."

"I want her, but if she connects the dots and it leads back to me, I could be ruined. I need to find her first."

"You said that McDonnell was working the case?"

Elijah nodded.

"I know him, and I can do a little digging around the office and see what he has."

"As long as it doesn't look suspicious."

"Never."

"Then do what you need to do, but let's keep this between us."

"Done." He then held up Jules' phone. "What do you want me to do about Jules?"

Elijah thought hard. That was a tough call, because right now, he needed that asshole for the next few weeks to facilitate scheduled shipments.

"Nothing just yet. I need a little more time to tie up some loose ends."

Elijah turned and faced the window. A winter storm was due to hit the area tomorrow morning. The clouds were moving in, giving the sky a dreary look, like his current mood.

"I will find her, Vargas. I know she is out there."

"Well, I will leave you to your business. As soon as I connect with McDonnell, I will be in touch."

"Thank you, Vargas. And, remember, this stays between you and me."

Vargas got up and made his way out of the office. Elijah continued to stare out the window.

"Where are you, Mia?" He mumbled as he took Mia's hoodie and took another sniff of the garment.

He would wait until Vargas called later with any information, but in the meantime, it wouldn't hurt to start his own investigation. He picked up his phone.

"Claus, I need you to look into Mia's family. I want to know everything, where they live, what they do for a living, and anything else you may find along the way. I need it ASAP."

CHAPTER EIGHTEEN

Detective McDonnell stood at the water's edge of the Hudson River while divers brought a woman's body ashore. Police had been alerted after a business nearby heard a woman screaming and called 911. After searching the surrounding area, personal effects were recovered along the road leading to one of the piers, triggering a water search. New Jersey police believed the personal items recovered belonged to the victim. Since the driver's license showed the possible victim had a Queens address, he had been called to the scene. Ironically, when he received the call, he was already in his vehicle heading that way to have a look around the area where Agent Larkin had found Mia.

"Do we know who owns the surrounding warehouses?" He asked one of the officers. The officer looked at his notepad.

"One belongs to a Seafood distribution company. Another belongs to a custom t-shirt and screen printing shop. The one behind you is registered to a veterinarian EJW in Manhattan. To your right, with the grey brick is a cleaning supply distributor, and the building one over with the mural of the mermaid painted on the front belongs to a clothing distributor in Europe."

The officer looked to have another four or five businesses listed, but only one piqued his interest. "Do you have a name for the veterinarian?"

The officer shook his head. "Not here, but I can get it for you."

"That would be great."

McDonnell couldn't shake the odd feeling he had right now. It made his gut twist. He would bet money that the EW in the name belonged to Elijah Walters. Why would a veterinarian in Manhattan have a warehouse across the river?

Just then, his phone rang, and he excused himself. "McDonnell."

"Detective, this is Ace, Mia's brother. Look, I'm sorry to bother you, but Alex just informed me of something that I think you'll want to hear."

"Go ahead."

179

"We just left Dr. Walters' office. Alex didn't want to bring attention to it at the time, but while we were there, Alex spotted Mia's hoodie lying on Dr. Walters' sofa in his office."

Since Mia worked at the clinic, the detective really didn't see what the big hoopla would be about that. He understood Ace's sense of urgency in wanting to catch the person responsible for what happened to his sister, but he needed to sit back and think through the details before throwing out accusations, although now with the Dr.'s warehouse in the close vicinity of a murdered woman, maybe it wasn't an accusation.

"She does work there, Ace. Could be she left it there."

"It's the same hoodie she was wearing the night she was abducted."

McDonnell felt his body vibrate with excitement. This could be the smoking gun they were looking for. He walked away from the crowd of people for a little more privacy.

"You're sure?"

"Positive. Mia said it was taken from her. Alex recognized it because she was the one who bought the hoodie for Mia last year."

The detective took a deep breath and released it. With this new information, along with the murder situation unfolding in front of him, he was pretty sure he could get a search warrant executed.

Detective McDonnell caught some of the other detectives discussing something then start walking towards him.

"This is huge news, Ace. I'm currently working an investigation right now. Let me give you a call back when I get back to the office as I may have some additional information to share with you."

"Yeah, sure. Thanks."

McDonnell disconnected the call and ran a hand down his face. He knew something was up with the doctor. Especially with the crew he had working for him. He approached the group of officers.

"What do ya got?"

"One of the witnesses just returned and gave us a description of a tan sedan they saw leaving the area around the time they heard the screams. They even got a plate number. We called it in, and it came back to a shell

180

corporation backed by Demitri Barros." The hairs on the back of Detective McDonnell's neck stood up. He knew the name very well. Every law enforcement agency had tried unsuccessfully to have him thrown in jail on various organized crime charges, but with a team of good lawyers with inside connections, the charges never stuck. Demitri and Elijah were close associates. Were those two working together?

McDonnell stared at the choppy, dirty water of the Hudson River. Something fishy was going on, and all the signs were pointing to Dr. Elijah Walters. Then an idea popped into his head. He pulled his phone out and called into the precinct.

"Yeah, Astor, McDonnell here. I need background on a couple of perps." He heard the man typing on a keyboard. Astor was somewhat of an odd man, but he was a genius when accessing information. He could get his hands on about any record needed.

"Sure. Give me the names."

"Dr. Elijah Walters, Claus Jenkins, and Marlon Zurek."

"How soon do you need it?"

"As soon as possible. It pertains to an extremely important case." His gut was telling him he was close to nailing the bastard.

"You got it. Let me finish up a report, and then I'll work on it. Tomorrow by noon good?"

Detective McDonnell grinned. "Perfect. Thanks, man."

CHAPTER NINETEEN

Stitch helped Mia off the ATV and led her along a trail through a small compost of trees. It was a trail that he created himself when he stumbled on the spot he was taking Mia to shortly after he had purchased the cabin and land.

It was the second-highest point of his property, and nobody but him came up here. His teammates knew about the sacred spot, and they all understood the importance to him and respected his wishes. Sure, the cabin was nice, but his spot was like heaven, though he never experienced heaven, but he imagined it had to be a close comparison. It was secluded and surrounded by nothing but nature and peacefulness. It was his spot to think and let his mind run free.

As they came to the small clearing that only yielded a small wooden bench that he made himself, Stitch inhaled deep, taking in the crisp, clean air.

He heard the faint gasp that came from Mia as he pulled her in front of him.

"Oh my gosh, Stitch…it is beautiful up here."

He cuddled close, wrapping his arms around her waist and resting his chin on top of her head. The sun was setting, and the sky was painted an array of colors. The purples and pink against the orange backdrop was breathtaking. The small peak where they stood offered a landscape that could be a painting—mountain peaks capped with snow could be seen all around.

"Welcome to my private haven. It's where I come to expel the demons trapped inside my body. I've seen a lot of bad shit, but this right here is what grounds me."

Mia turned in his arms, and he gazed down into her beautiful brown eyes. He saw the love and emotion and knew she understood what this place meant to him. She placed her hands against his chest.

"So, nobody knows about this?"

"Yes and no. The guys on the team know about it, but none of them have ever been here. They know its significance to me and respect it."

"It's so high up. You can see miles and miles."

There is only one spot on my property that's higher, and the only spot you can get a glimpse of this spot from."

"Where is that?"

He turned and pointed up and toward the left. "I thought about making that location my special spot, but it didn't offer the privacy and seclusion like this one does."

She turned in his arms and hugged him close.

"Thank you for sharing something so private and special with me. I promise always to respect it."

He nudged her chin up towards him and gazed into her eyes.

"I want to share everything with you, Mia. What is mine is yours, including this spot."

She snuggled into his chest. "I love you, Stitch."

"I love you too, babe."

He took another deep breath and exhaled. Yes, this was heaven, with his angel by his side.

CHAPTER TWENTY

Mia felt disgusted and shocked as she, Stitch, Derek, and Tink listened to Ace and Alex explain what they found out on their little jaunt to New York.

She and Stitch had arrived in the morning and invited the others to lunch. They opted for the small family diner just down the road from Stitch's parent's house.

"They think Dr. Walters is involved in puppy smuggling and my abduction?"

"They aren't a hundred percent, but it isn't looking good for him. When the detective called me back last night, he said that he was waiting on some information. But, Mia, how else would Dr. Walters have your hoodie?"

Mia shook her head. "I don't know. I mean, I just can't believe this."

Ace gave Alex a quick glance as if trying to communicate with her silently, but Mia hadn't missed the look.

"What else did you find out? How was my apartment?"

She got complete silence for a couple of seconds before she looked at Stitch, who shrugged his shoulders. He hadn't spoken with Ace yet either.

"Ace, was something wrong with my apartment?" God, she hoped not. That was all she needed, to owe her landlord for damages. It was bad enough she was going to need to break her lease.

Ace blew out a breath. "Your apartment was fine." He rubbed the back of his neck." However, we did run into an old acquaintance."

She scrunched her eyebrows together. Nobody but Danny had a key to her apartment, and he was a friend, not an old acquaintance.

"Jesus, Ace, just tell her." Alex blurted out.

"Terek."

Her eyes widened, and she looked at Stitch, who looked like he was thinking, but then his mouth opened slightly all too suddenly, and she knew he figured it out. He squinted his eyes as he looked right at her.

"The Green Beret? Your ex that cheated on you." Before she could answer, he looked over at her brother. "I hope you gave that asshole a piece of your mind."

Ace smirked, "Well, Alex gave him a good beatdown. Literally." He used his thumb to caress the scab that had formed on Alex's lip.

"You got into a fight with him?! He fucking hit you?" Stitch roared.

Alex shrugged her shoulders. "He didn't know who I was, and I didn't know who he was. Once we realized who was who, everything settled down."

"Why in the hell was Terek at my apartment? How did he even get in?"

Everyone just stared at her as if she asked the dumbest question.

"What? What did I say?"

"Terek was a Green Beret, remember? The locks on your front door are shit."

"Oh..."

Stitch chuckled and patted her shoulder.

"Why was he there?"

Ace took a deep breath, and Alex looked nervous, which only made Mia more anxious.

"Mia, there is something you need to know about Terek, and what happened the night you were abducted.

As Ace and Alex told her everything, she had so many mixed feelings. She was grateful, hurt, angry, and sad. She had tears in her eyes.

"Terek saved me and warned me. I don't understand why he was so secretive." They had left out the part of him being an undercover FBI agent.

Ace looked torn, but then Alex spoke up, "Ace, you need to tell her."

Mia looked at her brother. "Tell me what?"

"Terek works for the FBI. He's in New York working on an undercover assignment."

"What?" She put her hand over her stomach. *Had their whole relationship been a sham?*

"There's more."

Jesus, she wasn't sure if she could take more. She was ready to cry as it was.

"Terek never cheated on you." Mia started to speak, but Ace told her to let Alex finish explaining. "Because of his assignment and not blow his cover or endanger you, he had to—"

"Break up with you," Ace barked out. "Not that I agree with how he did it, but I understand."

"He staged the whole thing with the other woman you thought he was sleeping with. She works with him. He never slept with her. He just made it look like it."

Mia's head was spinning with the news. She put her hand on her head. She felt Stitch's hand on her back.

"He still cares for you, Mia."

Mia looked over at Stitch and could tell that hearing that little tidbit wasn't making Stitch any happier, judging from the scowl on his face as he stared at Alex. "But he knows you are happy with your life now."

Alex looked over at Stitch and smiled. Mia also smiled and reached out, taking Stitch's hand as she gazed into his eyes.

"I am happy. In fact, it's the happiest I've been in a long time." She felt a little more relaxed when Stitch's facial expression softened, and he squeezed her hand before bringing it up to his lips. Then he pulled her chair closer and kissed her.

"I love you."

Ace groaned, "Fuck, Stitch. Really? Save that shit until after I leave."

Stitch shrugged his shoulders and smirked at Ace. "Better get used to it, buddy."

Ace huffed out another groan, and everyone laughed. But then things got serious again when Ace squinted his eyes at Mia.

"Why didn't you tell me that your boss had the hots for you?"

"What?"

"According to Terek, your boss couldn't keep his hands off you at the gala." Ace gave Alex another look. "Mia, why didn't you say anything about Dr. Walters forcing himself on you?"

186

"What? Is that true, Mia?" Stitch asked.

Oh shit! With everything going on, she had pushed that incident aside for the time being. She touched her lips, remembering the way he took her mouth.

She must have zoned out, because Stitch gave her a little shake. She glanced over at Alex, who looked guilty.

"Alex? Why? You promised you wouldn't say anything. I handled it."

"I'm sorry, Mia. I know you trusted me with that information, but hearing Terek's concerns, I had to say something."

Mia glanced at Stitch, who looked confused and angry. He turned away from her, and that broke her heart.

"Stitch, look at me." She grabbed his face with both her hands turning his head to face her. The look of anger his eyes held destroyed her.

"Why didn't you tell me?" He whispered.

Tears formed in her eyes. The last thing she wanted was for Stitch to be upset with her.

"Because I knew you guys would be upset if you found out. Believe me; I handled it."

"Obviously not, considering that fucker may have been a player in your abduction!" Stitch's loud, boisterous tone had her pulling back.

"Stitch…" Ace said in warning, and Stitch shook his head.

Finally, after a long silence, Stitch turned back to her and gently pulled her onto his lap.

"He can't have you."

She looped her arms around his neck and smiled. "I don't want him; I only want you." She leaned forward and pressed her lips against his. It was a quick kiss, but she made her point.

"Mia, Detective McDonnell is trying to locate Willow, your friend from the clinic. Dr. Walters said she resigned over the holiday weekend. Do you know how to reach her?"

Mia scrunched her eyebrows together. "Willow quit?" She asked, and Ace nodded. "Dr. Walters showed Detective McDonnell the email he received from her. Your friend Danny said she had been acting strange the last couple of weeks."

"I wonder if that's why she wanted to talk to me. She and I were supposed to meet that night. All I have is her phone number."

"Yeah, she's not answering, and she hasn't been home."

"The envelope!" Mia blurted out and Alex looked at Ace.

"Ace, remember the detective asked you about an envelope? Danny mentioned it to him." Alex looked at Mia. "Did Willow give you an envelope?"

"Yes. It's in my backpack in the car. I completely forgot about it. Willow told me not to open it until she and I spoke." Mia looked at Stitch. "Do you mind running out to the car? It's a manila envelope in the middle zippered section."

While Stitch went to retrieve the envelope, Mia sat down trying to take in everything. It was overwhelming, not to mention confusing. It was like there were so many moving parts that you couldn't keep up.

Stitch returned and handed her the envelope, and everyone was silent while she slipped her finger under the seal and pulled out the papers inside. As she fingered through the ten or so pages, she was trying to figure out why Willow wanted to give her copies of vaccination and registration records, until her eyes landed on a page with the words "Blue French Bulldogs" written in blue marker across the top. She flipped to the next page, and she gasped when she read "Dachshunds." These were papers for the litters of puppies found in the city and brought to the clinic. All of them had prior dates of exams and vaccinations, along with certified AKC registrations. It was impossible. Her chest tightened, and she covered her mouth as tears built in her eyes. It was true. These papers with her testimony proved that Dr. Walters was operating a puppy trafficking ring. What made her feel even sicker was that she had helped him. She was aiding him and didn't know it. He betrayed her trust and loyalty.

She set the papers down on the table and slid them toward Ace. She felt a tear roll down her cheek and quickly wiped it away.

"There's your proof that Dr. Walters is trafficking puppies."

Ace picked up the papers. "What are these?"

She sniffled, trying to hold in her emotions. "Those are forged documents saying each of those puppies are certified AKC registered."

"How do you know they're forged?"

"Because I was there when those puppies were brought to the clinic. They had been abandoned on the street. Or at least that was what I had been told. Their vaccinations were done by me, not the person signing veterinarian on those documents."

She glared at Stitch. "He was smuggling in puppies probably from those puppy mill places you read about, and then selling them. He used me. He manipulated me and used me to aid his criminal activity." A thought then hit her, and she turned sharply to look at Alex and the guys. "Do you think Dr. Walters knew that Willow had caught on to his operation, and he did something to her?"

Ace looked at Stitch and then back to her. "It's possible, Mia."

Tink gathered all of the papers and tucked them back into the envelope. "I'll go give Detective McDonnell a call." He looked over at Mia. "He will probably want to talk to you, honey."

"I'll do whatever they need me to do. I'll even go back to New York if I have to."

A round of "no's" echoed around the table, then Stitch draped his arm over her shoulders and pulled her close. "You're not leaving my side."

189

CHAPTER TWENTY-ONE

The next morning Elijah was in a panic. He moved around his penthouse like a man on a mission. How could his men have been so stupid and careless? He nor Claus knew which one had abducted and murdered the girl found in the river because nobody was fessing up, but when he did find the person responsible, the next body the police pulled out of the river would be theirs. That was if Demitri didn't get his hands on the perpetrator first. Whoever it was had used one of Demitri's cars.

"Elijah, calm down. We got this. The police don't have any hard evidence on you. If they did, they would've taken you in for questioning last night, not wait until the morning and schedule a meeting with you." Lawrence, Elijah's attorney, said as he took a sip of coffee and laid down the newspaper.

Elijah couldn't understand how calm Lawrence could be. Detective McDonnell was due to arrive any minute to question him about the girl found last night in the river. And, since items belonging to the victim had been found near his warehouse, it was standard procedure that the police would want to question him.

He stopped and leaned against the kitchen counter. Christ, he was becoming paranoid. With the cops honing in on him, maybe, he just needed to cut his losses and ditch the operation. He'd made more than enough money to live off of.

A knock sounded at the door. He took a deep breath, knowing this wasn't going to be easy. At least Lawrence was here and could handle the Detective in case the questioning got out of hand.

Mia couldn't stop laughing as Stitch's dad told some funny stories from his days in the SEALs. Non-classified stories, of course. Mainly how the guys liked to pull pranks on one another. She could see where Stitch got his looks from. He was the spitting image of his dad. They were both very handsome men.

Things were off to a good start with his parents. She had been extremely nervous on the ride over to their house. It took Stitch pulling over on the side of the road and talking to her to calm her nerves. Well, that and kissing her senseless seemed to settle her down. She still wasn't sure why the nerves hit her because she normally dealt with meeting new people all the time in her career. But Stitch's mom and dad weren't just any new people. Stitch's parents were people that she needed to impress, considering she was planning on being with Stitch for the long haul.

"So Mia, Stitch tells us that you are a vet. Where about in the city is that located?" Robin asked as they sat around the living room talking. Mia sat on the sofa across from her. Stitch and his dad were pouring drinks for everyone.

"Not too far from Times Square." She noticed that Stitch had stopped what he was doing and was watching her. Mia wanted his parents to know her intentions. "But, I don't think I'll be heading back there."

Stitch's mom looked surprised. "Really? Why?"

Stitch sat down next to her and put his arm around her. "Because Mia has decided to look for a job here in town."

Robin's eyes twinkled. "That is wonderful news."

Stitch locked eyes with Mia. "Yes, it is the best news." He looked back toward his parents. "She and I are going to live in the rental I have until we find some property we both like."

"Well, then, Mia, you should consider stopping at the shelter and clinic I volunteer at."

"Mom is a big animal lover, especially dogs. She spends one or two days a week at the local animal shelter volunteering. Right, mom?"

Robin's eyes lit up. "Oh, yes, I could spend every day there. However, your father has a conniption every time I tell him I'm going there." She glanced over at Stitch's dad and winked, "he says it is a bad influence on me. It's hard when I have to leave the dogs."

It was magical seeing the love between the two, and Mia could see where Stitch got his romantic and gentle side from. There was still that spark of young love between them. Something she hoped to have after being married for as many years as they were.

"What type of shelter is it?" Mia found herself asking more about the shelter that Robin volunteered at.

"Oh, it is a wonderful place. A no-kill shelter, and owned and operated by a local vet. His name is Dr. Katz. When he expanded his practice a couple of years ago, he opened the shelter. He has a small staff to run the shelter. The manager there, I believe her name is Grace, she pretty much does everything around the place. She is a lovely young woman, a little on the shy side. She graduated college a year or two ago. She has really helped Dr. Katz grow the practice and shelter in just a short period. She has a knack for getting the dogs and cats adopted. I don't think I've seen a person come in there and not leave with an animal."

"That is quite impressive. Is she a vet as well?"

"No, but she is one very smart woman and keeps things running smoothly. Dr. Katz has full confidence in her. You know Dr. Katz is looking to sell the clinic."

Mia glanced over at Stitch. "Maybe I can stop by there before we head back to the cabin. I can take a look around and maybe speak to Dr. Katz."

"Yeah, that might be doable," he stated. He turned towards his dad. "Dad, I have to be present for a meeting tomorrow on base. Would you and mom have some time that you can drive Mia over to Dr. Katz's office?"

Hal smiled. His mom was a beautiful woman with the same light brown hair as her son's.

"Your mother has a get-together with her cooking club tomorrow, but I'd be more than happy to take you, Mia. I know Dr. Katz personally. I can introduce you to him."

"Thank you. I'd like that."

"Anything for the woman who has captured my son's attention," Hal said and winked at Mia, making her blush.

"Oh, for heaven's sake, Hal, don't embarrass the poor woman. We don't want to chase her away."

She was already falling in love with Stitch's parents. They reminded her of her family and how close they all were.

Mia felt giddy inside. As if someone just gave her a huge gift. This was it. This was the start she was looking for. If her visit with Dr. Katz went well tomorrow, she could have planted the first seed in starting her life in Virginia Beach.

ꙮ

Later that evening, Mia was in high spirits as she sat around the table at Bayside with her friends. It had been a great time catching up with Tenley, Autumn, and Bailey. She needed some socializing time with her girlfriends. She wasn't complaining about being cooped up alone with Stitch, however. It had been amazing getting more acquainted with him.

Earlier, Stitch had received a call from base. They had wanted him to come in today instead of tomorrow to present his findings. With him completing that task, it meant she had all day tomorrow to spend with him in town before they ventured back up to the cabin.

Mia popped a jalapeño popper into her mouth and moaned. Jesus, she'd missed food like this. Not that she was knocking Stitch's healthy habits, because she studied medicine and knew that healthy food was good for the body and all, but sometimes you just needed some good ole' greasy fried food to cure the craving.

"So, how long are Stitch and your brother letting you stay in town?" Bailey asked as she stuffed an entire cheese stick in her mouth. Mia wanted to giggle because as Bailey chewed on her own greasy delight, she looked like a chipmunk.

Mia shrugged her shoulders. "I think one more day. Stitch, and Ace don't think it's wise to stay too long, just in case whoever was involved with my ordeal was snooping around."

"What if Stitch has to stay longer? Ace mentioned that Stitch has a presentation he has to give tomorrow. You aren't going back to the cabin by yourself, are you?"

Mia smiled at her soon to be sister-in-law. Hopefully, Ace would get off his ass and realize that Alex didn't care if she got her fairy tale wedding.

193

The last time Mia had visited, she and Alex had gotten completely hammered one night, which led to Alex opening up to her when they broached on the subject of marriage. Alex had admitted that she didn't care what type of wedding she had; she just wanted to be married to the man she loved. Alex made her promise not to say anything to Ace about it, and Mia was a woman of her word. But that didn't mean she couldn't drop some hints along the way to her clueless brother.

"Stitch actually presented earlier today, before we came here. If he did, though, I was planning on staying with his parents."

"I'm shocked he didn't ask Bear or one of his guys from the team," Bailey said to Mia.

"I'm not," Autumn said, grinning. Autumn was Frost's wife, and she had beautiful long, flaming red hair and eyes the color of emeralds. Of course, she, too, has had her fair share of drama.

"Why aren't you surprised?"

"Because all of those guys are Alphas. Oh, come on, you've been around to see it; when one of them sets their sights on a woman, they don't let other men near the said woman if they can help it." Autumn beat on her chest like Tarzan. "You know. Me man, you woman." Everyone laughed, and then Alex chimed in.

"Yeah, but as soon as one of their women is thrust into danger, it doesn't matter whose woman it is. They all step up to the plate and protect her no matter what."

Mia thought it was funny that all the women sitting with her automatically thought she belonged to Stitch. These ladies didn't know what had transpired between her and Stitch the last week. Well, except for Alex, and she was pretty sure she hadn't spilled the beans. Alex wasn't one to gossip unless it was something really juicy and it didn't hurt anyone's feelings.

"What makes you all think Stitch and I are together?" Mia said and took a sip of her fruity drink. Stitch told her she'd be okay if she had one drink since she was still taking a pain pill at night. When she looked up, the women were staring at her as if she had two heads, and she started to blush, knowing she was busted. Well, it was worth a try, and she grinned.

"Oh, please, you aren't fooling any of us, sister," Tenley said as she rubbed her big round belly. Her twins were due in a couple of weeks, and everyone had been on baby watch for the last week or two, knowing that most women pregnant with multiples deliver earlier than their scheduled due date. The guys even had a pool going.

"Oh, hell, honey, by the blush spreading across your face, I think you are holding back on us. What exactly has been happening up at that cabin? Or should I call it the love shack?"

Mia couldn't help but laugh and threw a crumpled-up napkin at Tenley.

"It's definitely not what your dirty mind is thinking, Tenley. We have done a lot of talking. Plus, I'm still coming to terms with what happened. I guess you could say it has been more of a coming together for the two of us and a healing for me."

She felt the hands on her shoulders and knew it was Stitch before he whispered in her ear.

"Hey, beautiful. You doing okay?"

She turned and looked up over her shoulder and smiled. Man, she loved this guy with all her heart. She stood up and hugged him, and he chuckled.

"I'm going to take that as a yes."

She pulled back and looked at him. "I'm perfect. Especially now that you're here."

"You seem to be enjoying yourself with your friends. What have you all been chatting about?"

She grinned. "They're trying to get me to gossip about us."

"Us. What about us?"

"They want to know what exactly you and I have been up to at the cabin. You know, since we've had the place alone."

"Really?"

"Really."

His eyes twinkled with mischief. "Well, why don't we just show them exactly what we've been up to?" And, before she had a chance to say anything, he dipped her backward and kissed her deeply as everyone hooted and hollered and cheered them on.

When he pulled her back up, he hugged her close and nuzzled the skin just behind her ear. "I love you so much."

She gave his trim, muscular waist a good squeeze. "I love you too."

He gave her one more quick kiss before he disappeared out the back door with the guys. Derek had arrived a few minutes ago and summoned them all to the other side of the room. Hopefully, it wasn't a sign they were being called out.

When she turned back to the table, all the women were staring at her, but in a dramatic fashion; it was Tenley who was using her hand to fan her face. "Damn, chica, that was hot! Even I need a cold shower after witnessing that." Everyone, including Mia, burst into giggles.

Mia looked around. She was surrounded by everyone she loved; friends, family, and most importantly, Stitch, and she knew she wasn't making a mistake in wanting to move here. She was looking forward to meeting Dr. Katz tomorrow. Stitch's mom had called him right before she and Stitch had left their house, and he too seemed excited to meet Mia.

Mia started to take a step toward her friends when a strong smell halted her in her tracks. It was familiar, but very different and smelled awful. She inhaled again, and her eyes went wide. She felt her chest tighten, and suddenly everything around her faded into a blur as she was thrust into one hell of a flashback from the night she was attacked.

She couldn't see a damn thing. It was cold, and she shivered. The hard slap to her face had her jerking backward. She felt violated as hands roamed her body. "I'd love to get a test ride on this one," One of them said. She was breathing rapidly as the men continued to grope her despite her pleas to stop. Suddenly hands landed on her shoulders, jolting her out of the horrible memories.

"Mia?"

She blinked a few times to get her eyes to focus. Her body shook with fear. When she saw Alex standing in front of her with a concerned look, she realized others had seen her in the moment of the flashback. Before a tear could fall, she quickly wiped it away.

"Mia, are you okay?" Alex whispered to her.

"I just need some air. Excuse me for a minute."

Mia headed toward the back doors that led to the patio. She heard Alex call after her, but she didn't stop. If she did, she was afraid she would fall apart and make a fool of herself in front of everyone in the restaurant including Stitch.

As soon as she stepped onto the wooden deck, the ice-cold air hit her face, but it did nothing to calm her. She walked deeper toward a corner that overlooked the beach and was secluded by a couple of fake potted trees. She closed her eyes and tried to relax by taking a couple of deep breaths.

Stitch was watching Mia from across the room while he and the guys talked about a possible upcoming mission. He knew something wasn't right. A second ago, she was laughing and chatting up a storm with the other ladies. Now her facial expression was completely blank and looked to be zoned out. He saw her say something to Alex before she headed toward the back patio door. Why the fuck would she go out there? It was freezing outside. Then it hit him.

"Shit!" He said as he jumped from his seat and headed towards the door that Mia disappeared through.

He hadn't realized Ace and Potter had followed him until they caught up with him. "What's going on?" Ace asked.

"It's Mia. I think she just had a flashback."

Stitch heard Ace mutter something under his breath as the three of them made their way out the door. He scanned the empty area. This time of the year, Paul, the owner, only turned on enough lights for the smokers. He let his eyes adjust to the darkness, and then he saw her. Tucked into the far corner was Mia. She was crouched down with her knees pulled up to her chest and her head bowed.

Not wanting to scare her any more than she probably was, he called her name. What he wasn't expecting was for her to jump up and come running into his arms. He held her close and walked to a nearby table and sat down as both Ace and Potter stood to the side watching.

ॐ

"Mia…talk to me, honey. What happened?" Stitch asked her, but she shook her head as if trying to clear the pungent smell from her nostrils and the awful memories from her mind. She started to shake harder, and Stitch wrapped his strong arms around her, infusing warmth to her frigid body.

He spoke in a low and calm voice. "Breathe, baby—slow deep breaths. In one, two, three. Out, one, two, three. That's it, nice and easy. I've got you."

"Mia?" She heard Ace's voice and looked up, and tears poured from her eyes when she saw the worried look in her brother's eyes. She swallowed past the emotion clogging her throat. He stepped forward and placed his warm palm against her cheek, and she closed her eyes. She was safe. Her brother and Stitch were here, and they would protect her. When she opened her eyes, Ace gave her a soft smile. Stitch still had his arm around her waist, and she leaned back into him as she tried to gain back some normalcy.

"I'm sorry."

"Don't be. Can you tell us what happened?" Stitch asked.

"It's going to sound silly, but there was a smell."

"A smell?" Ace asked.

"Yeah, it was a cologne. Someone walked by, and I caught a whiff of it inside."

She looked over her shoulder up into Stitch's eyes, then brought them back to her brother. "It was the same cologne my attacker wore."

Stitch's armed tightened around her. "Are you positive?"

She turned in Stitch's arms, then nodded her head as a tear slipped out of her eye. "I'm positive. It's not one I'll ever forget."

Stitch used his thumb to wipe away the tear then hugged her to him.

"What if it was him? What if he found me and knows I am with you guys? Oh god. What about Alex and the others? The kids. I've put everyone in danger. I have to leave."

She tried pulling away, but Stitch held on to her. "No, baby. You are not going anywhere, and especially not by yourself. So, get any ideas of sneaking off out of your head right now. We won't let anything happen to you. Plus, it could be someone who just happened to wear the same cologne."

Mia supposed it could, but she wasn't willing to take a chance. She felt uneasy and exposed. She looked up at Stitch.

"Can we go back to the cabin tonight?"

Brushing her hair away from her face, he kissed her forehead, "Yeah. We can do that."

Mia prayed she hadn't just put her friends in danger.

Brice Vargas pulled his phone from his pocket and hit Elijah's name. He couldn't believe who he just saw standing just a feet away from him. On the second ring, Elijah's voice came through the phone.

"This better be good, Vargas. I've got a shit show happening around here right now. I've got that damn detective breathing down my neck, and I just heard they are issuing search warrants for all of my properties in the city and Jersey."

"Well, that is partially why I'm calling. You'll never guess who I just found."

"What? Hang on, let me step out of the room." He listened as he heard Elijah moving around. He heard other voices in the background.

"I'm not in the mood to play guessing games, detective, so just spit it out."

Vargas chuckled. He'd been on Elijah's payroll for years and knew the guy had no patience. "That lovely little doctor of yours that you've been worrying your head about."

He heard Elijah's voice hitch.

"You found her? Where?"

"Virginia Beach."

"Her brother lives there. I've had someone watching his place, and he hasn't said he'd seen her. Are you sure it's her?"

"Oh, yeah. It is definitely her. She even still has some bruising from Oscar and Jules' beatdown."

"Don't remind me. Those fucks won't be touching another female for a while. How did you end up in Virginia Beach?"

"Well, you asked me last night to do some investigating, and I did. I found out where her brother lived. While I was in the process of gathering additional information, my chief came into my office and informed me that one of the other detectives came down with the flu and couldn't attend a law enforcement conference, and that I had to go in his place. And you'll never guess where it is?"

"Virginia Beach?"

"Not exactly, but close enough. Norfolk. Anyway, during one of the morning sessions, I met some of the local SWAT guys from Virginia Beach PD, and they invited me out for drinks after the conference sessions today. And here we are. I would never have guessed in a million years the same person you are looking for is right here in the same bar."

"And, you're definitely positive it is her?"

"A hundred percent. I wouldn't have called if I wasn't."

"Is she with anyone?"

"Looks like her brother and some friends." Vargas watched three men follow Mia outside. He moved closer toward the door they went through to keep an eye on the situation. For a minute or two, Mia had looked like something had shaken her up. When he got to the door and looked out, he was shocked when he saw one of the men holding her on his lap. Judging from the guys' actions toward Mia, Vargas assumed there was something between the two. Then he saw the heated look the two exchanged before the guy kissed her, solidifying his belief.

He focused back on the phone call. "I hate to be the bearer of bad news, but it looks like you may have some competition."

"Like what?"

"It seems Mia has been busy while she's been in hiatus. I believe she may have a lover."

"A boyfriend? She wasn't seeing anyone."

"Well, I'm watching her right now with him, and I beg to differ. He is a big dude too."

Elijah was silent, and Vargas knew he wasn't taking Mia's indiscretion well. He still didn't know why Elijah was caught up with this chick. She seemed like more trouble than she is worth.

"I can see if I can get some information on the guy."

"She never saw you that night at the warehouse, right?"

"Correct."

"See what you can find out and let me know. Keep an eye on her. In the meantime, I'll make some travel arrangements and get down there. Just so you are aware, after the next hour, I'll be off the grid."

Elijah disconnected, and Vargas put away his phone. He took a swig from his beer as he watched the guy carry Mia inside, then down a hallway to what looked like an office.

It seeed like he was sticking around for a while. He took a seat at the bar and started chatting with some local guys from the police department.

Elijah threw his phone on the couch and ran a hand through his hair. He was in a state of panic. He had Claus helping him contact all of his associates across the country to cease all operations and purge all documents relating to his business. Whatever those locations had regarding merchandise, they needed to get it the hell out of the warehouses.

He didn't have time to waste. Depending on when they executed the search warrants, he was possibly facing jail time sometime today. He and Claus were tying up some loose ends and then they were getting out of town. The plan had been to fly out of the country, but knowing now where Mia was he thought maybe he would pay her a visit as she was considered to be a loose end now.

He now wondered what type of game her family and the police were playing, because it was no coincidence that she appeared in the same small town her brother lived it. Yes, she had to be silenced.

He had enough money saved to last several lifetimes. It was better to get out now before he was caught.

Claus emerged in the doorway.

"Is everything taken care of?"

"Yes, all operations after midnight tonight will be shut down. New Orleans, Portland, and Corpus Christi were the only three with merchandise. All three locations have moved any remaining dogs to shelters."

Claus stood there just staring at him and knew the look; something was on his mind.

"Is something bothering you, Claus?"

"I just went by Mia's apartment to look around one last time to make sure she had nothing there connecting you to your operation."

Elijah turned to face Claus and raised an eyebrow. "And did you?"

"No, but I did see a familiar face leaving her apartment before I got there."

When Elijah didn't say anything, Claus continued, "Terek Larkin."

"The guy who handles Demitri's distribution in New England and Canada?" Claus nodded. "Why in the hell would he be at Mia's place?"

"I thought the same, so I did a little digging and made a few phone calls. It appears that Mia and Terek used to date. According to my source, they broke up earlier in the year. I also found out that Terek doesn't have any ties in Canada or New England. But he does have several in Washington, D.C. and most of them are law enforcement."

Elijah rubbed his head. None of this made any sense.

"You think that Terek could be law enforcement?" Then a thought hit him. Could Mia have been playing a role in gaining information? She had access to everything in the clinic. He thought back to the night of the gala and the moment Demitri had introduced Mia to Terek. Terek couldn't take his eyes off of her. At the time, he couldn't blame any man for staring at her. She was radiant and a ball of positive energy. After the introductions, he remembered that Mia had remained quiet and resilient, which had been unlike her actions earlier on in the evening. Was Terek the reason she had clammed up?

"Bingo. My guy inside the police department said he'd heard a lot of rumblings about FBI agents infiltrating the city and going undercover to bust major organizations."

"You think Terek is an undercover agent?"

"I don't know for sure, but my gut is telling me yes."

"What about Mia? They could be working together."

"Mia? Do you really think Mia is involved?" Claus questioned, sounding like he wanted to argue. Elijah ran his hand through his hair. *Fuck!* Did he really believe she could betray him like this? Did she really have it in her to gather information on him? Sure she had access to anywhere in the office except for the basement, including his office, but he was very careful about what was brought and kept in his office at the clinic. It didn't matter; he couldn't take any chances.

"Shit, I need to call Demitri." He picked up the phone but looked back at Claus. "I think we all have been played. Have the car ready in thirty minutes. We're making a detour to Virginia before we fly out."

Claus raised an eyebrow in question, and Elijah explained the phone call he received from Vargas.

A grin appeared on Elijah's face. Demitri would love to get his hands on Mia. Maybe instead of silencing her, he could make some cash off of her. Demitri would pay major cash for her.

"Do I want to know what evil thought put that wicked grin on your face?"

Elijah looked at Claus. "Probably not." He stood up and walked over to the safe he had hidden inside a decorative pedestal. Punching in the numbers on the keypad, it opened, and he started throwing stacks of hundred dollar bills into a bag until the safe was empty. That would last a while until he got his overseas accounts settled. His destination was his private estate in New Zealand that he held in a different name. He'd make a few stops along the way to redirect their movements and throw off anyone who may be following. Suddenly, an image of Mia's luscious body laid out on one of the loungers along his private beachfront popped into his mind. He wanted her so bad. Instantly, he was changing his mind. Even if she was involved, he was going to keep her. She would be punished for undermining him, but in the end, she would be his.

He looked at Claus. "Let's do this and then get the fuck out of here."

CHAPTER TWENTY-TWO

Terek sensed the presence behind him right before he heard the swoosh sound of the bullet being fired. Luckily he had fast reflexes, and had been able to duck and take cover behind his car before his head got blown off. He felt the burn on his upper arm and winced. Blood oozed from the wound, but not enough to immobilize him. He had his gun pulled and ready to counter the attack. He waited and listened but heard nothing. A few moments passed when a voice echoed in the air.

"Did you hit him?"

"I don't know."

"Go check. Demitri said to make sure he can't talk."

"Why the fuck do I have to go?" The guy complained. Terek wanted to call the guy a pussy.

"Because I said so. Now go. Demitri said once the hit is done to let Elijah know."

"I thought he and Claus were heading out of the country."

"They are, after Elijah ties up some loose ends in Virginia. Now go fucking make sure that dude is dead."

Shit! Elijah was going after Mia. He needed to warn Detective McDonnell.

He heard footsteps approach the rear of the vehicle and moved into position. As soon as the guy rounded the rear bumper and was in Terek's eyesight, he didn't hesitate and fired off two bullets into the guy's chest. The guy jerked before falling to the ground, motionless. He heard another set of footsteps running. He readied himself for another attack, but instead heard a car door slam followed by tires squealing. He poked his head around the back of the vehicle and saw a small SUV racing away from the scene. He took a deep breath then got into his car. His arm hurt like a bitch. He pushed aside the pain. He'd had worse injuries in his days as a Green Beret. He put the car in drive and raced out of the city. He wasn't stopping until he got to Virginia Beach. He pulled his phone out to call his supervisor to report that his cover had been blown, and to call Detective McDonnell; however, all he kept getting was a busy signal. It was like his phone was jammed.

CHAPTER TWENTY-THREE

It was a quiet ride back up the mountains. It was like a damn convoy coming up the mountain. Stitch and Mia rode with Ace and Alex, while Potter, Tenley, Frost, Autumn, Irish, and Bailey all followed in their vehicles. Potter had wanted Tenley to stay behind because of her condition; however, she was adamant that she was going, come hell or high water.

Diego, Skittles, and Dino stayed behind to keep an eye on things in town. Derek and Juliet, with help from Tink, were keeping an eye on all the kiddos back home. Stitch had told everyone to stay in town and not get involved, but just as he suspected, not one of them budged, making comments that they were a team and would fight as one. Moments like that were why he loved his brothers in arms. Even off the battlegrounds, his team stuck together as one force to be reckoned with.

Stitch looked down at Mia who was sound asleep with her head in his lap. He couldn't stop running his fingers through her silky, raven-colored hair. The image of her with that haunted look on her face plagued him. He was familiar with flashbacks and how they could wreak havoc on a person, but he prayed he would never have to see that look again on her beautiful face for as long as he lived. It was heart-wrenching to watch when there was nothing he could do.

There were so many people milling around the area where Mia was, so it was hard to say who could've been wearing the cologne that Mia had smelled. Before they left, Paul said that he would pull videos from the cameras and see if he noticed anything. Derek and Tink were in contact with Detective McDonnell. According to McDonnell, the case was being turned over to the Feds because of the legalities involved. They were closing in on Dr. Walters as a suspect of a huge puppy trafficking operation that now expanded to other states. He hadn't told Mia that part yet.

Ace glanced at him in the mirror as he drove. Stitch knew Ace was worried about Mia. He'd been quiet since they got Mia into the car and started making the trek up the mountain. Alex had tried to make small talk, but she had given up when it was apparent Ace wasn't in the mood for conversation.

Once they arrived at the cabin, Stitch carried Mia straight up to the bedroom and tucked her into bed. She was out cold. With all the excitement and sudden movements, she had overdone it a little, and both Ace and Stitch thought it was best that she take a pain pill, which meant she wouldn't be waking up any time soon.

As he walked out of the bedroom, he almost collided with Ace.

"You okay?" Stitch asked, knowing it was a stupid question because he knew his friend was anything but okay. He could see the turmoil etched in Ace's expressions. The only other time he'd seen Ace this torn up was when Alex had been rescued and was fighting for her life.

Ace appeared to think before he spoke. "I don't think I ever want to see that look of fear on my sister's face again." Ace glanced over Stitch's shoulder into the bedroom. "I know she's asleep, but I just need to see she is okay."

"Go on in." The last thing Stitch wanted to do was stand in between Ace and his sister. Especially at a time like this. He was quite sure if he had a sister, he'd want to be as close to her as he could to keep watch over her. "What are the others doing?"

"Alex, Autumn, and Bailey are making up the beds in the other rooms. Tenley is pitching a fit because Potter won't let her help." Ace snorted a laugh. "On my way up the stairs, I heard Potter threatening to tie her to the chair."

Stitch raised one of his eyebrows. He found it hard to believe that anyone could tie Tenley down, although it would be Potter if anyone could accomplish that feat. Ace must have seen the question Stitch was asking himself because he smirked. "Tenley was refusing to listen to Potter, so he picked her up and put her on his lap. She isn't going anywhere."

Stitch just shook his head. "Who would've thought Potter would be so pussy-whipped."

"Shit, who thought any of us would be. Hell, we are all dropping like flies. If the trend continues, there won't be any bachelors on the team." Ace

then shook his head. "In all seriousness, I want to thank you again for everything you've done for Mia."

"You don't have to thank me, Ace. I love your sister and would move heaven on earth for her."

"I know you would, and that is why I am so damn happy for the both of you."

Ace's phone rang with an incoming call. He looked at it, then glanced at Stitch. "That's strange; it's Paul from Bayside."

Stitch didn't move from where he stood. Paul wasn't a very talkative man, so his calling wasn't to just shoot the breeze. He just listened to the one-sided call.

"Hey, Paul, what's up? He's there, at the bar? Yeah, I know him, and he is legit. Really?"

Stitch heard the floor creak behind him and saw Alex moving in with her phone to her hand, and judging from the expression on her face, she wasn't coming to deliver good news.

She looked at Stitch. "Who is he on the phone with?"

"Paul."

"He must be calling Ace about Terek." She looked up at Ace. "Terek just called me; you need to call him. But before you do, I need to show you something."

Ace finished up and disconnected from Paul. Alex hit some icons on her phone, and the video surveillance from Bayside appeared. Both Stitch and Ace looked down at Alex.

"What? I had Paul send me a couple of the video feeds. I wanted to take a look myself and see if I saw anything or anyone hanging around Mia."

"And," Ace asked.

"And...see for yourself, and you tell me."

Stitch leaned in to view the feed. Alex was able to manipulate the video a little more, but Stitch didn't recognize anyone. Ace, on the other hand, had. He looked back at Alex.

"Is that who I think it is?"

Alex nodded. "The guy that we passed coming into the clinic when we were leaving?"

Stitch asked them about the guy, and they explained. Stitch hardly believed in coincidences, and he stood his ground in this instance as well. What are the odds a guy seen at Dr. Walters office was at the bar in their small community?

"So, are we all saying this has to be the guy? Can we call Paul and see if the douche is still there?"

"Hang on and let me call Terek," Ace said and dialed his phone and put it on speaker.

"Hey, Terek."

"Hey, man. Alex wouldn't say, but please tell me you guys have Mia someplace safe."

Stitch looked at Alex, and she just grinned and shrugged her shoulders. He shouldn't be jealous of the guy, especially when he was only trying to help Mia out, but he couldn't help it. Even though he knew the reason behind their breakup, he still wasn't happy with how it all played out.

"Mia's safe. We left the beach and headed up into the mountains; what's wrong? I just got a call from the owner of the joint we hang out at. He said you were just there."

"Yeah. Look, things have taken a turn in the case I've been working on."

"What does that have to do with Mia?"

Terek explained about being ambushed and what he had overheard.

"Shit! Are you okay?"

"Just a minor flesh wound. I my damn phone just started working about thirty minutes ago or I would've called sooner. Look, from what I heard, Dr. Walters is looking for Mia. He has to be in Virginia. The police went to his penthouse to arrest him, but he's gone. His staff said he left with four bags. The police also picked up the two guys who abducted Mia. They confessed to everything and gave up a lot of information on Dr. Walters. Mia wasn't the intended target. It was Willow, the receptionist from the clinic. When Elijah found out that the guys had picked up the wrong woman, Claus, Elijah's second in command, apparently got rid of her."

Ace swallowed hard. Shit, he knew that Willow was Mia's friend.

Terek continued, "I found out Elijah has some inside help at the NYPD. One of them is in your town."

"I think I know who you are talking about. There is a guy we just saw on a video at the restaurant we frequent, and he is the spitting image of a guy Alex and I saw at Dr. Walters office."

Ace described him, and Terek agreed it could be the same guy.

"He's supposedly attending a law enforcement conference."

"Yeah, I know about it. It's over in Norfolk. A bunch of our friends from Virginia Beach PD were attending. Actually, we saw some of them tonight."

Stitch felt the goosebumps crawl along his skin. He met Ace's glare, and he knew Ace was thinking the same as he was.

"Terek, this is Stitch. Are you still at the bar?"

"Yeah, I'm sitting in my car in the parking lot."

"Alex is going to call Paul right now. Go back in there. He can pull up the video feed from tonight. There was an incident earlier. Mia suddenly had a flashback, and it wasn't pretty. She was able to tell us that it was a cologne someone was wearing that set it off. Can you take a look at the feed and see if it is the same guy you are talking about?"

"Sure. Whatever you guys need."

"He is wearing a ball cap with an American flag on the front. You'll see him walk behind Mia."

"Okay. I'm on it. Let me get in there, and I'll give you guys a call back once I take a look."

"We appreciate it."

Ace hung up, and Stitch ran his hand thru his hair.

"Ace, with Elijah looking for Mia, we can't let our guard down."

"I know Stitch, I know. If they come, we'll be ready. The good thing is that we aren't still in town."

"Yeah, but it only takes one person to say the wrong thing, and we could have trouble on the doorstep."

"Well, let's just hope that doesn't happen."

Within five minutes, they had their answer, and it wasn't good. The man in question at the bar was Brice Vargas, a detective for the NYPD and an inside informant for Dr. Elijah Walters. An arrest warrant had been issued for him as well.

Trouble was by the time Terek took a look at the video and walked around the bar searching for him; he was long gone.

Now, the team had to sit tight and wait.

CHAPTER TWENTY-FOUR

Elijah stared out the passenger window as Claus drove them through the mountains' winding roads toward the town where Mia was thought to be hiding. Thanks to Vargas' investigative skills, he was able to gather information on Mia along with her brothers and his friends who had been hiding her but insinuating to outsiders that she was missing. He knew Mia's brother was in the military, but he was surprised to learn that he is a Navy SEAL.

Vargas had called and said a buddy had contacted him, telling him that the Feds wanted to talk to him. He quickly made his way out of the city limits of Virginia Beach and was heading up towards the mountains following Mia. He was lying low, but said he would meet up with him once he got into town.

They entered Elkton, Virginia's city limits, which was only about forty-five minutes from where Mia was supposedly hiding out. He had a plan in place, but upon hearing that it was a large group that traveled with them, he needed to revisit and adjust those plans. Vargas had mentioned there were four other men and four women who had joined Mia and her lover. Knowing he was dealing with Special Forces soldiers, he needed to be smart and create a well-thought-out plan. These guys wouldn't fall for just anything, but he needed to find a way to draw their attention away from the women, specifically Mia.

Claus pulled the car into a run-down motel that looked like it had been abandoned, but the flickering vacancy neon sign said otherwise.

Elijah sighed. "There isn't anything else?"

Claus snorted. "Not unless you want to stay in a shed with pigs and cows. There isn't anything in this town. Are you sure you don't want to go elsewhere?"

"Shit. No, we need to play it safe and lay low for a day or two. At least with this place, I'm sure they won't worry about you showing any ID or paying with cash."

While Claus went inside to get their rooms, Elijah sent Vargas a text on the burner phone he had purchased to communicate. Vargas replied, letting him know that he had picked up some supplies he had requested. They agreed to meet up later after dark and go over the plan that Elijah was concocting in his mind.

Claus got back into the car and grinned.

"What are you smiling about?"

"We may have some luck on our side. There is a big rally tomorrow being held downtown Sugar Bend. A major corporation wants to buy up land around the National Park to build, and the people in the area aren't happy about it."

"And, that concerns us why?"

"A protest rally means heavy police presence. I can't imagine these small towns have a huge police force, which means—"

"They will be too busy to patrol the rest of the town."

"Exactly. And if Vargas is right, that cabin is about thirty minutes from town. As long as we have a good plan, that should give us plenty of time to do what we came to do."

"What about the guys that Vargas said were staying with them? We know that the brother is a SEAL."

Elijah smiled. "We create a distraction. Call Vargas and tell him to pick up some gasoline." Claus raised an eyebrow at him, and Elijah's smile grew, "I'm in the mood for a bonfire."

As Claus drove around to the other side of the motel where their room was, Elijah had made his final decision. He wasn't going to let Mia have the easy way out, death is too easy for what she's put him through. He was going to make her pay for her disloyalty by being his possession. She would live out the rest of her life under his control.

"You need us to do what?" Stitch asked, looking at his friend the Sherriff as if he was out of his mind. Two days had passed, and there had been no signs of Elijah or Brice Vargas. Not that they'd let their guard down either.

"I need you guys to help with crowd control."

"You do realize we hate crowds," Irish said, drawing nods from the others.

"I promise you won't be in the mix of the crowd. I just need some perimeter assistance. Several agencies from the neighboring counties who were scheduled to assist are now dealing with their own rallies in their towns. This land control shit is so out of fucking control it is a wonder we haven't had riots."

The Sherriff pleaded with his eyes, "I just need you guys for about an hour or two."

Stitch looked at Ace. It was funny that they still looked to their team leader for his thoughts first, even in their personal lives.

"What about Mia and the others? We can't take them to the rally."

Alex stepped up next to Ace. "Ace, we can handle ourselves for an hour or two. If it makes you feel any better, I have my gun with me."

"Look, if you'd be more comfortable, I can pull the deputy I have working dispatch and have him patrol out here. I can call my assistant and have her cover dispatch for that time. She's always looking for more hours."

Ace looked at the team. "This is a group decision. It's everyone's call. If you don't want to, I'll understand."

Stitch laughed out loud when Tenley pushed Potter forward and told the Sherriff that her husband would love to volunteer, which earned her a scowl from Potter. After speaking with Autumn, Frost stepped forward, followed by Irish after some reassurance from Bailey. That just left Ace and Stitch. Alex gave Ace a wink, and Ace turned and said he was in. Stitch glanced over at Mia. He was having a hard time with the decision, and as if she had read his mind, she answered for him.

"Stitch is in as well." When he looked over at her, she said, "Stitch, go and help your friend. We'll be fine. We will have the deputy, and Alex has her gun."

Though he was still unsure, he turned toward the Sherriff, "I guess you've got yourself a team."

"How does this even work? We aren't deputies." Ace asked.

Sherriff Prescott grinned. "Do each of you promise to uphold and enforce the laws of this town?"

With a resounding yes from all eight men, the Sherriff said, "Congratulations, you have been deputized under the laws of the town of Sugar Bend."

Stitch cocked his head sideways and eyed the Sherriff, "Did you just make that shit up?"

The Sherriff grinned, "Yep."

CHAPTER TWENTY-FIVE

The next morning after seeing their men off to the rally, Mia, Alex, Tenley, Autumn, and Bailey sat around the living room picking at the make-shift breakfast buffet they had set-up for the guys. There were platters of scrambled eggs, bacon, sausage, grits, toast, home fries, and fresh fruit.

Mia wasn't very hungry. Her stomach was still in knots from everything going on. She did manage to eat some toast with jelly to put something in her stomach so she wouldn't get sick.

As promised, Sherriff Prescott had his deputy stationed in the driveway. Mia had felt bad that the guy had been put on babysitting duty, so she had taken him a plate of food, which he thanked her for.

"So, Mia. What's next for you?" Bailey asked as she sipped on a cup of coffee.

"What do you mean?"

"Well, once all of this over, what are your plans? Are you going back to New York?"

She put her coffee mug down on the table next to her. "I am." She saw the surprised looks on her friend's faces, not to mention the frowns, and she smiled. "I am going back to pack my things. Stitch and I talked. I'm going to move in with him, and from there, we'll look for a place together."

"What about work?" Tenley questioned.

"Well, I was supposed to meet with the owner of that clinic and shelter that Stitch's mom volunteers at. He is looking to sell, and I might be interested in taking it over.

"Mia that is awesome news!" Bailey exclaimed.

"Well, nothing is set in stone. I still have to meet with Dr. Katz."

"I'm sure he'd sell to you."

"Is a business like that something you can afford?" Alex asked.

"I've looked into the process of taking out a business loan. Plus, with the practice also housing a shelter on site, there are grants available as well. Like I said, I'll see."

"Well, it sounds exciting."

"Where's Autumn?" Tenley asked, looking around.

"I thought she went to get a soda out of the fridge in the garage," Bailey said just as Autumn emerged from the bathroom using a towel to wipe her mouth, and Mia suspected she had just gotten sick. She didn't look so well.

"Damn, honey, you look like death warmed over you," Alex admitted getting up and heading into the kitchen to find some crackers or ginger ale for her.

"I think I have a stomach bug or something. I've been queasy for the last couple of days," Autumn said, dropping on the sofa as if she had all the energy zapped right out of her.

Mia eyed Alex, who glanced over at Tenley, who then looked back at Autumn with a sly smile.

"Autumn, could there be a possibility that you're pregnant?"

When Autumn's eyes widened with a look of shock, Mia could tell the beautiful redhead hadn't considered that possibility. She knew Autumn and Frost were trying, but from the deer in the headlights look, Autumn hadn't thought through that scenario.

"Oh, shit! I don't know. I mean, there could be a slight chance, but hell, I just went off the pill. Plus, I wasn't sick when I was pregnant with Cody."

"Every baby affects your body differently. Look at me; I was on the pill, now I'm knocked up with twins that already have their daddy's battle training, going by the punching and kicking my insides take every day."

"Well, there is only one way to find out," Alex said, looking at Autumn.

"What's that?"

"Take a pregnancy test. And, I just happen to have one with me." Alex dug through her purse and pulled out a pregnancy test kit.

Tenley gave Alex a funny look. "Do I even want to know why you're carrying around a pregnancy test in your purse?" Tenley's eyes shot wide open. "Oh, my, god! Are you and Ace trying to have a baby?"

Now it was Alex's turn to give Tenley a look. "No....I have to be married first before I'd consider having a baby. And with mine and Ace's luck at planning a wedding, I'll probably be the first eighty-year-old woman

218

to pop out a kid." Everyone laughed, but Mia could tell Tenley's comment hit a sore spot with Alex. Again, Mia saw that dawning look in Alex's eyes. She would definitely need to drop a hint to her brother to get his ass in gear and marry Alex.

"The pregnancy test was for one of the patients at the clinic. Well, it was for his wife. They have some financial issues at least until he can get his benefits and pension straightened out, so I bought the test for them and some groceries. I dropped the groceries off but forgot about the test."

Bailey clapped her hands together. "This is so exciting! Well, go pee on that stick," she told Autumn.

A few minutes later, Autumn came back. Her face was unreadable.

"Well?" Tenley questioned as she shoved another forkful of home fries in her mouth.

"I think I need to have Frost rework the addition on the house because he's going to need to build a nursery," Autumn said that part with a little squeal and was smiling ear-to-ear as she held up the stick that showed pink lines.

Everyone jumped up, were hugging and congratulating her, when suddenly Tenley doubled over and clutched her stomach.

Alex was right by her side.

"Tenley, what's wrong?"

"The babies..." She took another deep breath and exhaled.

"Ten...what about the babies? What's going on?"

"I think the babies are ready to escape."

"Seriously?"

"Oh god, my water just broke."

Mia looked down, and judging from the slight puddle forming around Tenley's feet; she told the truth.

"Alex, you need to call Potter. I need Potter," Tenley said in between breaths, and Mia couldn't help but be both excited and worried."

"Should I call for an ambulance?" Bailey asked.

"No, let's call Potter and see how fast they can get here. Tenley, let's get you over to the chair."

"No! I'll ruin Stitch's chair."

"Honey, Stitch isn't going to care about the chair. If he does, I'll buy him a new one."

"At least get a trash bag that I can sit on."

Mia wanted to laugh at Alex's subtle eye-roll. She ran and got the trash bag from the kitchen so Tenley would sit down.

"Mia, can you run out front and let the deputy know what's going on? That way if we need to get Tenley to the hospital before the guys get back, he could take her."

Mia nodded and headed outside. It was cold and dreary outside. She heard Stitch say this morning that there was a chance for snow later in the day.

As she started down the porch steps, she caught a whiff of smoke, and she looked around. Not seeing anything, she walked around to the side of the house, and she gasped when she saw a shed near the back of Stitch's property on fire. The hair on the back of her neck stood up.

She took off and ran toward the deputy's patrol car. As she approached, the window was half down, and she saw the Deputy was slumped against the steering wheel. His eyes were closed, but she knew on instinct that he wasn't asleep on his own doing.

She covered her mouth, spun around, and sprinted back to the house. She didn't even bother looking around to see if anyone was near. She was almost to the front door when a bullet struck the house just left of the door. She stumbled through the door, slamming it and locking it.

"Was that a gunshot?" Alex questioned, getting up and coming toward Mia.

Mia was too stunned to speak. She felt herself shaking. She had to warn the others. Someone was out there. Oh, god, that poor deputy, she thought to herself.

"Mia, what's wrong? You're shaking like a leaf."

Mia looked at Alex. God, she wished she had the strength that Alex had.

Mia was nodding her head when she found her voice. "Someone shot at me. The Deputy is knocked out or something, and Stitch's shed is on fire."

220

Suddenly, an explosion occurred nearby, and Alex ran to the kitchen window. When she returned, she started closing all of the window blinds and pulled the curtains closed.

"Bailey, did you get a hold of the guys?" Alex asked, and Mia stood there for a minute in awe as Alex took control of the situation. She reminded her of her brother when he was in commander mode.

"No, I keep getting a busy signal. It's weird. I can't even get through to 911."

"Okay, since we don't know who or what we are dealing with, our best option is to hunker down here. Autumn, help me get Tenley into the bathroom. Mia gather some blankets and pillows and brought them into the bathroom."

Just as Mia crossed the living room, the huge picture window shattered, and Mia screamed as she fell to the floor.

Alex came crawling out of the bathroom.

"Mia!"

Mia shook even harder than before. She couldn't move. Alex came up beside her.

"Mia? Mia, look at me." She took a few seconds to process Alex's words. She also saw that Alex had her gun in her hand. Mia needed to be strong and brave. She got through the ordeal back in New York alive.

She went to say something when they heard men talking just outside on the front porch. They said something about going around the back.

Mia's eyes widened. "Alex, the back door is unlocked." Before Alex could say anything, Mia leaped up and sprinted for the back door. When she got there, she knew she had to do something. She gasped when she recognized Claus, Elijah's employee standing to the right at the bottom of the porch stairs.

She had to protect the others. She wasn't sure how many bad guys there were out there, but if she could draw some away from the house, it would help Alex and the others. She eyed the woods that led to the trails. With her body still recovering from the incident in New York, she wondered how far she could make it before they caught up with her. Her main concern was her ankle. As long she could run, she could endure the other aches if it meant saving her friends' lives. She tested her ankle by putting weight on it and bounced a little. It was a little sore, but she could do it. She had to do it. The thought sounded good, and before she could question herself, she yanked open the door and took off to the right. As she made her way down the stairs and toward the tree line that led to the trails, she heard the shouting behind her, followed by gunfire, and she prayed the girls were okay and that this plan would work.

✎

"Stitch! Gather everyone up," Sherriff Prescott called out just as the team made their way back to the Sherriff's department. The so-called rally ended up being a dud with only a handful of protestors showing up.

They met the Sherriff by his patrol truck. "What's going on?" Stitch asked.

"A 9-1-1 call just came in. There was an explosion on your property. I can't get in touch with my Deputy. There are reports of gunfire. I've got other deputies en route now."

"Fuck!" Everyone scrambled into their vehicles and took off toward the cabin.

Stitch was scared, angry, and felt guilty. He banged his fist on the dashboard.

"Motherfucker! The bastard from the bar must have followed us."

"That, or he saw you all cozy with Mia and asked around and got your information from somebody. It is pretty easy to check a background, especially with his connections. Think about it, Stitch. We have a lot of cop friends. This asshole is a detective who most people would assume is a good guy. If he asked, it's possible someone said something."

Stitched glanced back at Irish, who was trying to call Bailey.

"I can't get through."

"Shit!"

Ace pressed the gas pedal to the floor, and Stitch held on. In record time, they made the turn up the driveway leading to the cabin with cop cars following. The truck skidded to a stop, and Alex emerged from the front door carrying her glock, but it wasn't so much of her presence that drew their attention. It was the blood all over her.

Ace got to her first, pulled her into his arms, and then started patting down her body and looking her over to find out where the blood was coming from. She swatted at his hands. "The blood isn't mine."

"Whose is it?" He barked, obviously shaken up by the scene.

"The guy who made a huge mistake by trying to attack us."

"Where is everyone else?" Stitch asked, looking around. He saw the flames shooting from the shed. Just then, the fire department arrived. He didn't care about the shed; all he cared about was that all the women were safe.

"Autumn and Tenley are inside along with two dead perpetrators." She looked at the Sherriff. "Sorry, I tried to warn them, but they fired first."

"Where are Mia and Bailey?" Irish asked.

"Mia took off towards the trails. I think she was trying to lure the other two guys away from the house. I think Bailey may have been with her. I don't know for sure, though. She definitely isn't in the house." She looked between Stitch and Ace. "I think it was Dr. Walters. One of the dead inside is the guy from the bar."

"Dammit!"

"Are you okay?" Ace asked, pulling her into a hug.

She looked at Potter. "I'm fine. It's Tenley I'm more worried about."

"Tenley's hurt?" Potter asked as he took off in a sprint toward the front door.

"Potter!" Alex shouted, making Potter stop and turn towards her. "She wasn't injured. Her water broke. She's in labor. She's in the bathroom downstairs with Autumn." He nodded his head and ran toward the house.

As Potter left to tend to his wife, Stitch and the rest of the crew all gathered their weapons and took off on foot toward the trails searching for Mia, and possibly Bailey.

Mia was sucking air big-time as she made her way through the trails. Even with her running regiment, she still struggled on the incline. Her bummed ankle wasn't helping as she hopped over branches and slipped on rocks and leaves. She could hear the footsteps of the men following behind her. They were yelling as if trying to intimidate her.

She had tried to pay attention when Stitch brought her up here, but she was so enthralled with what nature had to offer that she may have missed a few things he had pointed out. Mainly when he spoke about where certain trails led to.

She paused for a moment to rest against a tree. She bent over and took deep breaths. Her mind was still on Alex, Tenley, Autumn, and Bailey. She prayed they were okay and that the guys were alerted to what was happening. She looked around and noticed a clearing up ahead. It wasn't the same one that Stitch had taken her to, as this one wasn't up as high.

As she cleared the trees, a small area opened up. She heard a gunshot in the distance and prayed it hadn't hit anyone she loved. She looked around and noticed she had hit a dead end. The only way out was to go back the way she had come, or over the side of the mountain.

She heard the crunch of footsteps as she turned and gasped when she stood face-to-face with Elijah, holding a gun in his hand. He, too, was breathing heavily.

"Mia."

She shook her head as tears emerged in her eyes.

"How could you? I trusted you. I looked up to you."

"I could say the same about you. You betrayed me by working with the authorities who sent you to spy on my organization."

She was jerked back by his comment, clearly confused.

"I don't know what you are talking about. I never worked for anyone other than you."

"It doesn't matter now."

She took a few steps back into the clearing, being careful not to go too far or she'd go over the edge.

"I don't want to die," she told him. "I swear I didn't know about anything until after the fact."

"You don't have to die, Mia. Just come with me, then you and I can put all of this ugliness behind us."

She shook her head. "You almost had me killed."

"That was a mistake. Those responsible had mistaken you for Willow. You were never the intended target. I'd never harm you, Mia. I've wanted you ever since I first laid eyes on you."

"Where is Willow?" She asked, sudden realization dawning.

Elijah's face went blank, then he rubbed his forehead before looking her in the eye. "Willow crossed the line, Mia. She had to pay the price for her betrayal."

Mia placed her hand over her mouth to cover her sob. He had killed Willow. Oh, God, she felt sick to her stomach.

He took a step toward her, and she moved back. She didn't have much more room.

"Mia, don't test my patience. Come with me now."

In a surprise move, he stuffed his gun in the waistband of his pants then held his hand out to her. Without a gun being pointed at her, she felt a little reprieve.

Suddenly, Stitch's voice echoed through the trees.

"Mia!"

"Stitch!" She shouted, and Elijah ran toward her. She braced herself for the impending hit. He tackled them both to the ground. She swung her fists, hit him in the face, then got to her hands and knees and tried to crawl away. Elijah grabbed her foot and dragged her backward as he flipped her over onto her back. He straddled her body, and she cried out from the pressure on her still healing ribs.

"Stop fighting me!"

"Go to hell!" She told him and dragged her fingernails down his cheek, drawing blood. He cried out and grabbed her arm and slammed it against the ground. She felt the bone in her forearm crack, and she screamed. He latched onto her throat and squeezed until she could no longer breathe. Her lungs began to burn, and black dots started forming in her vision. It was the telling moment that she knew she was going to die. Her eyes started to close as death pulled her under its spell. Just as she took her last breath, a gunshot sounded, and then everything went silent. She felt free.

Stitch knew the direction Mia was in when he heard her call his name.

As he and the others charged up the trails, the group had started to fan out to surround the area. There was no way he was letting this asshole go. But Mia was his first priority. One of the deputies had taken out the other guy.

Stitch got to the clearing where he believed Mia was, and he became enraged when he saw Elijah on top of Mia choking her. He could see Mia was without a fight and losing consciousness. He raised his gun to take the shot, but suddenly, another shot came from another direction, and a bright red bloom appeared on Elijah's chest, and he fell over.

Stitch raced to Mia's side.

"Mia?" He said frantically as he shook her. Not getting a response, he checked her pulse—nothing.

"No!"

He started CPR as the others all came running towards him from all different directions.

Ace knelt beside him and took Mia's hand.

"He was choking her," Stitch said before giving Mia another breath of air.

"Got a pulse," Ace said right before Mia started sputtering and coughing. Stitch pulled her into his arms and held her close. He buried his face in her hair and cried.

He felt Mia move, and when he looked down into those brown eyes staring back at him, he almost lost it again. The others had all taken off their coats and laid them over Mia to keep her warm until help arrived.

The paramedics arrived and secured Mia to a backboard and loaded it onto one of the deputies ATVs.

Stitch never once let go of Mia's hand. She was quiet through the whole process, probably in shock and exhaustion. The paramedics splinted her arm, but other than her arm and bruising, she appeared to be okay. She squeezed his hand, and he bent down, so he was face-to-face with her.

"The others…are the others, okay?" She asked him. Her voice was rough and raspy.

He smiled. "Everyone is good."

"What about Bailey? I think she followed me."

Stitch's smile faded as he looked to Ace.

"Ace, did anyone confirm Bailey's whereabouts?"

Ace looked at the Sherriff, and he radioed down to some of the deputies who were at the cabin processing the crime scene.

When one of the deputies radioed back saying no, that she was not there with the others, Stitch saw the panic in Irish as he pulled his phone out. Stitch knew he was trying to call her.

Ace tried to calm him.

"Irish, if she is up here, she may have just gotten lost."

"Yeah, I've my deputies starting to search. We'll find her."

The Sherriff then looked over at Elijah's body that was now covered with a white sheet.

"Who fired the shot?" The Sherriff asked, turning back to the group.

The guys all stood there looking at one another as if waiting for the other to confess. Stitch knew the shot couldn't have come from anyone on the team because of their location. The shot had come from the other direction. He looked at the Sherriff. "Are you sure it wasn't one of your guys?"

The Sherriff shook his head slowly, then as if right on cue, there was rustling in the bushes to the right of them, followed a woman's mumbled curse.

"God damn, fucking thorns. Jesus, by the time I find my way out of here, I'm going to look like freaking cactus."

They all stood there wide-eyed as Bailey emerged from the thick brush, shaking her hair out and pulling out vines that were stuck to her clothing, all the while carrying a huge ass rifle that was slung across her small frame.

Stitch looked closer. If he wasn't mistaken, the rifle resembled Irish's sniper rifle.

227

When she had finally pulled the last vine from her shirt, she looked up, and Stitch wanted to laugh at the look on her face and the faces of the others.

"Oh, thank god. Can someone please take this thing?" She asked as she pulled the strap of the rifle over her head. Irish was there in an instant, taking the rather large weapon from her shaking hands. When nobody said anything, she said, "What?" Irish's eyes widened at first, but quickly narrowed as he found his voice.

"Why in the hell do you have my rifle?" When she grinned and her cheeks pinkened, Stitch wanted to laugh out loud. Hell, even he knew nobody ever touched Irish's rifle unless there was a damn good reason. For a while, until Irish found Bailey, the team was beginning to think that the only marriage Irish would have would be to his rifle. Stitch just shook his head as the little sprite batted her eyelashes at her husband.

Sherriff Prescott stepped forward and rested his hand on the butt of his gun. Stitch didn't miss the amusement in the Sherriff's voice when he spoke to Bailey as serious as the situation was.

"Darlin, would you like to explain why you are hiding out in the bushes with your husband's rifle?"

"Well, when the bad guys came into the house, I saw Mia slip out the back. I knew she was trying to protect the rest of us by leading those two guys away from the house. I knew Alex could take care of herself and Tenley and Autumn."

"So, you decided to follow her." Irish blurted out.

"Christ, don't get your flippers in a twist, husband of mine." Stitch was biting his cheek to keep from laughing, but the coughs covering the laughter he heard from the others didn't go un-noticed. He even saw Mia crack a smile.

"Anyway, I couldn't let her go off by herself without backup. I didn't know where you guys were or when you'd be back. I remembered when Irish brought me up here for a weekend, and we had spent a lot of the time hiking the trails. I wasn't really sure where Mia was leading them, but I remembered Irish taking me up to a deer stand that overlooked Stitch's property. You could see almost any spot from that vantage point."

"Sweetness, do you care to share how you even know how to shoot my rifle, let alone hit a perfect shot?" Even though Irish pretty much growled out his question, Stitch could also hear the pride in his tone. He knew deep down Irish was proud of his wife, but on the other end of the spectrum, she had taken someone's life, and they all knew the toll that could take on a person.

Stitch saw her lip start to quiver. Shit, he hated tears. Especially tears that belonged to his and his team's women.

"Are you mad at me?" She asked Irish just as the first tear breached her lower eyelid and slid down her cheek. Irish was a hard man. They all were, but Irish more so than the others and probably due to the fact he had racked up an impressive kill list, though he would never admit it or be proud of it. But, doing so, it takes what is inside to get through the guilt of having to take another life. But, seeing now how his face melted as his wife stood there asking if he was mad at her showed the true man Irish was. He was a true softy at heart.

Irish grabbed the front of her sweater and pulled into a crushing hug. "No, baby. I'm not mad at you. I'm damn proud of you for your quick thinking. Without you there to help Mia, we could be dealing with a whole other situation. But, you never answered my question. How do you know how to handle my rifle?"

"Well...Alex and I have been going to the shooting range the nights we have kickboxing. I expressed my interest in learning to shoot, whatever that is called. I told Alex I wanted to learn to shoot the same type of gun that you have. She laughed at me at first, but then she thought it was a great idea. I tried asking you, but you kept telling me that it was too much for me." Stitch heard Ace groan at the mention of Alex's name. Alex loved handling all types of weapons and could probably handle with ease any weapon put in front of her.

"We will be talking about yours and Alex's extracurricular activities later. I'm just glad you're safe. I was so damn worried about you."

The Sherriff chuckled. "You guys are some lucky bastards, I tell ya. My men and I will handle this scene. You all head to the hospital. Potter and

229

Alex took Tenley. From what I heard, she was in labor, and as my deputy put it, the woman can give a sailor some competition when it comes to her language. Frost and Autumn are waiting for you guys at the cabin."

Stitch took Mia's hand as the ATV started to move.

"What do you say we go say hi to the newest members of Team 2 and then head home?"

She smiled, "Home sounds good."

CHAPTER TWENTY-SIX

Standing by Tenley's side, Alex took deep breaths along with Tenley as she endured another contraction. By the time they arrived at the local hospital, she was already too far along for an epidural. Unfortunately, because of the delay from the fiasco back at Stitch's caused, they had no other choice than to admit Tenley to the closest hospital or risk delivering the twins in the back of their car.

She had gotten a message from Ace telling her that the cabin's situation had been defused, and they were on their way to the hospital. Thank god because she had been torn between going to the hospital with Tenley and staying to help look for Mia.

Alex had to bite the inside of her cheek to conceal her amusement when Tenley turned to Potter and spouted off the next verbal beatdown on the poor guy. But, Potter, because of the Special Forces soldier he was, took it all in stride, knowing that Tenley didn't really meant anything she had said.

"Potter, I love you dearly, but damn, if I will ever let you put another one of your super SEAL sperms up my vagina again." Her eyes got really big. "Oh shit, here comes another contraction. Motherfucker! Where in the hell is the damn doctor? The pressure is getting to be too much, and I feel like I have to push."

The nurse assigned to Tenley, who seemed more interested in Potter's comfort, looked at Tenley and told her by no means should she try to push until the doctor arrived. If looks could kill, that nurse would be six feet under by the death glare that Tenley gave her. Alex swore if the woman put her hand on Potter one more time to "reassure" him everything was fine that Tenley was going to come up off that bed pregnant or not and kick the woman's ass. Potter had been polite and calmly brushed the woman's advances off. He never left Tenley's side and constantly praised her as she got through each contraction.

Tenley leveled her stare at the nurse, and Alex knew that look and waited for it. "Well, how long does it take to get here? It's not like this a huge town.

231

Unless instead of cars, you all get around by horse and buggy. If that's the case, then you better suit up because these babies are coming out."

To ease some of the tension into the room, Alex got the nurse's attention. "Why don't you go check and see where the doctor is? If Tenley says she needs to push, shouldn't that indicate we need a doctor, like yesterday? And, if he's not close, maybe they can send a doctor from the ER up.

Thankfully the nurse had a sliver of brains and agreed. As soon as the woman was gone from the room, Tenley relaxed then turned to Potter. Alex was shocked to see tears streaking down Tenley's face. Potter pushed the loose strands of hair that had escaped Tenley's ponytail from her face and tucked them behind her ear. He took her face between his large palms and placed a kiss on her nose. For anyone who knew Potter, they only saw the large, serious, and broody man. Rarely did anyone get the glimpse of the gentle giant that he was on the inside. Alex knew when it came to Tenley; the man would bend over backward to give her what she needed.

"Honey, what are the tears for?" Potter asked her.

Tenley sniffled. "I'm sorry for yelling at you. I love you so much. Please don't be upset with me."

Potter's expression softened. "Oh, baby. I love you too, and I could never be upset with you for expressing your emotions while giving birth to our children. I would take your pain if I could." He leaned down and kissed her. Alex felt a little awkward listening to such an intimate conversation between the two of them. She tried looking away, but then she felt Tenley grab her hand. When she turned back, Tenley was looking at her. "Alex, thank you for what you did. That twatwaffle was starting to test my patience, and I was afraid that I would lose my cool and have to get out of this bed to deal with her. And, oh my goodness, wouldn't that have been a sight. Me going all cavewoman on the nurse with a baby dangling from my lady bits."

Alex couldn't hold back her laughter. She laughed so hard that she cried. Even Potter was laughing. Then he bent down and whispered something in Tenley's ear, and Alex thought it was a good time to give the parents a couple of minutes to themselves. As she excused herself from the room, promising Tenley she would be right outside, she couldn't help but notice the black mass making an appearance between Tenley's legs. Alex quickly stepped outside and went in search of a doctor. Thankfully, the search didn't take long. By the time she got to the nurse's station, the doctor was walking in. She quickly explained, and the doctor seemed a little agitated. On the way back to Tenley's room, he apologized for his delay and explained that the details he was given made it seem that Tenley still had a while before she would go into full labor. Needless to say, Nurse Barbie wasn't welcomed back into Tenley's room.

After the doctor did a quick introduction with Potter and Tenley, he suited up and started barking orders to the staff that filled the room.

Looking up from between her legs, he gave Tenley a warm smile and said, "Okay, sweetie, I think these little rascals of yours are in a hurry to meet you." Alex was pleased to see Tenley smile. Potter, on the other hand, looked ready for battle. But that didn't surprise Alex at all. His eyes never left his wife. "On this next contraction, I want you to push. Push like you have to poop."

The room went completely silent, and Alex wanted to laugh at the expression on Tenley's face.

"What happens if I actually poop? Oh my god. That is disgusting, not to mention embarrassing. Tenley looked down at the doctor that sat between her legs. "Is there another way to get these little hellions out?" Alex couldn't hold it in any longer and burst out laughing. It must have been contagious because soon, everyone in the room was laughing, including Tenley. "Well, shit, let's just get on with it because if I have endure this much pain any longer, I think I might just pass out."

Alex held Tenley's hand as another strong contraction hit Tenley hard. She pushed and grunted, and the doctor motioned for Potter to look at the action happening between Tenley's legs.

"What is that?" Potter asked as his face took on a little bit of a green, sickly look.

The elderly doctor just smiled and said, "That, son, is the top of the head of your first baby."

Alex really wasn't sure what she was expecting from Potter, but what she damn well wasn't expecting was for Potter's eyes to roll back in his head and his large body to collapse to the floor.

"Oh shit!" Alex blurted out as Tenley just sat there staring at her husband sprawled out on the floor, then started laughing hysterically.

By the grace of God, Juliette entered the room. "What happened?" She asked, all concerned as she stepped over Potter to get to Tenley's other side and held her hand.

"Well, my big badass SEAL husband apparently can't stomach a baby coming out of my hoo-ha." She started sobbing. "He's the one that put them in me. And, it's not like he's the one having his vagina stretched the length of the Grand Canyon."

Jesus, Alex didn't know if she wanted to cry for Tenley or to laugh at her and the mayhem that was taking place in this room. They could win America's Funniest Home Videos, hands down. Potter would never forgive himself if he missed the birth of babies. Well, as long as he wasn't working for Uncle Sam. Alex looked at Juliette. "Can you handle Tenley? I'm going to go get Derek and Ace, and they can help get daddy here up."

At Juliette's nod, Alex took off running down the hallway to the waiting room. When she got there, the whole team was now there, and she explained what happened. She could see they were all trying to suppress their amusement with the situation, and honestly, she couldn't blame them one bit because as soon as all of this was over, they were all going to sit around having a drink and laughing their asses off.

When Alex, Ace, and Derek hit the door to Tenley's room, Alex heard the most amazing sound. The sound of life, double time. Her heart melted as she opened the door and saw Tenley and Potter both sitting on the bed, each of them holding a bundle of pink.

When Tenley raised her head and looked at Alex with unshed tears in her eyes, Alex couldn't be any happier for her best friend. She was envious of her. She had the perfect family. A husband who loved her unconditionally, a seven-year-old daughter who they brought life to again after her parents were killed, and now these two precious bundle of joys they welcomed. She looked up at Ace, who seemed to have the same look on his face as she did. But when he looked down at her, she saw guilt, even though nobody else would recognize that look. It was a look that Alex was pretty sure Ace made a point not to let many people see.

He wrapped his arms around her and pulled her close to his chest. He then whispered the word "soon" to her, and she felt her heart kick-start. They had been trying to get married for almost a year now. But life got in the way, and things got postponed. But her friends weren't letting life slow them down. Maybe it was time to take a different approach to marriage. Maybe she didn't need the big fairy tale wedding she'd dreamt of. Maybe all she needed was just the man.

CHAPTER TWENTY-SEVEN

Stitch couldn't wait to get to Mia's side. He smiled, and even found himself whistling as he walked through the emergency room department as he headed to Mia's room. Seeing Tenley and Potter's twins had been a bright spot on the events that occurred today.

As he rounded the corner, he caught sight of a man entering Mia's room. He was on full alert with everything that had happened today and became suspicious and hastened his walk. As he neared the open door, he heard Mia's soft voice, followed by the guy's.

"Terek."

"Hey, Mia."

"What are you doing here?"

"I was told you were here, and I wanted to come and make sure you were okay."

Stitch stood at the door enough to where he could see in. He felt horrible for eavesdropping on a private conversation, but he wondered why her ex-boyfriend would come all this way just to see if she was okay.

"I'm good—some bruises and a broken arm. But it could've been worse." She tilted her head sideways as she looked at him. "Terek, you could've called to see how I was. Why are you really here?"

Stitch heard him sigh. "I needed to talk to you before I headed out, and I wasn't sure if you would take my call."

"Terek, Ace explained why you did what you did. I can't say that I agree with your style of execution, but I do understand why you did it."

"Mia, I'm so sorry. I really wish things could've worked out between us. You are an incredible woman."

She shrugged her shoulders. "Things happen for a reason."

"So, you're happy?"

She smiled, "I am."

"Then, that's all that matters."

"You said you were headed out. What's next for you?"

"Well, since my cover was blown and my target skipped the country, my career in the bureau is pretty much over unless I want a desk job."

"That doesn't sound like you," she teased.

He chuckled, "No, definitely not. I spoke with a buddy of mine from the service. He just opened a private security company in Florida. He offered me a job, so maybe I'll head down that way and see how it goes."

"Well, I wish you all the best."

"Thanks, Mia."

He leaned forward and kissed her cheek. "Take care, Mia."

Stitch didn't want to be seen, so he slipped into the vacant room next door until Terek passed. Once the coast was clear, he entered Mia's room and saw her wiping her eyes. He knew everything had to be taking a toll on her.

"Hey, you okay?"

She looked up and smiled, red eyes and nose. "Yeah, just a very emotional day."

He grinned, "Yeah, it was. I saw Terek was here. Everything okay with him?"

"Yeah, all good. He just wanted to see how I was and say good-bye. He's taking a job down in Florida. Some security business a friend of his from the service opened."

"Good for him."

Mia snorted a laugh. "Stitch, you don't give a rat's ass about him."

He gave her a boyish smile. "True."

He took her hand. "All your paperwork is taken care of. You ready to get out of here?"

"Yeah, can we make a quick detour? I'm dying to see those babies."

Stitch's smile grew, and he kissed her lips. "They are so cute. Come on, a quick stop; then I want to get you home."

237

CHAPTER TWENTY-EIGHT

Mia locked the doors to the clinic and smiled as she admired the new signage on the door—*Virginia Beach Animal Hospital and Rescue Center – Mia Chambers, DVM.* With Stitch's mom's help, Mia was the new owner of the town's veterinarian clinic and rescue shelter.

A lot had happened in the last three weeks since the incident at the cabin. After Mia was released from the hospital. She had flown back to New York to meet with Federal Investigators regarding Dr. Walters. During those discussions, Mia found out that Dr. Walters held several properties around the country to import and export puppies illegally. In the end, the FBI had arrested a little over forty people in connection with the operation, and they were working with international law enforcement to crack down on the growing business of puppy smuggling. She had made arrangements with the FBI to have all of the puppies that were still in Dr. Walters' possession to be shipped to Virginia Beach and housed at her rescue center until they could be adopted.

During the meeting with the investigators, she had asked about her friend Willow. While Dr. Walters had claimed he had killed her, there was no solid evidence to back up the claim, so the police considered her a missing person, though Mia had her doubts knowing now what type of person Dr. Walters was.

Stitch had been by her side the entire time. Her brother and a couple of the others from the team traveled to New York to help pack up her apartment and move her "home."

The biggest surprise had come when she and Stitch arrived in Virginia Beach. Instead of going to Stitch's apartment, Mia was puzzled when Stitch pulled the moving truck up in front of a house. It had been dark by the time they arrived, and she had been asleep the last leg of the trip, but once her eyes had time to focus, she realized it was the same house that she had seen when she and Stitch had come to town. It was a quaint home just down the road from Stitch's parents' house. She had seen a 'for sale' sign in the front yard and looked it up on the internet and had fallen in love with it just from the pictures alone. With the help of his mom and dad, Stitch had contacted the realtor and started the process of purchasing it. With their connections, they had pushed the sale through very quickly to surprise her.

Not only did he surprise her with a house, but he had it newly furnished. Stitch owed Skittles and Diego for helping pull off that part, along with Alex and Autumn, who had helped pick out the furnishings since they knew Mia's style.

She pulled her coat a little tighter around her as she walked to her car. It was the day before Christmas Eve. Though she had been over the moon with all of the positive changes in her life, she'd admit that she had felt a little depressed because Stitch wasn't sure if he'd be home for Christmas, but she understood. He and the team had gotten called up a few days after they returned from New York. And, of course, with his assignments, there was no timeline on when they would return.

On a positive front, she had been cleared by her doctor to resume all strenuous activities. She had started running again, and even started joining Alex for kickboxing, though she still had a cast on her arm. But she was due to have that removed in three weeks.

As she pulled into their driveway, she sighed, looking at the dark house. She hadn't even put up Christmas decorations. Hell, she still had boxes all over the house to go through and unpack. With the clinic closed for the next couple of days, she'd have a lot of time to spend working on getting the house organized. It would be a nice surprise for Stitch for when he got home.

She unlocked the door, and when she stepped into the foyer, a white light flicked on, and she dropped her bags as she covered her mouth. Tears began to flood her eyes as Stitch stood next to a fully decorated Christmas tree.

She was speechless but began to walk toward him.

He smiled and met her halfway.

"I thought it would be nice to surprise you."

"You did," she said, looking between him and the tree.

239

She couldn't stop crying. She was still emotional over everything that happened, so the slightest little thing could send her into a fit of ugly tears. But these were tears of happiness.

"I'm sorry I don't have the house cleaned. I've just been so busy with trying to get the clinic running in the direction I want it to go."

"Mia…"

She looked up at him as he wrapped his arms around her waist and pulled her close.

"Stop apologizing." He leaned down and covered her mouth. He kissed her deeply and with so much passion that she relaxed and gave over all control to him.

As he released her lips, he smiled. "I missed you."

"I missed you too."

She smiled then looked at the tree. "The tree looks beautiful." She touched some of the ornaments. They were all ornaments that they both had collected over the years.

"I saved the angel for you to put on the tree."

He picked up a shoebox and brought it over to her.

"Really?"

"Your mom mentioned how it's always been your thing."

She was excited because she and Stitch had picked out the Angel together. She wanted an angel that held meaning for them.

When she stood beside him, he looked down at her and smiled as he ran his knuckles down her cheek. She was so in love with him.

She removed the lid to the box and gasped. In place of the rustic Woodland Angel was a stunning white gold band with a diamond embedded into the band.

Stitch took the ring box out of the shoebox and dropped down on one knee, and took her hand in his.

"Mia, since I met you; you have always been the source of joy and happiness in my life. No matter where I'm at in the world, when the sun shines, it reminds me of your beautiful smile. I want my heart to be your shelter and my arms to be your home. Will you marry me?"

"Yes," Mia whispered with tears streaming down her cheeks. She was so overcome with emotion, she dropped to her knees next to Stitch. He slipped the ring on her finger and pulled her into his embrace. He was absolutely right; her home was in his arms.

EPILOGUE

"Mia, this is gorgeous!" Alex said as she admired Mia's engagement ring.

"Thank you," Mia replied and then winked at Stitch. "He did a good job picking it out." Because the diamond was embedded in the ring, it gave it a smooth surface so she wouldn't snag it on anything while at work.

The gang was once again gathered at Ace and Alex's celebrating the holiday. Stitch couldn't stop smiling. There was so much to celebrate besides Christmas. He glanced over and wanted to laugh at Potter as he sat back in the chair with his new daughters, one in each arm as they slept the day away.

"So, did you and Mia talk about wedding plans yet?" Frost asked Stitch.

"Some. She wants a small event. Similar to what you guys had," Stitch said, looking at Frost, Potter, and Irish.

Just then, Sienna, Irish, and Bailey's little girl walked into the kitchen and grabbed a cookie off the tray in the table, and Stitch smiled, seeing how Irish morphed into daddy mode. It was heartwarming, and Stitch couldn't wait for the day that he would become a dad. Mia had told him last night that she had been cleared by her doctor. It had been killing him not to be able to make love to her, and the last thing he wanted was to cause her more pain. But she better be ready because tonight, he was going to show her what she meant to him as he explored every inch of her body.

"Sienna, where are Cody and Alejandra?" Tenley asked.

"Oh, they're in the game room playing with Cody's balls."

The room went silent, and Stitch wasn't sure what was more amusing—the blood draining from Frost's face, or Potter spewing his beer all over his newborn twins. Everyone else thought it was funny as shit.

Before Potter blew a gasket and Frost keeled over from lack of oxygen, Bailey asked Sienna while trying to keep a straight face, "Honey, what balls are they playing with?"

"You know, the squishy ones." She said as she squeezed and relaxed her fist.

"Oh hell!" Potter exclaimed as he leaped up and handed the twins over to Tenley before high-tailing it out of the room.

Everyone else laughed their ass off when Sienna clarified that the squishy balls were the stress balls that Alex kept around the house.

Once the amusement died down, Stitch turned toward Dino, who had been on the quiet side for most of the day. He noticed he kept looking at his watch as if he had some place to be.

"Dude, what has been with you the last two weeks?"

Dino looked up with his forehead scrunched up. "What do you mean?"

"You've been skipping out on drinks at Bayside, not to mention hauling ass out of the base, and just like you're doing now, you keep looking at your watch. What gives, man? You got a woman waiting on you or something?" Stitch joked, but Dino didn't reply.

"Wait a minute. Have you been seeing that neighbor of yours?" Diego asked.

Judging by the death stare that Dino gave Diego, Stitch knew Diego had hit a nerve.

"Are you seeing someone?" Alex asked, and Stitch smiled to himself. He knew that Dino couldn't and would never lie to Alex. Although he could skate around the truth, Stitch knew Dino respected Alex too much.

Dino just shrugged his shoulders. "It's really nothing. I have a new neighbor that moved in next door, and we've been....talking."

"Oh, well, talking is good, I assume."

Dino just nodded his head, and Stitch could see that the conversation was becoming uncomfortable for Dino, so he changed gears.

"Hey Alex, I heard that Arianna was coming back to town in a few weeks."

Alex smiled at the mention of their old high school friend. "Yeah, Paul said she was due in between Christmas and New Year's. It will be great to catch up with her."

As they all discussed the impending arrival of their old friend, Stitch couldn't help but hope everything was okay with Dino. Whatever was going on, he hoped it all worked out for his friend.

Dino and Arianna's story is coming in April 2021!
Pre-order available now!

BOOK LIST

The Trident Series
ACE

POTTER

FROST

IRISH

STITCH

DINO

SKITTLES

DIEGO

A TRIDENT WEDDING

The Trident Series II – BRAVO Team
JOKER *(2021)*

BEAR *(2022)*

DUKE *(2022)*

PLAYBOY *(2022)*

AUSSIE *(2022)*

NAILS *(2022)*

SNOW *(TBD)*

JAY BIRD *(TBD)*

ABOUT THE AUTHOR

Jaime Lewis, a *USA TODAY* bestselling author, entered the indie author world in June 2020, with ACE, the first book in the Trident Series.

Coming from a military family she describes as very patriotic, it's no surprise that her books are known for their accurate portrayal of life in the service.

Passionate in her support of the military, veterans and first responders, Jaime volunteers with the Daytona Division of the US Naval Sea Cadet Corps, a non-profit youth leadership development program sponsored by the U.S. Navy. Together with her son, she also manages a charity organization that supports military personnel and their families, along with veterans and first responders.

Born and raised in Edgewater, Maryland, Jaime now resides in Ormond Beach, Florida with her husband and two very active boys.

Between her day job, her two boys and writing, she doesn't have a heap of spare time, but if she does, you'll find her somewhere in the outdoors. Jaime is also an avid sports fan.

Follow Jaime:

Facebook Author Page: https://www.facebook.com/jaime.lewis.58152
Facebook Jaime's Convoy: https://www.facebook.com/groups/jaimesconvoy
Goodreads: https://www.goodreads.com/author/show/17048191.Jaime_Lewis
Instagram: authorjaimelewis

Made in the USA
Coppell, TX
17 February 2022

73710548R00152